HARPER BLISS

IF YOU

Kiss

ME LIKE

That

lady lit_ publishing

Copyright © 2020 by Harper Bliss
Published by Ladylit Publishing – a division of Q.P.S. Projects Limited -
Hong Kong
ISBN-13 978-988-74415-5-7

Chapter One

A sh quickly paid the driver and hopped out of the taxi. She was only fifteen minutes late. Very acceptable by her own standards. But her own standards didn't matter tonight. A swell of laughter came from behind the fogged-up windows of the party venue across the street. The place looked packed already. Of course it was. She couldn't think of anyone else who would be there tonight who'd had to commute from London on a Friday night—most people at the party would be retired.

She took a deep breath and went inside. Mercifully, Adrian was standing close to the door and he was the first person to greet her.

"Hello stranger," he said. "You made it."

"Was there ever any doubt that I would?" Ash gave her brother a hug.

"Maybe you were hoping to get disowned." Adrian held her at arm's length and gave her a once-over. "You look like you work too hard."

"I do work too hard," Ash said. *As well documented by my ex-wife*.

"And for what?" Adrian grinned at her.

"I'd better go find Mum before she actually does disown me for being late on this very special birthday."

"You can't miss her. She's the one with all the airs and graces." Adrian winked at her.

Before Ash found her mother, she had to make her way through a throng of family members she hadn't seen in a long time. Uncle Bernard hugged her like she was his own long-lost daughter. Auntie Mabel asked if she had a new girlfriend, emphasising the 'girl'—as though she'd never been to Ash and Charlotte's wedding. At least Auntie Joan told her she looked good; that was something.

"Darling." Her mother opened her arms in a dramatic gesture as Ash approached. "There you are."

"Happy birthday, Mum." Ash hugged her mother, who held on to her as though she would never let her go again.

"I haven't seen you in ages."

"I was in town just last month." Ash still stood squeezed in her mother's embrace.

"It's not enough." Her mother finally let go of her. "Now that I'm officially retired, you'll need to spend more time with me. What else am I going to do?"

"That's why I got you this." Ash reached into her jacket pocket and got out an envelope.

Her mother smiled widely, then tore it open. "Exchange this voucher for a night on the town with your only daughter," she read aloud. "Oh, darling, I'm already looking forward to it." She kissed Ash on the cheek. "This is just for me, right? Your father's not invited?"

"Just the two of us, Mum." Ash had racked her brain for a suitable retirement-slash-birthday present until she came to the conclusion that the best thing she could ever give her mother was her time. "No men allowed."

"You won't be taking me to one of *those* bars, will you?" Her mother grinned.

"We'll see," Ash teased. "Speaking of men, where's Dad?"

"Probably by the bar." Her mother only half succeeded in suppressing an eye-roll. At least she hadn't said anything about Ash being late. She had probably been too busy luxuriating in all the attention.

"I'm going to find him. I'll talk to you later."

Ash waded through the sea of people, trying to find her father. She grabbed a glass of lukewarm Prosecco on the way. Her dad was probably ordering a pint. Prosecco would be too girly for him.

"Ashley." Before Ash was able to find her father, Aunt Daisy, her father's only sister and Ash's godmother, grabbed her by the arm. "Come here."

Ash dutifully hugged her godmother. It had been a long week and it would be capped by a very long night. Not that Ash didn't appreciate spending time with her family, but all of them concentrated in a room like this was a bit much. The last time all these people had gathered, had been at her and Charlotte's wedding. Even though it had been the middle of July, it had rained all day, and the whole event had to take place inside. A bad omen if ever there was one.

"How are you?" Aunt Daisy's tone was full of compassion— or was it pity?

"I'm fine. And you?" Aunt Daisy was well into her seventies now and getting her to list all her physical ailments would distract her from her goddaughter's failed marriage for a while.

Ash emptied her glass of Prosecco while listening to her godmother, who, instead of discussing her health, raved about her grandchildren. Ash wasn't sure which was worse.

She caught a glimpse of her father, his elbow propped onto the bar. Ash managed to free herself from the conversation, with the promise that they would continue it later, and finally went to greet her father. That burly man who couldn't stop tears streaming down his cheeks on his daughter's wedding day.

3

Ash didn't know if his cheeks had remained dry on the day the divorce had been finalised. She guessed not, but she would never ask.

"I could murder one of those." Ash pointed at her dad's pint.

"Hi, darling," her father said, as though he had just seen her a few hours ago. "Coming right up." He gestured to the barman first, before curling an arm around Ash's shoulders. "How are you?" He gave her shoulder a squeeze.

"Fine." *Fine, fine, fine.* The number of times Ash had uttered that word since she and Charlotte had separated. As though it had to be repeated often enough to reassure everyone around her that she was, indeed, fine.

While she waited for her pint, it was as though everyone's gaze was aimed at her, as they wondered where Ash's wife was, and why Ash was there alone. What had gone so horribly wrong between the couple they had witnessed getting married only a few years ago?

"Here you go." Her dad offered her the beer. Ash gulped it eagerly. She had wolfed down a pack of crisps on the train so she wouldn't have to drink on an empty stomach. Because drink, she would. Facing her entire family for the first time since she and Charlotte had divorced would not happen without an alcoholic beverage firmly clasped in her hand throughout the evening. "How's work?"

"The same," Ash said. It was as though arriving at this party had catapulted her into a parallel universe. Even though Murraywood wasn't too many miles from London, to Ash it always felt a bit like travelling to a different time and a vastly different place.

Her dad grunted, just the way she had expected him to do. Ash and her father didn't have many in-depth conversations. Sustained silences didn't make them uncomfortable. They excelled at this very thing in each other's company. When she needed a break from it all, there was no place Ash would rather be than in the pub, next to her dad, with a cold pint in her hand. He didn't require any explanations from her. He didn't need her to express her innermost feelings to him. Just being there was always enough.

Of course, tonight, they weren't in The Horse and Groom, the pub her father had frequented all his adult life. They were at her mother's sixty-fifth birthday party at The Pavilion, Murraywood's prime venue-for-hire. There wasn't a lot of peace to be found, what with the endless parade of family members and friends of her parents milling about. The only younger people there were Ash and Adrian and his wife, whom he had miraculously managed to hold on to for almost fifteen years. Another case of her younger brother outperforming her in the feats of life. He and Lizzie had also managed to procreate, as straight people tend to do, and had produced two adorable grandchildren for their parents to dote on.

When she and Charlotte had got married, Ash had believed that, finally, she had done something right by the standards this world still seemed to operate on. Until the divorce, of course.

"Ashley Cooper." Ash heard her full name being boomed behind her. "As I live and breathe." A cold hand squeezed her neck. Christ. Some people were just too loose with their touch. "Look at you."

"Gloria Young." An instant smile formed on Ash's lips. She had always liked Gloria.

"Is this really your daughter, Alan?" Gloria bumped her elbow into Ash's father's arm. "Did she really make it down to little old Murraywood tonight? If Mary is to be believed, your daughter hardly ever does."

Ash could have hugged her dad for the very impressive way in which he rolled his eyes. He had lived with her mother's flair for exaggeration his entire marriage.

"Don't believe a word that comes out of my wife's mouth," he mumbled.

"How long has it been, Gloria?" Ash tried to remember, but she came up empty. "You look good."

"Must have been years," Gloria said, ignoring the compliment. Instead, she briefly touched her hand to Ash's arm. She must have heard about the divorce.

A piece of cutlery tapped insistently on a glass.

"Time for your mother's speech," Ash's dad said.

Her mother kept it brief, however—surely she would give another, much longer, speech later—and invited everyone to find their assigned seats.

"Let's talk later," Gloria said.

Ash watched her go off in search of the table she'd been placed at.

"Time for something heartier than a pint, darling." Her father put his empty glass on the counter, looking quite sad that he had to leave his spot at the bar.

Chapter Two

❧

G loria had hoped not to be relegated to the singles' table at this party. Yet, when she finally found her designated seat, she instantly knew she had been, because of Karen Lloyd's presence. Gloria had shared a table with Karen too many times since George had died ten years ago. She knew all about Karen's life, which wasn't dull per se, but it had become dull to Gloria because she'd had to listen to Karen's stories over and over again. She knew them all by heart by now.

Miraculously, none of Mary and Alan's siblings had become widowed, and therefore placed at the singles' table, even though they were all at least a decade older than Gloria. And at least two decades older than George when he had lost his long battle with cancer. But Gloria had stopped blaming other people for simply continuing to live a long time ago. If you started holding their very life against another person, it ended up not being much of a life for yourself.

"We meet again so quickly." Ash's voice sounded in Gloria's ear.

"Welcome to the exile table for widows and divorcees." Gloria was glad to have Ash's company. It gave her someone to talk to other than Karen. Gloria had learnt not to expect too much from life anymore and a small mercy, like sitting next to Mary's daughter during dinner, could actually make her happy these days.

"I'm neither, but hello," Karen said, while giving Ash a very obvious once-over. Truth be told, she did stand out in this particular crowd, with her platinum-blonde hairdo that looked striking against her tan skin. The sides of her head were shaved so close to her skin that you could make out a birthmark above her ear.

"You've got it all wrong," Adrian said. Ash's brother and his wife, Lizzie, had ambled up to the table. "This isn't the singles' table at all. This is the younger-than-sixty table."

"I barely made the cut then," Karen said.

"Bless you, Adrian, for seeing things that way." Gloria took her seat.

Ash sat next to her. Gloria knew Lizzie well because they were colleagues. This dinner wouldn't be too bad at all. In fact, she'd rather find herself at this table, Karen included, than at any of the other ones, where, no doubt, health ailments would be the main topic of conversation. Gloria got enough of that during the day.

A waitress approached with open bottles of white and red wine. Gloria covered her glass with her hand; it was automatic now. She noticed Ash glance at her hand. Didn't she know? Maybe Mary wasn't as big a gossip as Gloria believed.

"How's the money business?" Gloria asked Ash, before any possible untoward question could be uttered. To not drink at a social gathering, especially with people of Mary and Alan's generation, was still seen as quite the oddity.

Ash just shrugged.

"Are you usually happy when Friday evening rolls around or does it make you itch for Monday morning?" Being a district nurse, Gloria was very skilled at making conversation. Some of the patients she visited only ever had her or one of her colleagues to talk to. She always made sure they got their money's worth when it came to a proper chat.

"It depends," Ash said.

"That's pretty vague, even for you," Adrian butted in.

"I love my job, but my dedication to it has been held against me before, you know."

Gloria tried to read the look that passed between Ash and her brother. Held against her by whom? Her family? Or... oh yes, of course. Her ex-wife. Gloria had to admit she'd never actually met a divorced lesbian before. Same-sex marriage had only been legal since 2014. But why would things automatically work out better between two women or two men, anyway?

"How's life in London, then?" Gloria asked.

Ash sipped from her glass of white wine. "It's London. The greatest city in the world. It's not that far from here, you know. Just hop on a train and you'll be there in thirty minutes."

Was that a touch of defiance in her tone? Was Gloria pushing too hard? When had Mary told her about Ash's divorce again? It wasn't that long ago. Maybe Ash was still grieving for the marriage. Gloria knew a thing or two about grief. About that ache in the pit of your stomach that never let up, that didn't seem to diminish with time, but only grew fiercer for the first couple of years. At least that was her experience. She suppressed her nurse's reflex to pat Ash on the shoulder and decided to cut her some slack instead.

"I do take the train up to London once in a while for some shopping, or just to soak up the atmosphere," Gloria said. "Remind me to ask you for some tips later."

Ash reached for the bottle of water that stood in front of her. "Do you want some water?"

Gloria nodded and let Ash pour her a glass.

"Good luck getting through tonight without a drop of booze," Ash said.

"It's really not a problem for me." Gloria gave Ash the practiced smile she reserved for that kind of comment.

"I tried dry January this year." Ash took a sip from her wine again, as though she was trying to prove a point. "I lasted a week."

"To each their own." Another well-practiced phrase, even though Gloria hated platitudes like that. They stood in the way of a real conversation. But sometimes platitudes were the only possibility.

"I'm sorry," Ash said. "I don't mean to be insensitive. Drinking alcohol is practically a required skill in my job. There isn't a cliché about bankers that isn't actually true."

"That might be so, but I bet you're quite different from your co-workers."

Ash's face lit up a little. "The amount of testosterone in our office is through the roof." She shook her head. "You would honestly not believe some of the things these guys say—and some of the women as well, of course. Equal opportunity, political incorrectness and all that."

"How about you?" Gloria saw how Ash came alive when she talked about her work. This skill of Gloria's was one of the reasons she'd had the same job all her life—she knew the merits of persisting in getting certain conversations off the ground.

"I give as good as I get. And, of course, these days, when one of the guys does go too far, I just have to hashtag-metoo him." She chuckled.

From the corner of her eye, Gloria could see Karen's face pull itself into a frown.

"Ash has always suffered from too much testosterone," Adrian said.

"I've always had more than you," Ash said.

"I got myself a woman and spawned two kids," Adrian said. "What more can a man achieve these days?"

"I tried to make him pee sitting down," Lizzie said. "But it didn't work. He's got that Cooper stubbornness in him."

"You have to leave a man some dignity," Gloria said.

"Christ, almighty," Karen said. "And the first course hasn't even come out yet."

They all chuckled heartily.

"Why did you never get married, Karen?" Ash asked.

"Why would I?" Karen said.

"No man or woman has ever tempted you?"

"I've always been perfectly happy by myself," Karen said matter-of-factly, and Gloria admired her for doing so.

"I loved my husband dearly," Gloria said. "But I've been single for a very long time now, and it does have its advantages." Not that Gloria wouldn't trade everything she had for one more day with George. But she had her children. Once she'd emerged from beneath the rubble of her grief, she'd found she still had a life left. A job she loved. Life-long friends. The persistent kindness of her family and people she had shut out for months and months.

"Like what?" Lizzie asked.

"Why are you so keen to find out?" Adrian threw an arm around his wife.

"Just curious, sweetie." She blew him a kiss.

God, how they reminded Gloria of her and George when they'd been in their thirties, free of disease and worries.

"Now that my girls have flown the nest, I can do whatever I want. I don't have to consider anyone's opinion on how I choose to spend my time."

"If you have children, you'll never be truly free," Ash said flatly.

"That might be true, but I will always have them, so..." Gloria's mind drifted to Sally, her oldest daughter, who was in her last year of university in York. Would she move back home after she graduated? Gloria had no idea. Her youngest daughter,

Janey, had just started university and Gloria wondered what she would be up to tonight. Some nights, she preferred not to wonder about these things at all.

"I will always have an ex-wife," Ash said. "No matter what happens next in my life, Charlotte will always be a woman I once married. A person I stood next to in front of all my family and friends and vowed to be with for the rest of my life." She shook her head more vigorously this time. "I'm never doing that again. Not ever. The utter foolishness of the whole thing." She looked at the table where her parents and aunts and uncles were sitting. "Can you believe that they're all still in their marriages? As are all our cousins? What is it with this family?"

"Dumb luck," Karen said.

"It's not really something to bemoan, though," Gloria said. "I think it's wonderful."

"Try being the only divorced one of the lot," Ash said. "First, I made them all come to my big, fancy lesbian wedding. Then, it turned out to be all for nothing. We didn't even make it to five bloody years."

"Have you eaten at all today, Ash?" Adrian asked.

"I had a bag of crisps on the train," Ash said.

"That's it?" Lizzie sounded appalled.

"Why would you not eat?" Gloria couldn't believe what she was hearing.

As if on cue, their starters arrived.

"I'm about to tuck in." Ash picked up her cutlery. "And before anyone gets their knickers in a twist, it's called intermittent fasting. It's not an eating disorder." She held a forkful of smoked salmon in front of her mouth. "Yes, I should have eaten more today because I knew I would be drinking, but time just got away from me. If I had taken the time to buy more food before I got on the train, I would have missed it." She put the salmon in her mouth and started chewing.

Gloria hadn't seen Ash in years, but she had known both her

and Adrian for a long time. Ash had been like this as a girl as well. Feisty and stubborn to a fault.

"Intermittent fasting." Karen said the words as if they were the dirtiest she'd ever spoken. "Whatever will they invent next to torture women with?" She looked at Ash, but Ash didn't reply. She kept on shovelling salmon into her mouth. Gloria was sure she would be doing the same if she hadn't eaten all day.

"Ash has been doing it for years. Since long before it became trendy," Adrian said, earning himself a shut-up look from his sister.

"As much as I'd love to regale you all with the benefits of fasting, I'm too busy breaking my fast right now," Ash said. Her plate was nearly empty, while Gloria had yet to start.

"I don't drink alcohol," Gloria said, "and Ash doesn't eat food before a certain time of day. I'm sure we each have our own habits." She glanced sideways at Ash, while finally scooping some food onto her fork.

"Don't get me started on Adrian's quirks." Ash grinned. "We'll be here all night. Oh wait, we are going to be here all night." She turned her head and shot Gloria a wink, which Gloria hadn't expected at all.

"The salmon's good," Lizzie said, probably to keep Ash from spilling the beans on Adrian.

Gloria nodded, even though she'd barely tasted it. Ash's wink was just that. An acknowledgement of what Gloria had said just before, which, in a way, could be interpreted as coming to Ash's defence. It was nothing. Just a wink. Still, for a reason she couldn't explain, it felt like something to Gloria.

Chapter Three

"Sorry about earlier." Ash pushed her chair back and leaned a little closer to Gloria. "Being hangry makes me feel very sorry for myself." She threw in her widest smile.

"Understandably." Gloria smiled back.

"My belly's full." Ash patted her stomach. "I can handle anything now. Even this lot..." She made a sweeping gesture with her arm. She'd have to do the rounds of her family soon, have a chat with every aunt or uncle she only saw once or twice a year. Give them all the same rundown of her life. Work's busy. No, I'm not seeing anyone new. Yes, yes, yes, I'm doing just fine. She'd stay in her chair a bit longer.

"Look at Mary," Gloria said. "She's positively beaming tonight."

Ash cast her glance to her mother. Gloria was right. Her mother had a huge smile plastered across her face. "She's officially a lady of leisure now. Wouldn't you be beaming if you were?"

"I'd be climbing up the walls if I didn't have a job," Gloria said. "Wouldn't have the foggiest what to do with myself all day."

"Mum will just get on Dad's nerves, I presume." Ash turned her chair so she could see more of Gloria's face. "How long before your retirement party?"

"Oh, decades." Gloria slung an arm over the back of her chair and fixed her gaze on Ash.

"It was my very convoluted but discreet attempt at trying to find out your age," Ash said. "But yeah, sure, decades. I can see that. You don't look a day over forty." Ash held Gloria's gaze.

"Nor do you, Ashley." Gloria narrowed her eyes a fraction.

"I just turned forty-two, so thank you kindly."

"Oh, gosh. No way, Ash." Gloria held up a hand at chest height. "Do you remember I babysat you and Adrian when you were this high?"

"I have zero recollection of that, to be honest."

"Hm." Gloria crossed one leg over the other. "Must be all the fasting. Are you sure it's good for your memory?"

Ash enjoyed the mischievous expression on Gloria's face. "I bet Adrian gave you hell."

Gloria shook her head. "No, Ade has always been well behaved. You on the other hand. The tantrums. Goodness me."

"Now you're pulling my leg. My dad keeps telling me what a good child I was."

"Maybe Alan's a bit biased."

Ash sniggered. "I think you're making the whole thing up. You never babysat us at all. I think it's *your* memory that's been affected and you're confusing us with some other children."

"Ask your mum," was all Gloria said.

"I will." Ash truly couldn't remember any of it. They'd had so many babysitters when they were children, they all blurred into one authority figure, whom, Ash could admit, she probably would have had a problem with. "Excellent deflection technique, by the way. I still don't know how old you are, but I might be able to figure it out." Ash racked her brain. She seemed to remember that Gloria was at least ten years younger than her mother, possibly more—or was it less?

"I'm fifty-four," Gloria said. "It's really not a secret at all. In fact, I have no idea why women feel compelled to be so coy about their age. I love getting older."

"No midlife crisis for you, eh." Ash stuck out her bottom lip and nodded approvingly.

"I am on hormone replacement therapy. Maybe that helps." Gloria patted her upper arm. "A fresh patch every few weeks keeps me going."

Ash admired how easily—and lightly—Gloria spoke of her menopause. She remembered the drama of her mother going through menopause, although, truth be told, she hadn't been present for most of it. She'd been too busy building her career and falling in love with Charlotte.

Ash didn't immediately have a reply to this and a short silence fell between them. Adrian had left the table earlier to have a chat with the DJ and Lizzie had taken the opportunity to sit with her parents for a bit. Ash had no idea where Karen was. But it was just her and Gloria at the table.

"Now that we're throwing it all out in the open." Gloria leaned forwards a few inches. "Do you mind me asking about your divorce? I sense some bitterness around the subject. I take it the whole thing wasn't very amicable?"

Ash almost did a double take. She hadn't expected Gloria to ask her that question. "Not very, no." She locked eyes with Gloria for an instant, then averted her gaze. She didn't know why her divorce still invoked such shame in her. Maybe because she believed it was all her fault.

"What happened?"

Ash heaved a big sigh. "I guess... we grew apart. We fell out of love and there wasn't enough to replace it. Although, if you were to ask Charlotte, she would tell you that I was never there when she needed me because I preferred spending time at work to spending time with my wife. Which was true to a certain extent, especially near the end." Ash reached for her wineglass. She needed a sip. "If I had to sum it up, I'd say it just didn't work out. We weren't the amazing match we thought we were."

"These things are never easy to sum up in a few words. I bet it's much more complicated than that." Gloria's voice was so soft and soothing now, it made Ash want to have another look at her face.

The background music that had been playing throughout dinner was interrupted by a screeching microphone.

"Oh Christ, don't tell me Ade is going to do a speech," Ash said. "I swear to God, nobody ever tells me anything in this family." *Because you're unavailable, Ash.* She heard Charlotte's voice in her head. *Because you don't want to know.*

But Adrian just passed the microphone to his mother, who thanked everyone for coming, and urged them onto the dance floor.

Ash pushed her chair a little closer to the table so she didn't impede any of the older guests who wanted to dance. In doing so, she suddenly found herself sitting very close to Gloria.

"You still owe me some tips," Gloria shouted into her ear. "For things to do in London."

"Give me your number," Ash shouted back. "I'll text you all you need to know."

Chapter Four

G loria watched Ash dance with her brother. They were making silly moves and, as siblings tend to do, each one was trying to be sillier than the other. She had witnessed it in her own girls. She had experienced it with her own sister and brother. Always wanting to outsmart the other. It was a thing of the ages and no one who had a brother or sister could escape it.

"It's good to see them like that," Gloria said to Alan, who was sitting silently beside her, nursing a pint. She wasn't one for long silences. Alan Cooper was the silent type, but Gloria had always known a way in with him: ask him about his offspring. "They're having fun."

Alan nodded. "I worry about Ash so much." He slurred his words a little. It was getting near that time when most people in the room would be getting quite merry. Gloria had got used to it. It didn't bother her anymore. And if it did, she left. "I wonder if she will ever land on her feet."

"What does that mean, though, Alan?" Gloria asked. "Landing on your feet?" Look at me, Gloria thought. Surely, her friends would consider her to have landed on her feet, even though it had taken her years to find some sort of balance after

George died. "You don't necessarily need to be with someone to be happy. Some people prefer to be alone."

"Well, yes, I accept that." Alan peered into his pint. "But having to go through a divorce. I just wish she hadn't experienced that. It's a vile business." He expelled some air. "Charlotte is such a lovely girl. I just don't see why they couldn't make it work."

"We can't all be as lucky as you and Mary," Gloria quipped.

"I thought Mary and I had set a good example." He sipped from his pint again. Gloria was beginning to see where Ash got her wallowing-when-drunk streak from. "Clearly, we didn't do a good enough job."

"Cheer up, Alan. Look at her." Gloria waved a hand at the dance floor. "She's doing fine. We could spend all our time striving to spare our children from heartache, but the truth is we can do no such thing. No one is spared, Alan."

"But she's in her forties now." He let his gaze rest on his children. Ash and Adrian were still at it on the dance floor. They tried to involve more people, but everyone seemed reluctant to join them.

"So? I'm in my fifties and my mother still hasn't given up hope." She bumped her elbow into Alan's arm.

At least she got a chuckle out of Alan. "Never give up hope."

Gloria cast her gaze back at the dance floor. Ash was wearing skinny jeans and a really tight floral shirt. While she excelled in goofy dance moves, her brother had much more natural rhythm. However, Ash didn't seem to care one bit about that. She danced as if no one was watching. Until she spotted that Gloria was looking at her. She waved, then mouthed, "Come here." Gloria couldn't hear, but the beckoning gesture Ash made with her hands was unmistakable.

"Go dance, Gloria," Alan said. "Go have fun."

"I think I just might." Gloria's legs were getting stiff from all the sitting down she'd been doing all night. She shuffled onto the dance floor and joined Ash and Adrian.

"Christ," Adrian said, when the song ended. "I'm the father of two children. I can't be doing this anymore. I give up, Ash. You win." He sank down in a chair.

"Just you and me now, Gloria," Ash said.

Gloria couldn't fault the DJ, one of Ash's cousins, for trying a different strategy to fill the floor. Yet, she didn't immediately know what to do when she recognised the intro of Eric Clapton's "Wonderful Tonight".

"What do you say?" Ash held her arms wide. "Will you dance with me?"

"It would be my pleasure." Gloria stepped closer. "I'll lead, though."

"Will you now?" Ash put her hands on Gloria's shoulders. She was a little shorter than Gloria, but not that much. Gloria rested her hands on Ash's hips. They started to gently sway to the lazy beat of the song.

Gloria was having none of that millennial slow-dancing. If she was going to lead, she was going to do it properly. "Just follow my lead," she whispered in Ash's ear.

"Yes, boss." Ash shot her a grin. "Take it away."

Ash was a little unsteady on her feet, but she did a good enough of job of following Gloria, who was used to manoeuvring much larger bodies in her day job, although not around a dance floor.

When she looked around, Gloria noticed, for the first time, that the DJ's strategy had worked. They weren't the only twosome on the dance floor. They were the only two women dancing together, though.

"I know I'm a really shit dancer," Ash shouted in Gloria's ear. "I take after my dad in many respects."

"You're doing just fine." Gloria held Ash a tad closer. She

could feel her hip bones jutting into her flesh. It wasn't an unpleasant feeling.

"I hope you're not going back to London tonight."

"God no. I'm staying with Mum and Dad," Ash said. "I might even stay for the weekend. Not much waiting for me back home."

"I'm sure you have a busy social life." Their faces were so close together, Gloria couldn't actually make out any of Ash's expressions. "Or at least a date to go on."

"I'm so done with dating," Ash said. "Did you... ever date again?"

The question threw Gloria. She took her time to reply. "I tried, but it never really worked out."

"How come?" Ash pressed herself into Gloria's embrace.

"I don't know. I guess..." Gloria slowed their pace. "No one ever really lived up to my expectations again. Maybe I was expecting a second George and of course there was only ever one of him, so I made it impossible." Gloria had thought about this a lot and this was the only possible conclusion she could draw. She had gone out with a few decent men. One of them, his name was Richard, had been very dashing—much more handsome than George, if you could look at that sort of thing objectively—but she'd never felt that spark again. She'd never been interested enough to allow anyone new into her life in that way.

"I figured it must have been down to you," Ash said. "A woman like you... surely a line of men would be queuing up all the way around your house." Gloria couldn't see, but she could hear the smile in Ash's voice. A bead of sweat trickled down her spine. Gloria wasn't much of a blusher, but if she were, her cheeks would have coloured at Ash's comment.

"The same could be said of you." She quickly turned the tables on Ash. As much as Gloria loved a chat, she didn't like to get too personal. "All the lesbians in the land must be throwing themselves at you." She felt Ash's body convulse against her hands as she burst into a giggle.

"Of course," Ash said. "Every single last one of them."

Gloria laughed with her. She tried to picture Charlotte, but she couldn't remember if she had ever seen her. She hadn't been able to go to the wedding; the reason why escaped her. Mary must have shown her pictures—she used to be the type to organise a viewing party to show off her holiday snaps—but, for the life of her, Gloria couldn't recall.

The song ended and they stepped away from each other.

"Thank you for this dance." Ash curtsied. "It's easily the best one I've had all night." She winked at Gloria again and, just like the first time earlier that night, it gave Gloria pause. She watched Ash saunter off to the table where Mary was sitting, clearly uninterested in dancing any more. Gloria could do with a sit-down herself. Then she felt a tap on the shoulder.

"What do you say, Gloria?" Jim, Mary's youngest brother, asked. "Shall we show them how it's done?"

"Sure." Gloria gave him a smile. Out of the corner of her eye, she looked at Ash, and saw her looking back at her.

Jim took the lead and twirled them around the dance floor. They exchanged pleasantries and Gloria tried to give him her full attention, the way she had done during the previous dance with Ash. But it seemed to her she had little attention left to give. Either she was tired—or she'd spent it all on Ash.

The sensation of being led around the dance floor by a man was nice enough. It even brought back some memories of better days. George loved to dance. At any party, he'd be on the floor from the first song to the last. And Gloria had adored dancing with him. They'd regularly danced in their living room. Often, without any music to guide them. George would scoop her up and draw her near and they'd sway to an imaginary beat, one that only they could hear. No wonder Gloria had never fallen for another man again. She couldn't picture hearing that soundless beat with anyone else but George.

As she spun around, Gloria's gaze caught Ash again. She was still eyeing her. Or maybe she was just looking at the goings-on on the dance floor. No. Her glance was solidly aimed at Gloria. Gloria could feel it, the way you can feel someone looking at you even when your back is turned to them.

On the next go-around, Ash smiled at her, taking away any doubts Gloria might have had about the direction of her gaze. Gloria swung her hips extra fancifully when she had her back turned to Ash. She didn't really know why. It was just something she felt like doing in the moment.

Chapter Five

L ewis could not look less like a hedge fund manager. He
    wore a suit all right, but it wasn't the kind any other
banker wore. It wasn't the obligatory navy or black suit that
made you fit in. Her boss wore what Ash called 'chat show host
suits', with loud flowery patterns and made out of shiny, gaudy
fabrics.

"You always look so fresh-faced when you've spent a
weekend in the country, darling," Lewis said, after he had
air-kissed Ash.

"Murraywood is hardly the country. It's half an hour on the
train."

"Imagine what actually going into the countryside would do
to your complexion." Lewis pushed the button of the automatic
coffee machine. Just like her, Lewis didn't believe in lunch. Not
eating throughout the day kept him sharp. In fact, Ash had
picked up the habit from him. "Here you go, darling." He
handed Ash the tiny espresso cup.

Ash knocked back the coffee. It was her third of the day.
Some days, she could take four, but most days, three of these
tiny but awfully strong beverages was her limit. "You keep

promising to get yourself a country pad. How about putting your money where that big mouth is?" Lewis wasn't just Ash's boss. He had also become her best friend.

"I'll have to get my trophy husband on to that." Jonathan was anything but a trophy husband. He ran a company that imported Japanese sake and whiskies into the UK and was more often than not on a business trip to Asia. If Lewis and Jonathan actually had a house in the countryside, neither one of them would use it. Ash would use it, though. Although, if she needed a hit of country-ish air, she could just go home to her parents.

Ash's phone buzzed in her back pocket. She fished it out and read the message.

Still waiting for those London tips.

A smile spread across her face. Gloria hadn't been at the forefront of her mind since the party. On Saturday, Ash, like the rest of her family, had battled a nasty hangover. She'd hung out at home, watching the Chelsea game with her dad, and eating her mother's chicken pie—an excellent cure for hangovers and post-divorce-blues alike. On Sunday, when she'd felt fresh as a daisy again, she'd spent the day with her nephews.

"What's that smile about? Did Charlotte flee the British Isles?" Lewis asked.

Ash shot him a look, then asked, "What smile?"

"I hate to be the bearer of bad news, darling," Lewis said, "but you've hardly been a barrel of laughs since the whole divorce debacle. I'll make do with the tiniest hint of a smile on your gorgeous face."

"Oh, please." She wanted to give Lewis a good comeback, but her brain was too occupied forming a reply to Gloria's text. "I'm well and truly over the divorce," she lied. Ash had stayed with Lewis and Jonathan, in their lavish town house in Kensington, after she and Charlotte had first split up.

As she looked up, she just caught Lewis's exaggerated eye roll. "Is there someone new on the scene?" he asked. "You know you can't keep vital information like that from me." Since Ash had found a new flat and had moved out of Lewis's house, he'd tried to set her up with no less than three women he vaguely knew, one of which he had only suspected of being interested in women. For some reason, maybe because he'd been with Jonathan for decades, Lewis was very interested in Ash's love life. He hadn't had much to sink his teeth into. Ash simply wasn't interested. Why would she even try? To end up divorced again?

"You'll be the first to know if ever there is something to know again."

"You're not going to tell me who just texted you then?" Lewis insisted.

"It's just a friend of my mum's, looking for some tips on what to do when she comes to London next. It's nothing. Sorry to disappoint you so immensely on a Monday."

Lewis briefly pulled a face. "Just remember. It's all well and good to not want a relationship. I totally get that, but you don't want to get any cobwebs down there. You have to keep the juices flowing, if you catch my drift."

"It's utterly impossible not to catch it, darling." Ash shook her head. "And we've had this conversation a dozen times before. A prolonged period of abstinence will hardly kill me, as hard as that is to believe for you." She tapped her fingers against her phone screen. "Now if you'll excuse me. I have to get back to work so I can make you some more money."

"You are the perfect employee, Ash," Lewis shouted after her, his voice dripping with honey.

It was an in-joke that had started after Ash told him she knew so much about Lewis's private life, he could never fire her.

Back at her desk, Ash replied:

27

It's only Monday. Give a girl a break.

On the train back to London, her mind had drifted back to the dance she'd had with Gloria. She'd watched her dance with Uncle Jim afterwards and Ash could have sworn Gloria hadn't had the same sparkle about her as when she'd danced with Ash. Of course, Ash had been quite plastered and her memories of the night were subsequently hazy. Gloria's reply came quickly.

Sorry. I have Wednesday off and I was thinking of taking the train up. Didn't mean to rush you. xo

Why had Gloria included 'xo' in her message? Maybe that was just her usual sign-off. But, hadn't she just said she'd be in town the day after tomorrow? Ash checked her schedule. There was no way she could take a day off, but she could surely blow off the monthly Women in Finance networking drinks she'd planned to attend after work and, perhaps, take Gloria out for dinner instead. Even though that was not what Gloria was asking for. She was just asking for tips on what to do in London. Nevertheless, the sudden prospect of having dinner with Gloria sparked something in Ash.

I promise to send you some suggestions tonight. One of them will be to have dinner with me in the evening.

Gloria didn't reply so quickly now. Had Ash put her off? It was just dinner. It didn't mean anything. She liked Gloria because she was so easy to talk to and so much fun to be around. Ash craved people like that around her right now. Besides, her mind wouldn't even dare to venture anywhere else. Gloria was a friend of her parents. Maybe she could be her friend as well.

Ok. Look forward to it. xo

Look forward to what? Ash thought. Getting the message or having dinner with me? And was that a yes? She took it as a provisional yes. Her stomach growled. Ash drank a glass of water. Then she put the message out of her mind for the rest of the afternoon—she ignored it, just like the pangs of hunger that sneaked up on her—and focused on her work. It was how she had got through the divorce. Ironically, she'd started working even more, as if trying to disprove Charlotte's allegation that her working too much was the cause of their divorce.

Chapter Six

"You're being rather rude," Sindhu said. "What happened to no phones at the dinner table?" Ever since Janey had left for uni, Gloria cooked dinner for her two best friends on Monday night.

Sindhu's husband worked the late shift at the fire station and Fiona was more than happy to have dinner with her friends instead of her husband one night a week.

"I'm sorry." Gloria had trouble putting her phone away. She was expecting a message from Ash. "Bad habit, foisted upon me by my daughters."

"I don't see any youngsters here." Fiona scratched the side of her arm. A gesture familiar to Gloria.

"Fresh patch Monday?" Gloria asked.

Fiona nodded. "Bring on the hormones. I'm ready for them."

They all chuckled, because you had to laugh, really.

"How was Mary's party?" Sindhu asked. "Not an eligible bachelor in sight, I suppose." She speared a piece of sausage onto her fork.

Gloria couldn't help but chuckle again.

"What's so funny?" Sindhu sounded too innocent to not be in on the joke.

"They put me at the singles' table, with Karen." Gloria played with the gravy on top of her mash.

"If you were fighting over bachelors with Karen, you likely didn't stand a chance." Fiona waggled her eyebrows.

"There were no bachelors. Both Mary and Alan come from very sturdy and loyal stock. Not a widower or divorced man in sight." Not if Ash was to be believed, at least. "Not that I was looking."

"Did you dance into the wee hours?" Sindhu's voice sounded as though she would like to do exactly that sometime soon.

"Pretty much." Gloria scooped more mash onto her plate. "It was a pretty lively do, especially if you consider the average age of the people there." Gloria had left not long after dancing with Ash and Jim. She had worked the afternoon shift on Saturday and needed to get her beauty sleep.

"You must have been the youngest guest," Fiona said.

"Apart from Mary's children. Yes." Gloria eyed her phone. She'd put it on the sideboard next to the table. No message alerts. How late did Ash work?

"Simon has Adrian's youngest in his pre-school class. He's just the cutest child you've ever seen. Quite well behaved as well, I hear," Fiona said.

"How was the hotshot from London?" Sindhu asked.

The question made Gloria glance at her phone again. "Ash is doing well, I think. She sat next to me at dinner. She's a lovely girl." *A lovely girl.* What did that even mean? And why did Gloria feel so flustered talking about Ash?

"Has she digested the divorce?" Fiona asked.

That was the thing about living in a small town like Murray-wood. Even if your children lived miles away, everyone still knew a little about their private business.

"I think so." Gloria suspected this wasn't entirely true, but it wasn't for her to say. Ash had made some bitter comments about her new status as a recent divorcee. "When I go up to London this week, I might meet up with her," she blurted out.

"With Ash Cooper?" Fiona sounded surprised.

Gloria nodded.

"Are you switching sides?" Sindhu would say something like that. "Is she taking you to a lesbian bar?"

Gloria huffed out a nervous chuckle. "Of course not. We just had a nice time at the party, so why not meet up? It's not as if I have a family waiting for me at home. I might as well go out for a meal in London."

"I don't want to imply anything, Gloria," Fiona said, "but as one of your best friends, I feel like I should tell you that you just sounded a touch defensive."

"You just sounded as though you're really enjoying that bottle of red you brought," Gloria was quick to say, and, in doing so, confirmed her defensiveness to herself.

"It is pretty good." Sindhu topped up her glass and took a sip, as though she had to prove the point there and then. "But you're totally right, Gloria. Go out. Have fun. Make new friends. We don't have to tell you that life can be bloody short."

Gloria wondered what George would make of all this. As he lay dying, he had made Gloria promise that she wouldn't stay alone. He wanted her to be happy again. To not mourn him for the rest of her life. She was still so young—barely forty-five when George had died. And Gloria had made the promise. Not because it was what she wanted, but because it was what *he* wanted.

A few years later, she had remembered George's deathbed request, and she had tried. Little had she known that she was actually much happier single than when she tried her hand at the old dating game. George couldn't have known either, of course. They'd been happy together. One of those couples other people envied—and their daughters called gross because

33

they kissed each other on the lips in their presence all the time.

"Thank you for your permission." Gloria smiled at her friends. She knew they meant well. Cooking them a weekly dinner was the least she could do after the endless hot meals Sindhu and Fiona had provided for her and the girls in the first months after George's death. She could never repay them for their kindness, but she knew she didn't have to.

Just then, Gloria's phone buzzed on the sideboard.

Sindhu looked at her as if to say: don't you dare.

"It's probably Ash," Gloria said. "Confirming our plans for Wednesday."

"By all means," Sindhu said. "Don't let us keep you from arranging your date with the young lesbian."

Gloria got up with as much dignity as she could muster. She reached for her phone and there was, indeed, a message from Ash.

It's going to rain Wednesday, so I would recommend a museum. There's a really great Turner exhibition at the National Gallery. I've been and it was really fantastic.

Gloria had barely had time to read and process the message when a second one came in.

Am I safe in thinking I have carte blanche to pick the restaurant?

"She's keen." Sindhu wasn't letting it go, despite what she'd said earlier.

Gloria put her phone away. She would reply later, when her friends had left. But she was happy to have heard from Ash, who could have easily not bothered to reply when Gloria had texted her earlier today. She could have decided to forget all about last Friday and forget that Gloria existed at all. And why wouldn't she?

But she hadn't. They were going out to dinner in London. It would make a nice change from all the meals Gloria had enjoyed on her own while going into the capital. She didn't mind. She was used to it. But the prospect of sitting across from Ash filled her with giddiness nonetheless.

"When are *we* going for a big night on the town?" Fiona asked. "It's been too long."

Fiona always said things like that, but they all knew their truly epic nights on the town were long behind them, which was just fine with Gloria.

Chapter Seven

A sh took a large bite out of an apple. The first bite of anything solid she'd had all day—and it tasted like the most delicious morsel of food she'd ever had in her life. It was like that every day when she broke her fast. She checked her watch. She'd only be a few minutes late. Meeting a friend of her mother's was unchartered territory for Ash. If this were a date, she'd deliberately arrive at least ten minutes late—not that Ash ever had to actively try to be late anywhere. It always seemed to happen of its own accord, no matter how early she set off.

She threw the apple core into a bin just before she arrived at the bar she'd chosen to meet Gloria. Ash hadn't been there before because bars that only served alcohol-free cocktails weren't really her thing. She'd just missed out on being a millennial, and sometimes, Ash thought it really showed. All these youngsters who preferred to go to the gym instead of the pub after work. Ash didn't get it. But she did understand that Gloria didn't drink alcohol, and she wanted to make her feel as comfortable as possible.

Gloria hadn't arrived yet and Ash wondered if she could quickly sneak off to the pub next door to have a shot of something. Just to take the edge off after the work day had ended. She either needed sufficient time to shake off the stress of her day job, or a stiff drink. Tonight, she wouldn't have either. Meeting Gloria like this was turning out to be stressful in a way Ash hadn't expected.

Whenever her phone had lit up with a text during the day, Ash had found herself hoping it would be from Gloria. Something about her soothed Ash in a fundamental way. She was curious to see if that feeling would remain with her tonight.

She picked a table in the corner of the bar and studied the drinks menu. Alcohol-free gin was all the rage these days, it appeared. She checked her phone to see if Gloria had been in touch. But this was rush hour in London. It was a miracle when anyone arrived anywhere on time.

Then the door opened and there she was. A smile appeared on Gloria's face when she spotted Ash. Ash stood to greet her and they exchanged a quick peck on the cheek. Gloria took off her long black overcoat and sat opposite Ash.

"Cosy," she said.

"All the cocktails are alcohol-free." Ash beamed her a smile.

"Really?" Gloria jutted out her bottom lip. "You really didn't have to pick a place like that on my account. I can deal with it." She smiled back at Ash. "Nevertheless, the sentiment behind it is greatly appreciated."

"Zero percent G and T?" Ash tried to sound suave, but she didn't seem to be in possession of her full confidence. There was something about the way Gloria had walked into the bar— something about her posture and how regal and self-possessed it was. Maybe Ash hadn't expected that, even though she didn't really know why.

"Sure." Gloria put down the menu without having properly glanced at it. "I hope you're not planning to transition into a career as a weathergirl any time soon." She grinned. "The sun was shining all afternoon."

A waitress came by to take their order. Then Ash asked, "You didn't go to the museum?"

Gloria shook her head. "I walked around a lot, to soak up the sun and the energy of the city. There's something to see on every corner."

"So much for my stellar tip." Ash leaned back in her chair. She was beginning to feel more comfortable again. And she wanted to get a good look at Gloria. For someone who'd been traipsing around the streets of London all afternoon, she looked very well put together. Her curly dark-brown hair was always a little wild, so she had that working in her favour. She'd applied a fresh coat of lipstick. She was wearing a dark-blue blouse with white dots. Ash couldn't help but smile when she looked at her.

"Admittedly, I was expecting a little more from you than the suggestion to go to a museum. Especially because I'm really not much of a museum person."

"I'm deeply sorry. I hope I can make it up to you somehow."

"You can try." Gloria narrowed her eyes. "I don't mean to pry, but have you eaten anything today?"

Ash chuckled. Gloria kind of sounded like her mother now. "Yes. No *hangriness* tonight. I promise."

"Good. I'm starving, actually. Maybe we can order some snacks." She opened the menu and did look at it this time.

"So you're not much of a museum person?" Ash asked.

"What can I say? I like lowbrow entertainment. Give me a musical over a play any day of the week."

"Next you'll tell me you watch *EastEnders* every night."

Gloria pulled a face that could mean either yes or no.

Their drinks were brought over and Gloria ordered a small cheese platter with sesame seed crackers.

"How was your day?" Gloria asked, after the waitress had left their table.

"Unremarkable." Ash sipped from her faux gin and tonic. It

tasted just fine, but it didn't give her the hit of booze she craved —that she was so used to having with a moment like this.

"Care to enlighten me about what you do all day?" Gloria took the cardboard straw out of her glass and put it to the side. "Don't feel you have to. I'm curious, but I understand if you don't want to talk about work."

"I love my job, but I often find that when I do talk about it with anyone outside of work, they'd like me to shut up as soon as I start explaining it to them." Ash flashed Gloria another smile. "It's also very easy to loathe my industry."

"Explain it to me as you would explain it to your nephews." Gloria was so unflappable. She didn't give the slightest hint that she might find what Ash just said conceited—a chance her brother never passed up.

"At the very core of it, I make rich people even richer. It sounds gross, but that's really it. That's what I do."

"You must be responsible for insane amounts of money." Gloria peered at her over the rim of her glass.

"Oh, yeah." Ash did feel a touch uncomfortable now.

"That must be quite stressful."

"Sure, but it's also quite exciting. And, of course, we always spread the risk."

"Have you ever lost an obscene amount of money?" A smile curled on Gloria's lips.

Ash nodded. "Of course. It comes with the territory."

"How did you deal with that?"

"I tried to make the money back, but, in the end, I had to let it go. Losses are inevitable. It's a bit like life. It's statistically impossible to make the correct decisions all the time. Because some events are just utterly unpredictable."

"Tell me about it." Gloria's smile had weakened. "Does it attract a certain kind of woman? When you're in the money business?" She seemed to quickly regroup.

"You mean like hedge fund groupies?" Ash chuckled.

"I'm probably imagining all sorts of things that aren't real." Gloria sipped from her drink. "Your job is probably the complete opposite of mine."

"You take care of sick people." The snacks were brought to the table, cutting off what Ash meant to say next. Maybe it was for the best because she was about to say something sappy.

Gloria reached for a piece of cheese immediately. "I barely had lunch. I meant to get a slice of carrot cake this afternoon, but time got away from me." She held the piece of cheese in front of her mouth. "I'm really intrigued by you not eating all day. How do you do that? I could never." She popped the chunk into her mouth.

"You get used to it. Over the years, I've very slowly extended the hours of my fast. Now, it's really no bother anymore. Except when I drink on an empty stomach. That's a massive no-no."

"Over the years?" Gloria's eyebrows jumped up. "How long have you been doing this?"

"About five years now, I think. I started researching it not long after Charlotte and I got married."

"Did she join you?"

"Charlotte?" Ash shook her head. "No way. It's not for everyone. Charlotte needs her slice of toast in the morning and she considers not having lunch a huge wasted opportunity." It was one of the things they'd fought about, but, all things considered, their different way of eating had only been a minor issue.

"I think I might be with Charlotte on that." Gloria pierced a piece of cheese with a toothpick.

"You're not alone." Ash popped some cheese into her mouth. She was definitely hungry. But she had learnt to manage her hunger a long time ago.

"Are you, um, getting over that? The divorce, I mean." It was the first time that Gloria really hesitated when she spoke.

Ash exhaled deeply. "Getting there, I guess." She sipped from her drink again and wished even more fervently for a splash of real gin in it. "It's just... hard to get rid of the feelings of guilt. Because I feel like it's my fault. I can't shake the feeling that if I'd tried a little harder, we would have made it. It's easy enough to say that we had grown apart, but there's a reason why two people who were previously nuts about each other suddenly don't get along anymore. In our case, that reason was me. I fucked it all up and it has left a very bitter taste in my mouth."

"Why do you think you're the one who fucked it up?"

Ash hadn't meant to swear, but she was relieved that Gloria didn't mind her more colourful use of words.

"It's a very long story," she said.

"I have time and I'm interested." Gloria leaned back but she also looked as if she'd just caught herself saying something she shouldn't have. "But I don't want to push you, Ash. I respect that you don't want to talk about it."

"Does Mum talk about it with you?" Ash asked, partly because she wanted to deflect and partly because she was curious about what her mother said to her friends about her daughter's divorce.

"She has mentioned it, of course. But she has never gone into any details. She's just worried about you, I think. As any mother would be."

"A divorce is just so... It's like failing at love. Because there was a time when we stood in front of the registrar all loved up, making silly promises for the rest of our lives, and it all felt so right at the time. And then it all falls apart and it's just so gruelling, because not only was Charlotte my wife but she was also my best friend. She was the person who knew everything about me and liked me despite it all, and now she's just gone from my life."

Ash paused, trying to formulate her thoughts. "The actual divorce was kind of a relief. A sort of full stop after all the agony we'd been putting each other through. But the aftermath has just been so painful. I lie awake at night thinking of all the times I could have made a better decision. When I could have said something nice to her instead of something mean or nasty. When I could have left work an hour earlier so we could have had a much-needed conversation. There are a lot of missed opportunities leading up to a divorce and sometimes it's hard to deal with, because I just really feel like I could have done better as a wife."

"My gosh, Ash." Gloria leaned over the table. "I'm so sorry you've had to go through that." She fixed her gaze on Ash. "That you're still going through that."

Ash hadn't really meant to be so forthcoming. Gloria seemed to have that effect on her. Maybe it was the kindness in her gaze. Or the softness of her smile. Maybe it was because Gloria was a nurse and there was something inherently healing about her.

"I didn't really mean to lay all that on you."

"Hey." Gloria's hand shot forwards on the table. "I asked for it."

Ash looked at Gloria's hand. Her nails were painted a dark shade of red. "I feel the conversation has revolved around me way too much so far." If Gloria ever got fed up with nursing, she should join the police force. She would make an excellent interrogator. She obviously knew how to catch people unawares.

"Feel free to ask me anything you like." Gloria had slanted back, her hand retreating with her. Had she intended to comfort Ash by putting a hand on her arm?

"Anything?" Ash did have a burning question. "You're sure?"

"Well, if you're going to put it like that, I'm not at all sure. But try me."

"Have you never drunk alcohol? Or did you stop more recently?" Ash vaguely remembered something her mother had said about Gloria joining Alcoholics Anonymous, but she didn't

know any of the details. And she had time and she was interested too.

Gloria emptied the dregs of her drink, as though she needed
some fake courage to tell the story. "After George died, I went
through a bit of a dark period." She paused. "We were both
always heavy drinkers. Nothing untoward, but we could really
tie one on when the mood struck us." She briefly bit her
bottom lip. "Then he died and I found myself drinking alone
more and more. But I had two young children to take care of
and a life to get on with. Even though, at first, it felt like I had
died right alongside him. But I hadn't. I was still alive and I
couldn't justify waking up hungover every other morning any
longer. I had to live. If not for myself, then at least for my children. So I got some help. Joined AA. I've been sober for more
than eight years now."

"That's really impressive. To pull yourself together like that
after such loss."

"When you have children, you really have no choice. My
daughters had already lost their father." She went quiet for a
moment and Ash let the silence between them smooth the
emotions that had visibly welled up. If she liked Gloria before,
she now admired her even more for her strength. If only she
could borrow some of it so she could put her divorce behind
her once and for all.

"Thanks." Gloria took a deep breath. "I think I'm going to
find the loo."

While Gloria was in the ladies', Ash asked for the bill. She
considered how open Gloria had been with her. And how easy it
was to open up to her. Ash had to really rack her brain to find a
moment in the recent past when she'd had a conversation like
this. She loved Lewis, but they didn't talk to each other like
this. Lewis was there for her in a very different way. He offered
light relief when things got too heavy. Gloria, on the other
hand, coaxed her into facing herself in a way she'd probably

been afraid to do since divorcing Charlotte. Maybe because Gloria had had her own grief to deal with.

Just as Gloria returned to the table, the waitress brought the bill.

"I'll get that." Ash handed over her credit card.

"I take it you can afford it." Gloria looked as though she had touched up her make-up. She also looked much more defiant than the woman who had just left to use the ladies'. She shot Ash a sly smile.

"Tonight's on me," Ash said. "Let's go eat."

Chapter Eight

"Who's your favourite singer?" Ash asked, as though they were teenagers on their very first date.

"No way." Gloria shook her head.

"What? Why won't you tell me?" Ash's face was already pulled into too gleeful an expression. She had taken Gloria to a fancy Kashmiri restaurant that didn't serve any alcohol.

"Because, Ashley Cooper, when I look at you, with your blonde hipster haircut and your skinny jeans, I know for a fact that you're going to mock my choice."

Ash pulled her lips into a pout. "You know that? How do you have that much knowledge?"

"I noticed you and Adrian roll your eyes at the music played at your mother's party. I think, musically, I belong more to the same generation as your parents."

"So? Excellent music has been made throughout the ages." Ash filled both their glasses to the brim with sparkling water. If she was trying to make the point tonight that not drinking alcohol wasn't a problem for her, she had surely succeeded.

"Fine," Gloria said. "I absolutely adore Celine Dion. In fact..." Gloria pursed her lips. "She's going on a world tour this summer and I'm still gutted that I couldn't get tickets for the London show."

"For the record," Ash said, "I'm a little old to be called a hipster. I'm a forty-two-year old divorcee, although, granted, I don't dress like one." She grinned at Gloria again—that same disarming grin she'd been throwing around all evening. "But I did kind of miss the Celine Dion boat and I will admit that it's hard for me to not be cheeky right now, but for you, Gloria, I will hold in all my cheek."

"Why, thank you. That is so very kind of you."

"It's really no bother, you know." Ash flashed her a proper smile now. "I can be quite a nice person. Very accommodating and all that. Respectful of others' tastes and opinions."

"I've never understood why Celine Dion is so controversial. Objectively, not one single person on this planet can claim that she's not a good singer." Gloria had had to defend her Celine Dion fandom a few too many times in her life, most recently to her daughters, who insisted on listening to the most mind-boggling hip-hop music—if you could even call it music—in the car.

"It's just all a bit... overly sentimental, I guess. Maybe that's what it is. Too over the top."

"So she's not cool enough." Gloria shrugged. "Once you're over fifty, being cool really stops being of any concern at all." *Or once your husband dies and leaves you with two young girls to raise on your own.*

"Do you think I'm cool?" Ash asked.

Gloria chuckled—and gladly pushed the previous thought from her mind. "I don't know what the right answer is to that."

"There is no right or wrong answer."

"That haircut must have set you back a few bob," Gloria joked, while wondering what Ash was really asking her. Did she want to know if Gloria liked her? Wasn't it obvious already, because they were having dinner together right now. Or maybe she was reading too much into it—again. Maybe part of her wanted Ash to wonder if Gloria liked her.

"It's not about a haircut, though, is it?" Ash leaned back—and she looked kind of cool as she did.

Gloria ran a hand through her hair. Her unruly mop of curls that she didn't know what to do with half the time. So she just kept it at the same length and let it fall where it may.

"Is it even possible to be cut up about your divorce and be cool at the same time?" Gloria had no idea why that exact question had come out of her mouth. "Sorry. You don't have to answer that." She took a quick sip of water.

"Strangely." Ash seemed unperturbed by what Gloria had just said. "I was much cooler right after the divorce. At first, it was a relief. Because all the fighting was officially over and done with. That had ended when the relationship ended. The thought of being married to someone who doesn't like you very much anymore is quite horrific. It all really seemed to hit me a few months after the fact. That it was all over and I'd lost Charlotte for good." She swallowed hard. "I'm doing much better now, but, to answer your question, I'm not very cool about it yet. I guess it will take time. Who knows, maybe Char and I will be friends again one day."

"Any loss takes time," Gloria said. "And even time is never enough. It may smooth out some of the rougher edges, but... It's not like I still miss George's presence every single day, but it can really creep up on me sometimes. I'm just going about my day and it hits me that I will never speak to him again, that I will never see him again, never put my head on his chest again, and a raw kind of pain slices through me all over again."

"Please don't think I'm equating my divorce to the death of your husband," Ash said. "It's not the same."

"Oh, it's very different. George's dead, and I know that I can't blame myself for that. But death is much more final than divorce, which is more painful in one way, but it also makes it easier. Because there's nothing I can do to bring him back. It should make it easier to move on."

"Have you moved on?" Ash rested her light-brown eyes on Gloria. There was such kindness in her gaze. Gloria wondered if it was because she was meeting with her at this exact time in her life—a time in which Ash was searching for some peace, where she was trying to make sense of what had made her marriage fail. Maybe that's what made her such a good listener.

"Not so much in the romantic sense," Gloria admitted. "But of course I've moved on with my life. And I have a good life. I really can't complain. My daughters are doing really well now. I love my work. I have a bunch of really good friends that I can always count on. It could all be so much worse."

"I truly admire your resilience," Ash said. "Your spirit. I can see it in your eyes." She curled the corner of her mouth into a half-smile. "There's something in them that just... I don't know." Was that a sudden blush on Ash's cheeks? The low lighting in the restaurant didn't allow Gloria to fully appreciate it, but she believed that Ash had just made herself blush. Gloria allowed herself an inner smile, because she must have contributed to it, although she didn't really know how. And Ash had just paid her a compliment as well.

"Maybe it's the company I'm keeping." Gloria kept her gaze firmly on Ash. At least, she wanted to, but she had to avert it after a few moments. Things had taken a turn for the intense.

Ash chuckled and Gloria joined her to break the tension between them a touch. Had they just crossed over into flirting? If so, what was Gloria doing flirting with someone like Ash? Sure, she was very attractive and engaging—maybe charismatic was the best word to describe her—but Gloria was not in the habit of flirting with anyone, especially not with another woman. And especially not if that other woman was the daughter of one of her friends. But if Ash, like she had just claimed, thought there was something about Gloria and Gloria equally believed there was something about Ash, then, yes, perhaps this was flirting.

"What time's your last train?" Ash asked, breaking the spell of the moment.

"Oh, sugar." Gloria checked her watch. "It's in half an hour." She had completely lost track of time. "I'd best get going if I don't want to miss it." For a brief instant, she wondered if she'd prefer to miss her train. But then what? A prolonged night on the town with Ash? Maybe if she'd been fifteen years younger.

"We'll get a black cab to the station." Ash was already asking for the bill. She was efficient like that. "I'll drop you off."

Chapter Nine

"What's your favourite Celine song?" Ash asked when they were in the back of the cab. She believed she'd had a good handle on the night. She'd taken Gloria to the right places. She'd abstained from drinking any alcohol. They'd had a good conversation. But fifteen minutes before they'd left the restaurant, Ash had felt like she'd lost her grip on things altogether. This was the only question she could come up with on the way to the train station.

"'It's All Coming Back to Me Now'," Gloria said without thinking. "Best song ever made, in my humble opinion, which, when it comes down to it, no one ever respects." She slung one leg over the other and, in shifting, skated her arm against Ash's. "You didn't have to drop me at the station. I'm a big girl, in case you hadn't noticed. But I'm grateful, nonetheless."

"Maybe I didn't want the evening to end." Ash looked out of the window, in which she could see Gloria's reflection. She couldn't really make out the expression on her face, but she did notice her smile. Ash quite liked the sensation of saying exactly what she meant in this context. It was thrilling to speak the absolute truth—because Ash truly didn't want this evening to end—and get a kick out of it, instead of entering into another endless argument.

"I've had a lovely time too." Ash felt Gloria's arm against her own again.

What Ash really wanted to ask was whether they could do it again some time, but there was something final about being in this taxi on their way to the station. As though the train that Gloria was about to board would carry her right out of Ash's life. Maybe the only reason Ash had said the thing about Gloria's eyes—had effectively resorted to blatant flirting—was because of this anticipated finality. Gloria could never be a proper love interest to her. It just wasn't a viable option for many reasons. Which left the door wide open for some harmless but immensely fun flirting.

Ash turned to Gloria. Her smile was broad, but there was a touch of sadness to it. "Let me know when you're in London next."

"Why? So you can give me another rubbish suggestion on what to do?" Gloria's smile transformed into a cheeky grin.

"Maybe I should only give you tips on what not to do."

"Okay. In that case, I'll let you know." Gloria patted Ash's knee briefly. "Thanks for tonight. Next time will be on me. I'll take you somewhere you can have a proper drink."

Next time? Ash shook off the thought. The cab pulled up to the kerb.

"This is me." Gloria leaned over, kissed Ash lightly on the cheek, gave her knee another quick squeeze, and exited the cab. Just like that, she was gone.

Ash gave her home address to the cabbie. As he pulled back into traffic, she tried to catch another glimpse of Gloria, but she had disappeared into the station.

"Beautiful lady." The cabbie had suddenly turned chatty. "Good date?" he asked.

Ash was taken aback by his question. It was quite forward

of the man to assume they had been on a date. They hadn't. Objectively speaking, it had all the trappings of a date, but that didn't make it one.

"It wasn't a date," she said.

"My daughter came out to us last year," the cabbie said. He found Ash's gaze in the rear-view mirror.

"How wonderful." She looked away.

"My wife and I told her we love her just the same."

This was turning into one weird taxi ride. But at least it took Ash's mind off Gloria.

When Ash didn't immediately respond, the driver said, "I've been doing this job a long time and it kind of looked like a date to me."

Ash wasn't sure how to reply to that, so she propped her chin on her hand and stared out of the window, hoping the cabbie would take the hint and leave her in peace for the rest of the ride.

Ash had barely unlocked the door to her flat, when Gloria texted her.

Thank you for tonight. Gloria xo

By the time she'd hung up her coat, there was another text message with a link to a YouTube video. Ash clicked the link and landed on a live performance of Celine Dion singing "It's All Coming Back to Me Now". She couldn't help but smile.

She sat to watch the video, but then received another message.

Your eyes aren't half bad either.

Ash sniggered. What was this? Had the evening with Ash made Gloria so gleeful that she was texting on the train like a giddy teenager? Ash would happily play along. After all, the evening wasn't over yet. Tomorrow, when she woke up, in the cold hard light of the morning, she would put a stop to whatever this was. She texted back.

Shh! I'm listening to Celine.

While listening to the song, which was all bombast and long held notes and not that much to Ash's taste—but she kind of liked it anyway—she anticipated a reply from Gloria. None came. She didn't have the patience to listen to the entire song— it went on forever. Instead, she texted:

After you got out, the cabbie asked if I'd had a good date.

Ash got up and poured herself a glass of cold wine. Gloria's reply came quickly.

Did you say yes?

Ash burst into a giggle.

Should I have?

Were they still flirting now? Gloria surely wasn't holding back. They had the advantage of distance. It was easier to say these things with the subtraction of body language and the occasional lingering glance. Ash waited for Gloria's reply with bated breath.

Do you like the Celine song?

Disappointment coursed through her. But one of them had to be the wiser one. Maybe it was only befitting that it was Gloria, seeing as she was older than Ash.

I already can't get it out of my head. Thanks for that.

Ash waited for Gloria to reply, but she didn't. It was late. She had a busy day tomorrow—a day that would allow her to forget all about tonight. Ash went to bed, but she took her phone with her nevertheless. All the self-help books she'd read post-divorce had one rule in common: keep your phone out of your bedroom.

She bet the authors weren't newly single. Sometimes, when she woke up in the middle of the night, Ash indulged herself and scrolled through Tinder to see if any of the women on there could pique her interest. But she wasn't ready for any of that. Sometimes, her heart would leap all the way into her throat when she thought she recognised a picture of Charlotte. But Charlotte wasn't the type for dating apps. Or maybe she was now. Ash didn't know. And she wouldn't be asking her any time soon.

Just as she was about to turn off her phone, it buzzed with an incoming message.

Made it home safely. Sleep tight. xo

Gloria wasn't stingy with the virtual kisses and hugs. The text left Ash so elated she feared she might not be able to sleep. But she turned off her phone regardless of sleep coming quickly or not. It was time to nip this in the bud before it turned into something she might find hard to control.

Chapter Ten

Gloria always slept with her phone on her bedside cabinet. That's how it was when you had children, even if they'd left the house. She woke early on Thursday morning, even though she was working the afternoon shift.

She reached for her phone and scrolled through the messages she'd exchanged with Ash last night. Now that she'd slept on it, it was quite clear that they had well and truly flirted. There were no two ways about it. They had flirted in the restaurant, continued furtively in the taxi, and not-so furtively in their texts to each other. Gloria was holding the evidence in her hand. If any of her friends showed her a text message thread like that, she would be the first to confirm that some heavy-duty flirting had happened.

Now that she was able to acknowledge this, Gloria asked herself what it meant. And how innocent it was. Despite their differences in about every area of their lives, they had one big thing in common. They'd both lost someone they'd loved. But whether having something like that in common would ever be enough to bridge their differences wasn't even a question Gloria could ask herself.

Because, as far as she knew, she was straight. But if she was, why had she flirted with Ash? And why was she looking at her phone as though willing a brand new message from Ash to appear on its screen?

She told herself to get a grip, got out of bed, and took a long, hot shower. When she emerged into the kitchen, she couldn't help herself. She played the clip she'd sent to Ash via text last night.

She sang along to Celine Dion as she prepared breakfast and, again, her thoughts were pulled into Ash's direction. Did she really never have breakfast? Gloria tried to wrap her head around that. No breakfast and no lunch? Gloria waited for a slice of toast to pop up as the kettle boiled.

Something in the music brought her thoughts back to what Ash had said about her eyes. Gloria wasn't easily flustered, and she'd been able to hide it last night, but she was definitely having a delayed reaction this morning. Or maybe it was a hot flush. She opened a button on her blouse and pulled it away from her skin. Maybe it was the menopause that had made her reciprocate Ash's flirting. She shook her head. Gloria didn't believe in the notion that a change in hormones could have that kind of power over her. If she'd flirted back—and she had—it had been with use of her full faculties. And it wasn't as if she could blame the drink either. Nor could Ash for that matter. Even though she never asked anyone to refrain from drinking in her presence, it had been very thoughtful of Ash to take her to two alcohol-free establishments. She seemed like a very considerate person in general. Easy on the eye as well. All the Coopers were olive-skinned, and the light colour of her hair made Ash's tan stand out even more.

Gloria truly believed that a woman like Ash was a catch, once she felt ready to be caught in the claws of romance again. She couldn't help but wonder what had truly happened in her marriage. Ash seemed to be shouldering most of the blame.

Her toast popped and she spread some salty butter on it. She should really stop thinking about Ash now. There was shopping to be done and a lawn to be mowed. She had patients to visit all afternoon, which was good. Keeping busy would keep her mind off things. Or maybe what Gloria needed was a strong incentive to stop flirting and allowing images of Ash to flood her brain. She should pop round Mary and Alan's. That should snap her right out of it. She made a mental note to do so as soon as possible—maybe later, on her way home from the supermarket.

Then her phone buzzed and her good intentions flew out the window. But the message wasn't from Ash. It was Sindhu, asking about her time in London. Maybe, instead of going to see Ash's parents, as some kind of aversion therapy, she should stop at Sindhu's. Her friend was as straightforward as they came. She would set her straight. But what would Gloria even say to her? *I flirted with Mary's daughter. We had a wonderful time. There was a moment in the taxi, just before I got out, that I thought I might kiss her.*

She munched on the last of her toast. Gloria wasn't going to say any of that to anyone. She would keep that very private— and momentary—inclination fully to herself for the rest of her life.

Gloria texted Sindhu back. She still had her phone in her hands and, as if on auto pilot, she scrolled to Ash's messages again. Should she text something? Ash hadn't replied to her last message. And why would she? More often than not, Gloria's own daughters didn't reply to her messages. Ash was an adult with a busy job and life—or so Gloria presumed. Why would she waste her time replying to Gloria now that their evening had ended? It had just been some harmless flirting. Best to leave it at that.

Chapter Eleven

"Are you humming Celine?" Lewis asked.

Ash hadn't been aware she'd been humming that particular tune, but damn, was it hard to get out of her head or what? No wonder it wormed its way out of her mouth at inopportune times like this, when Lewis was around to grill her about it.

"Got some romance planned for tonight by any chance?" He tapped a finger against his two o'clock shadow.

"Nope. You?"

"Yep. Jonathan's back from ten days in Asia." He waggled his eyebrows. "So you know what I'll be doing this weekend."

"No brunch invitation for your best friend then?" Ash sounded more disappointed than she actually was. She'd been toying with an idea of what to do over the weekend.

"I made things out to be much raunchier than they actually are, darling. Jonathan's parents are coming down for the day on Sunday. Of course, you're welcome to join us. In fact, as your best friend, I might even insist you do."

"No way. I'm out. You're on your own with your in-laws."

Ash had let Lewis lure her into spending time with Jonathan's family one too many times.

"Thanks for that. I'll remember it come bonus time." He winked at her good-naturedly. "Any other wild plans for the weekend apart from avoiding my in-laws?"

"I thought I'd go home. Spend some time with the family." Ash sipped from the espresso she had just made. Its intensity made her wince.

Lewis arched up an eyebrow. "Weren't you just home last weekend for Mary's big do?"

Ash nodded. "Mum's retired now. Maybe I feel it's my daughterly duty to spend more time with her."

"Do you?"

"Yes." It wasn't exactly true. Ash didn't mind spending more time with her family and she knew they'd welcome her with open arms, no matter how impromptu her visit. Her dad would take her to the pub and her mum would ask her to join her on her daily walk, and it would all be very low-key and undramatic and just simply *nice*. But that wasn't the real reason Ash was contemplating a visit to Murraywood.

Lewis squinted at her. He had a nose for things like this. He was the first person to ever dare ask Ash about the state of her marriage—long before Ash even realised how badly things were going with Charlotte.

"That party last weekend... did you run into an old flame or something? The first girl you ever loved? Nostalgia can be so overwhelming. Especially in the throes of heartbreak." He had broken out his compassionate newsreader voice.

Ash giggled like a teenage girl, then shook her head. "First of all, I'm really no longer in the throes of heartbreak. I'm fine. But, no, nothing like that. It was just a bunch of family at Mum's party."

"Not at the party itself then. But you were there all weekend. Plenty of opportunity to run into someone you used to lust after. That's what that song you were humming is all about, you know."

"I'm sorry to disappoint you," Ash said. "But I have no juicy gossip for you today. I've provided you with plenty of divorce drama over the past year, though."

"True." He took a step closer to her. "Still, this gay can tell, darling. You seem to be treading a little lighter in those comfortable shoes of yours this week."

"Maybe it's just time passing. Another week since the divorce. As you once said, I can't mope about it forever."

"Just promise me I'll be the first to hear about it when there is something to say."

"Who else would I tell first?"

"Baby, baby," Lewis sang. "When you whisper like that..." He let his off-key singing devolve into laughter and exited the kitchen.

Ash finished her espresso, then texted her mother that she was coming home this weekend.

♥

Ash woke up to unfamiliar sounds—or was it to the complete absence of any sound? Her flat in London was in a brand new building with triple glazing, but despite the quality of the insulation, it was never really quiet in her bedroom. More often than not, she woke to the loud blare of an ambulance or the invasive roar of a too-fast motorcycle.

She hadn't searched long for her new digs. She'd picked the building because it was walking distance from work. She'd had to make a swift decision. Flats in that building, because it was fancy and new and made a peculiar shape in the skyline, weren't available very often. Truth be told, she'd also taken it because if Charlotte had cast even one eye on it, she would have declared it utterly soulless.

65

Ash could hear Charlotte's voice in her head, "This is not a place to be lived in, Ash. Can't you feel that?" But Ash was very much living in her soulless flat, or at least spending the time there when she wasn't at work or out and about, which, most days, really only amounted to sleeping there. And being woken up by the incessant sounds of the city.

But not this morning. This morning, she stretched her limbs in her old bed, in her old room. Adrian's old bedroom had long been converted to a guest room, most often used by his own children, but Ash's room had remained pretty much intact, which she was grateful for. She and Charlotte had slept—and done plenty of other things—in this bed. Still, it was easy enough to replace the memories she'd made here with Charlotte with older ones, from when Ash was a teenager.

Ash was glad she'd taken the train last night, so she could wake up here this morning. Because weekend mornings were still the hardest when she had no one to wake up with any more, no one who turned towards her and automatically put a smile on her face. It had been a very long time since that had happened. The absence of that kind of warmth, a warmth she had long taken for granted, was easier to deal with in the bedroom of her youth. And all she had to do was go downstairs and she'd be greeted with all the warmth she needed. It was exactly what Ash had made the journey from London for—albeit not necessarily the one bestowed upon her by her family.

She put on socks and pulled a sweater over her pyjamas before padding down the stairs, into the kitchen. She was greeted by the smell of toast and eggs and coffee. Even though it would make her feel sluggish all day, Ash knew trying to fast would be futile this morning. Her mum wouldn't have it. She'd want to feed her. That was absolutely fine with Ash.

"Morning, darling." Her mum looked at the clock on the kitchen wall. "I heard you rumble upstairs so I popped in some toast."

Ash followed her mum's gaze. It was almost ten. She must have been really knackered.

"I slept so well."

"It must be the air here. It makes you sleep much deeper." Her mum put a steaming mug of coffee in front of her. "I'm so glad you're here, darling. Let's take the opportunity to plan our night out in London together."

Ash smiled at her mum and sipped from the coffee. It was nowhere near the strength of the double espressos she was used to, but she enjoyed the mildness of it, as she did the mildness of the entire morning. No alarm clocks. No work. No busy city streets. She didn't even have to shower. She could just hang out at the house all day and have her mother dote on her—Ash knew she loved it.

"Here's some toast," her mum said. "Eggs coming right up, just the way you like them."

"This is better than any hotel I've ever been to." Ash flashed her mum a wide smile. "Best watch it, Mum. I might come home every weekend if you keep this up."

"I wouldn't mind that one bit." Both their attention was drawn to the sounds of a car on the driveway, followed by a door slamming shut.

"Are you expecting a visitor?" Ash didn't really care that she was in her pyjamas. She was pretty sure that whoever was stopping by would be able to deal with her relaxed appearance.

Her mum had already walked to the kitchen door to peer through the glass. "It's Gloria. Lucky I just made a fresh pot of coffee."

Chapter Twelve

Gloria had wanted to stop at Mary and Alan's earlier in the week, but something had always come up. And then she and Ash had stopped texting—because what else was there to say, really?—and she no longer needed to get a brutal reality check. Until this morning. Now, she wasn't sure if she was here for a reality check or for something else entirely, like a small thread of connection with Ash. She could casually ask Mary how Ash was doing and, in the process, find out if Ash had mentioned their outing at all, and if so, if she'd said anything nice about her.

It was borderline childish behaviour, Gloria knew this, but there she stood, knocking on Mary and Alan's kitchen door. It wasn't that unusual for her to drop by. Mary always seemed to have a pot of coffee on—and she kept plenty of biscuits in the house for when her grandchildren visited.

Mary opened the door and, instantly, Gloria's gaze was drawn to the person sitting behind her at the kitchen table.

Ash was home.

Gloria hadn't banked on that. She wasn't prepared for it, but it didn't matter. She could handle herself. She pecked Mary on the cheek and gave Ash a quick wave.

"We have a surprise guest this weekend," Mary said.

"I can see that." Gloria couldn't help a full-on smile forming on her lips, as though they'd developed a mind of their own at the sight of Ash. She'd obviously only just got up. It made her look ten years younger than she was, in that jumper that was way too big for her, and with her very unkempt hair. "How are you, Ash?"

Gloria had no way of knowing if Ash had told Mary about their dinner. In theory, there was no reason at all why Ash wouldn't tell her parents. But in reality, if Gloria was being very honest with herself, there might be a very good reason to keep it hidden. Not just because of the flirting, which could easily be catalogued as harmless enough, as two single people just having a bit of innocent banter, but because of what it could imply. But maybe Ash didn't feel so self-conscious about any of this at all. After all, she was the one who had stopped replying to Gloria's messages. If it had been up to Gloria, they would have texted like that for the rest of the week. Every time her phone had buzzed since Wednesday evening, she'd hoped it was Ash. But it had always been someone else.

"Chuffed to be treated like a proper princess at Hotel Mummy." Ash held Gloria's gaze for an instant. If she was taken aback by Gloria's sudden appearance in her mother's kitchen, she didn't let on.

"I don't get to spoil you nearly enough." Mary gave her daughter's shoulder a quick squeeze. "Would you like some coffee, Gloria?" She pointed at the chair next to Ash. "Sit with us for a minute."

Gloria did as she was told and gladly accepted the offer of coffee. As Mary was busy fetching a cup, Gloria looked at Ash. Ash's reply was to just grin at her.

"Just a social call then?" Mary asked as she poured Gloria

and herself some coffee. She also planted a plate of eggs in front of Ash. Gloria guessed she wasn't fasting on weekend days then —knowledge that pleased her.

"I was just driving past and though I'd pop in. See how you're settling into retirement."

"Alan has fled the house already," Mary joked. "He's spending the morning working in Adrian's vegetable patch, with two young helpers by his side. He'll be exhausted when he gets back."

Gloria and Mary continued their conversation about this and that and while doing so, Gloria was very much aware of Ash's presence at the table. Ash didn't say anything. She piled eggs on a slice of toast, ate them, and drank coffee.

Gloria had been coming to the Cooper house for as long as she could remember—since Ash and Adrian had been children. Sitting there now it sort of felt like she had gone back in time, with the way Ash was being mothered by Mary, and how she silently observed their conversation, as if they were the grown-ups in the room and she the child who'd been told not to bother the adults.

Then Mary's phone started ringing.

"Guess who," she just said, then picked up.

Gloria took the opportunity to look at Ash again. She had finished her late breakfast and was sitting with one leg pulled up onto her chair.

"Are you okay?" Gloria whispered. "You're awfully quiet."

"Still waking up, I guess."

Mary ended her call. "Your father asks if you can drop by Adrian's before lunch and bring him that special kind of Super Glue he uses," Mary said to Ash.

"What does he need glue for? I thought they were working in the garden?" Ash even sounded a bit like a petulant teenager.

"One of the kids broke something," Mary said matter-of-factly.

Gloria remembered what it was like to have two children below the age of ten. Objects had a nasty habit of breaking all the time.

"Okay," Ash said.

Without thinking, Gloria said, "I'll give you a ride. Adrian lives around the corner from me."

"That's ever so nice of you, Gloria," Mary said. "You can get a ride back with your dad, Ash."

"I'd best put some clothes on then." Ash placed her dirty plate in the dishwasher and disappeared from the kitchen.

⚜

It was barely a ten-minute drive to Adrian's house, and Gloria had spent three of those minutes wondering what to say to Ash. She didn't really know where all of this sudden tension was coming from. She certainly hadn't banked on it when she'd offered Ash the ride.

"Do we... need to talk or something?" she finally asked.

Ash nodded. "Yeah, um..."

Gloria glanced at her. Ash was looking straight ahead.

"Do you still want to have dinner again?" Ash asked. "Or lunch. Or coffee." She turned to face Gloria.

Gloria concentrated as she overtook a cyclist and had to pay extra attention to the road, but she could feel the intensity of Ash's gaze on her. Gloria huffed out a nervous giggle. Every cell in her body wanted to scream yes.

"Do you want me to come to London again next week?" she asked.

"I'm here all weekend."

Gloria glanced at Ash. She was about to drive past her house. She made a quick decision. Before dropping Ash off at her brother's, she wanted to have a proper conversation with her. She pulled up in front of her house.

"Meaning?" Gloria asked, turning to Ash.

"We could meet up tomorrow," Ash said. "Or did you want to invite me in right now?" She sat there grinning.

"I'll drop you at Adrian's in a minute... I just, I don't really know what to think of any of this."

Ash sunk her teeth into her bottom lip for a moment, while she regarded Gloria intently. "I was hoping to run into you this weekend."

That didn't really ease Gloria's confusion, but she was pleased to hear it nonetheless. "Well, you did."

"I don't really know what's going on here either, Gloria. But I do know that I very much enjoyed your company on Wednesday. And that it was an experience worth repeating. Maybe we can talk about it when we see each other tomorrow?"

Ash wasn't going to take no for an answer—and it was also the very last answer Gloria wanted to give her. She mentally scanned her calendar for any activities tomorrow. It came up empty.

"I'm free tomorrow," she said. "Any time you can make it."

"How about I stop by on my way to the train station and then just take a later train back to London?"

"What time were you planning to go back?"

"After the Chelsea game," Ash said. "But I'll try to get out of that without disappointing my dad too much. I'll text you." Ash already had her hand on the door handle.

"Okay," Gloria said. "Don't you need a lift?"

"I'll walk. I need some time to process," Ash said.

Gloria needed some time to process as well, although she would never admit that out loud to anyone, contrary to what people of Ash's age did these days.

Chapter Thirteen

A sh almost had to physically fight off her brother, so dead set was he on driving her to the train station. She could have just told him that she was dropping by Gloria's before returning home, but something stopped her. She didn't want to have to deflect her brother's dozen questions about that. Moreover, Ash had an inkling that Adrian might put something together that she herself wasn't ready to admit to yet—most certainly not out loud.

She walked down the street. She'd reach the corner soon. Once there, she could still decide to go in the direction of the station. She could hop on a train and go home, the way she had told her family she would. Her dad hadn't seemed too disappointed when she'd told him she was going to see Adrian and the kids first and then head home from there. Spouting half-truths to her family wasn't as hard as she had expected. Maybe because of all the times she had told them in the not too distant past—straight-faced but dying a little inside—that she and Charlotte were doing just dandy.

She could even have told her mother about her little outing with Gloria. On the face of it, there was really nothing to it.

They'd chatted—and danced!—at the party. Gloria had told Ash she was planning a visit to London. They'd had dinner together. It sounded perfectly acceptable. There was nothing to it. Yet, Ash hadn't said a word to her mother. Because there *was* something to it. Something as of yet undefinable. Or no, if she was being truly honest with herself, and a moment of truth would soon be presenting itself when she came to the fork in the road, she knew exactly what was going on.

She liked Gloria. Not merely as an old friend of her mother's, but as something else. But none of this was all down to Ash. Granted, she could be misreading things spectacularly, but she knew in her gut that she wasn't. Her instinct told her that Gloria had felt something too. It had started at the party, maybe when they'd danced, and had continued on their night out. Ash had let the text messages between them peter out because she felt that she had no choice, no matter how alive a bit of flirting made her feel—it really didn't take much these days. But she had been the one to get on the train home on Friday. She was the one who had got herself invited over to Gloria's house this afternoon.

She reached the corner of the street and her legs just kept walking. Going straight to the station wasn't even an option. Gloria was expecting her. They had to talk about this. Surely, Gloria would make her see sense. She just needed a dose of reality. She was probably only getting sucked into this because she was so desperate for a distraction.

There loomed Gloria's house. Ash didn't recall ever having been inside. She'd never had any reason to. Gloria was a friend of her mother's. They'd known each other for decades. Ash focused on that. That would snap her out of it.

She went straight for the back door. An acquaintance of Adrian's might recognise her ringing the front doorbell and Ash didn't need anyone questioning her brother about that. She knocked and ran a hand through her hair while she waited to be let in. Her hair was getting long. She needed to make an appointment with her hairdresser this week. She made a mental note. Then the door swung open.

The smile on Gloria's lips was welcoming and warm. It felt like such a long time since someone had smiled at Ash like that, with so much possibility and kindness.

Gloria ushered her in. Ash looked around the kitchen. She noticed the typical country-style wooden cabinets she always disliked so much when she caught an episode of *Escape to the Country*.

"Come through." Gloria led them to the living room. "I made tea." They sat and Gloria poured tea and pushed the tray of biscuits in Ash's direction, but Ash ignored them. This all felt very formal. Ash pictured her mother sitting in this exact same spot, holding the same teacup—not ignoring the biscuits.

"How was the rest of your weekend?" Gloria asked.

"Fine. Mum really spoils me when I come home." She peered at Gloria over the rim of her cup. She was wearing the same shade of deep red lipstick she'd worn on Wednesday, but her attire was much more relaxed. She was dressed in jeans and a loose-fitting sweater.

"It's what mothers do when their daughters come home," Gloria said.

This reminded Ash of Gloria's daughters. The thought was another nail in the coffin of her desire—because wasn't that all it was? Just a silly bout of desire, ludicrously aimed at the first person who'd flirted with her in a while. Then magnified by the sheer surprise of it all. And here Ash sat, a slave to her own whim. The atmosphere that had slowly built between them at the restaurant was nowhere to be found. Not a flicker of it. So, in that respect, Ash was glad she'd come. It was working. Reality was hitting her around the head enough to snap her right out of it.

"Do they come home often? Your daughters?" Ash heard

herself ask even though she wasn't very interested in the answer.

"I don't think you came here to discuss my daughters' schedules," Gloria said.

"No." Ash shuffled around in the over-stuffed chair she was sitting in. "Um, yeah. I'm not sure I should have come. Yesterday, in the car, things got intense for a minute..."

"You said you were hoping to run into me this weekend." Gloria flashed that smile again. "And you did." When she said it like that, Ash had no trouble tapping into that feeling again.

Ash nodded. "I had also hoped it wouldn't have been at my mother's breakfast table." She put her teacup on its saucer.

"You looked adorable, Ash. You were awfully quiet, though." Gloria leaned back in her chair and slung one leg over the other.

"You'd come to see Mum. I didn't want to butt in."

"Hm." Gloria just nodded. "Did you tell anyone about having dinner with me?"

"No," Ash admitted.

"Why not?" Gloria sipped from her tea.

"It seemed... somehow weird to tell anyone in my family."

Gloria nodded as if she understood. "I told my closest friends, but it didn't feel like something I should share with Mary either."

"I'm glad you didn't."

"But, um, Ash... what is it that we're actually talking about here?" Gloria locked her gaze on Ash.

"You're asking me as if I'm the authority on this sort of thing?" Ash chuckled. She had to do something to break the mounting tension.

"Yesterday, before you got out of the car, you were the one who suggested we get together again."

"Did you not want that?" Ash was quick to say.

"What happens if we go to dinner again?" It was much more

78

an insinuation than it was a question. Gloria was at it again. She was flirting with Ash.

"Maybe there's only one way to find out." Ash couldn't stop herself. The dose of reality she'd been after was being relegated to the furthest confines of her mind.

"It's a bit early, but you're very welcome to stay for dinner tonight." Gloria had a way of lightening the mood.

"What should we do until then? Hang out?"

"*Hang out?*" Gloria arched up her eyebrows. "Does that actually mean just spend time together?"

Ash nodded. "Yeah. We can chat. Eat some biscuits. Drink more tea."

Gloria laughed now. "Oh, Ash. Do you know how hard it is to get a straight answer out of you?"

"Well, duh. Maybe because I'm a big old lesbian." Ash felt so silly then. She might as well have been back on the school playground, although there would hardly have been talk of how lesbian she was. Not back then.

"I'm so intrigued by you." Gloria's tone was sincere.

"Really?" Ash hadn't expected that kind of frank admission. Maybe because she herself excelled more in the cowardly art of coyness.

"Truly fascinated, to be honest." Gloria put her cup and saucer on the table between them. "Ever since you asked me to dance at Mary's party."

"I asked you?" Ash pulled her lips into an indecisive pout. "I believe it was the other way around."

"No." Gloria vehemently shook her head. "I don't drink, remember? I wouldn't even think about having that argument with me."

A blush rose hotly and swiftly up Ash's cheeks. She liked this very-sure-of-herself Gloria. Of course Gloria was right. Ash had asked her to dance, although she couldn't remember why. Maybe just because she had been there.

"There's really not that much that's intriguing about me." Ash reverted to being coy. She honestly had no idea how else to behave.

"You can't really be the judge of that yourself."

"Fair enough." Ash watched as Gloria refilled their tea cups. God, she could murder a very large pint right now. "I like your forward and very warm personality. It speaks to me. I find myself responding to it." Or unable not to respond to it, but that sounded too flirtatious, and Ash had already given away far too much. But it was the effect Gloria had on her.

"Does that mean you're staying for dinner?" Gloria's grin looked rather triumphant.

"I find myself quite unable to say no." Ash couldn't think of a better way to end her weekend than to spend the evening with Gloria.

"Then you might as well say yes." Gloria beamed her another smile.

Chapter Fourteen

✻❧✻

Gloria had expected to feel more out of her depth. But she didn't. That was the thing with Ash, she made Gloria feel so mighty good about herself. Like she was special. What Ash had said earlier about her personality had made Gloria want to jump right out of her chair and sit next to Ash. To touch her, put a hand on her arm, or ruffle her fingers through that perfectly styled hair of hers. She hadn't done that, of course. Just as she had refrained from trying to kiss her in the taxi. But that didn't mean she hadn't allowed her mind to wander. Since Ash had ended up in her car the day before, Gloria's mind had wandered and wandered, until Gloria had said stop—out loud.

She was preparing a salad to go with the pizza she'd put in the oven. She wasn't going to be cooking Ash a full-on healthy meal, although she did have the urge to feed her now that she was apparently eating everything presented to her.

Her levels of confusion were still exactly the same as yesterday. Gloria was perfectly willing to admit that she liked Ash and that she would like to get to know her better, but what did it say about her? What did it say about Ash that she was more than happy to linger at Gloria's house on a Sunday afternoon? Only that she had nothing better to do with her time, or was there something else to it? Was this friendship or was it already way past that? Gloria didn't speak to her friends the way she spoke to Ash. But she hadn't made a new friend in a while. Did budding friendships include flirting? And wasn't it different already simply because Ash liked women?

"You're tossing the hell out of that salad." Ash had ambled into the kitchen.

"I was lost in thought," Gloria admitted.

"Penny for them then." Ash's eyes rested on Gloria. She could be so smooth about things, make things sound as though they were utterly perfect for the moment. Gloria could just picture her in a club, a throng of doe-eyed women around her, hanging on Ash's every word. Because there really were no two ways about it. Ashley Cooper was gorgeous. This had been confirmed to Gloria when she'd clasped eyes on a just-out-of-bed Ash yesterday morning. Even with her hair all over the place and in an old pair of pyjamas, Ash had that thing about her that almost made it impossible for Gloria to look away.

"When did you know you were a lesbian?" Gloria wasn't about to give her thoughts away so easily.

Ash chuckled. "The better question would be: when did I not know? Look at me. I was born a tomboy. Whenever Mum tried to make me wear a skirt, I cried so hard the neighbours must have been tempted to call child protection services. I've never had the slightest thing for boys." She shrugged. "I've known for as long as I can remember."

"You're lucky Mary and Alan were so understanding then," Gloria said, because she thought it was what she should say. She noticed something in Ash tense up. Gloria racked her brain for any memories of her friends having issues with their oldest child being gay, but she couldn't find any.

"It's not a matter of luck. They're my parents. They're supposed to love me no matter what." She expelled a deep sigh. "It drives me nuts when someone says I got lucky. What do parents think when they procreate? That they get to choose how their child will be?" She was almost bristling now. Gloria had obviously hit a nerve.

"Okay," Gloria said. "I get what you're trying to say, but being a parent is complicated. It's not always as straightforward as children think it is."

Ash's eyes were still shooting daggers. Gloria didn't know why she was defending shitty parenting—apart from the fact that all parenting was, at one point or another, utterly shitty.

"Do you think it's 'complicated' for someone to beg her parents to come to her wedding just because she's marrying another woman?"

"No, Ash—"

But Ash wasn't done yet. "It's the grossest level of self-centredness human beings can achieve. You are not who I wanted you to be so I will not attend one of the most important events in your life. I don't care that it's the one day you stand up in front of your loved ones and declare your complete love for another person."

Gloria finally put down the spoon and fork she was tossing the salad with. "Is that what happened with Charlotte's parents?" Ash wouldn't have had such a strong reaction if it wasn't.

Ash nodded. "The worst part is that now that we're divorced, they get to gloat. They get to say 'I told you that marrying a woman wouldn't work out'." She shook her head in disgust. "It makes me so angry."

"Did they attend the wedding in the end?"

"Nope." Ash put her hands on the kitchen counter. Her fingers pressed so hard against the top that they were going white. "Do you have any idea what that does to a person? To have your parents disapprove of something so fundamental to you?" She relaxed her hands a little. "Of course, it didn't help Charlotte one bit that she was marrying me. She claimed she understood her parents and that she could accept it, but I could never let it go. There's just no way I can let something like that go." Ash painted on a wry smile. "One of the many differences between us."

"I'm sorry, Ash." With the way Ash could rage about her divorce—and marriage—Gloria's only conclusion was that Ash had not come to terms with any of it yet. "Do you have someone to talk to about all of this?"

"I have friends." The word friends seemed to spark something in her. "When you told *your* friends you were meeting me in London, how did they react?"

Gloria cocked her head. "Talk about a conversational U-turn."

"I don't want to talk about Charlotte. I really don't. I'm so utterly, completely, absolutely done with talking about Charlotte. Tell me something about you." She gave Gloria a crooked grin. "Delight me with a tale from your life."

"They teased me a little, because that's what friends do, I guess," Gloria said.

"Because you were going to dinner with me? Because I'm such a lez?"

Gloria chuckled. "They didn't put it like that."

"I am, though." Ash's little outburst earlier seemed to have melted away some of her defensiveness. "How do you feel about going out with a lesbian?" Ash's glare had softened to a playful glance.

"I wouldn't exactly call it going out. I'm having you over for dinner. I have Sindhu and Fiona over for dinner every Monday."

"Come on." Ash blinked slowly. "You know what I mean. It's not the same."

The oven started beeping. The pizza was ready.

"You might be saved by the bell now," Ash said. "But do not for a second think I'm letting you off the hook so easily."

Gloria took the pizza out of the oven. "Dinner's served."

Chapter Fifteen

W hile they ate, Ash decided that what she enjoyed almost as much as Gloria saying nice things about her, was teasing her. She didn't blush, but something in Gloria's cheeks twitched, and it made Ash melt a little bit more every time she could make it happen.

"You buy excellent frozen pizza." Ash wished she could wash it down with a sip of beer.

"It's a good skill to have with young daughters in the house."

"Thanks for having me over. I will return the favour some time, now that I know that the cooking standards are not very high." Ash couldn't help but chuckle at her own joke.

"Watch it." Gloria narrowed her eyes. "I'll cook you a proper meal one of these days." She paused. "Then again, I don't think you invited yourself over to sample my culinary skills."

Ash clasped a hand to her chest in fake surprise. "How dare you even insinuate such a thing."

"For someone so young, you have a terrible memory. Or is it just convenient for you to forget certain things you've said?"

"Hm." Ash acquiesced easily. "Maybe we should start having

the conversation I came over here to have." She tapped her watch. "Time is a-ticking."

"Since we just established that *you* invited yourself over here, why don't you start." Gloria heaped some salad onto her plate.

Ash sniggered. "It's quite hard to put into words. I've been here a while now and I still haven't found the right ones."

Gloria didn't make any attempt to eat the salad. She put down her cutlery and glanced at Ash. "To answer your earlier question," she said, "and to come back to what I also said earlier about finding you intriguing." She averted her gaze briefly. "Of course, in my case, that has to do with you being a lesbian."

Ash's hackles went up a fraction. She wasn't about to be anyone's experiment, not even the lovely Gloria's.

"Maybe..." Gloria continued. "If you weren't a lesbian, I wouldn't be so, um, drawn to shamelessly flirting with you."

"Now you make me wonder what my excuse is," Ash blurted out. She didn't want to give Gloria a hard time for being more honest than either one of them had been all afternoon.

"I wonder as well." Gloria narrowed her eyes further.

"I like you," Ash admitted. "I like spending time with you." She glanced at her watch again. "In fact, I don't want this day to end." Gloria had somehow done it again. She'd pushed Ash to a level of honesty that bordered on oversharing. But time really was ticking away. Ash would need to get to the train station soon if she wanted to catch the last train to London. She'd already been at Gloria's house much longer than she'd expected.

"Why me?" Gloria asked. Was she really feeling insecure? Or did she want Ash to continue to sing her praises? Ash found her gaze—definitely the former, then. "I don't mean to put you on the spot, Ash. I'm sorry." Gloria was obviously beyond flustered. Maybe Ash had said too much. "I just don't really know what to do about how I feel."

"How do you feel?"

"I feel like I want to spend more time with you, but at the same time, I also feel like that's the exact opposite of what I should be doing." Gloria expelled a small sigh.

"Yeah." Ash tried to find Gloria's gaze again, but it was harder now. Not only because Gloria kept looking away, but even more so because looking into Gloria's eyes right now could suddenly take on a whole other meaning. "Maybe..." She had given this some thought. Despite trying to dismiss it, Ash hadn't just ignored her attraction to Gloria. "...that's exactly why we want to, because we shouldn't."

Gloria shook her head rather adamantly. "No. That's not what it is for me. But I do understand that it might be for you."

Ash nodded. "You're curious." It sounded more like a statement than the question it was meant to be.

"Aren't you?" Gloria asked.

Ash huffed out a small chuckle. "You think I've never kissed a straight woman before?" *Argh.* She shouldn't have said that. It made her sound so smug—which was the opposite of what she felt at the moment—and she really shouldn't be uttering words like 'kissing' right now either.

"I make absolutely no assumptions about you. For all I know, you've done it all." Gloria peered at the wilting mountain of salad on her plate.

Ash chuckled again. She'd most certainly never kissed a woman like Gloria before. She hadn't kissed anyone in a very long time. She'd said the word and, now, it suddenly served as some sort of password that had unlocked something in her.

"How about..." Ash stood. Gloria looked up at her expectantly. Oh, God. It had been a split-second decision and it had quite possibly been the wrong one. Ash had intended to be all smooth and suave about it, but there was nothing suave about how she stood there now. If Gloria didn't meet her halfway, she was ready to bolt.

Ash witnessed how Gloria swallowed slowly, then pushed

herself out of her chair as well. Gloria took a step towards her, then leaned her hip against the table.

"Are you leaving?" Gloria asked, her voice low, the words barely coming out.

Ash shook her head. The tip of her tongue flashed over her bottom lip.

"Then what are you doing?" Gloria whispered.

Ash bridged the last of the distance between them. Now that Gloria was standing so close to her, all the reasons for this being a bad idea fell away. They didn't matter any longer. Ash's heart pounded against her ribcage as she slowly brought up her hand and touched a finger against Gloria's cheek. She looked deep into Gloria's eyes. Gloria didn't look away.

I think I might kiss you. Ash didn't say it out loud. What if Gloria pulled away? She didn't look like she might. Instead she was pushing her cheek against Ash's finger.

Then Gloria put her own hand over Ash's and moved it along her cheek, towards her lips. She touched her mouth briefly to the side of Ash's finger, but it was enough to move Ash into further action. She brought her other hand to the other side of Gloria's face and pulled her as close as she could possibly come.

Then, she finally did what she had come here to do in the first place. She pressed her lips against Gloria's. Ever so softly at first, exploring, feeling her like that for the very first time. Then Gloria's hand was on Ash's neck, drawing her nearer.

Ash still had her eyes open, but their faces were so close together she couldn't really make out anything apart from the texture of Gloria's skin. This was no time for looking, anyway. This was a time for feeling, for enjoying the sensation of Gloria replicating the motion, of their lips touching again, their lips slightly opening for each other. The first hot breath of air that passed so closely between them. Ash's heart wasn't just pounding in her chest any longer, it was somersaulting. It was doing a happy dance. And it was spurring her on to skate the tip of her tongue over Gloria's bottom lip.

Gloria pulled away a fraction, but Ash knew instinctively that she wasn't turning away from the kiss. She was getting a better vantage point. She wanted to get a proper look at Ash. Ash took the opportunity to do the same. Her lips still slightly agape, she peered at Gloria, and saw the intention all over her face. Ash had no idea what it felt like to kiss another woman for the first time when you were in your fifties, but if the look on Gloria's face was anything to go by, it must be pretty damn spectacular.

Gloria closed the gap between them and this time brought both her hands to the back of Ash's head. She pressed her lips against Ash's with much more insistence than before. When their mouths opened again, Ash let her tongue dart much further into Gloria's mouth. Gloria pushed her entire body against Ash's as she held her close.

Ash let herself be held like that and while the kiss was utterly delicious, it was the way Gloria pulled her so near to her that made her heart leap all the way into her throat.

Chapter Sixteen

G loria wondered if she was having a meltdown. Or a stroke. She'd had patients explain to her exactly what had happened to them—or what they recalled happening to them—when a blood vessel in their brain burst. This was not that. This was Gloria pulling Ash towards her. These were Gloria's lips, willingly opening up for Ash. This was Gloria's desire on full display.

Of course she had been curious, but this was much more than curiosity. Ash's soft, cool lips on hers sent a shiver all the way down her spine every single time they touched. If it had been just curiosity, it would be satisfied by now. Gloria would know what it felt like to kiss another woman—to kiss Ash. She could remove that from her bucket list and consider it done. But kissing Ash was not something she wanted to stop doing anytime soon. So she pulled Ash a little closer, even though she was already pressed all the way against her. Gloria could feel the swell of Ash's breasts against her own. She already had her hands in Ash's perfectly styled hair. She didn't seem to mind too much.

Gloria flicked her tongue over Ash's lips and into her mouth and she heard a tiny groan escape her throat. What was happening to her? She certainly wasn't under the influence of any substance—only under the influence of Ashley Cooper's easy intoxicating charm, perhaps. It must be a psychological thing then. Or another symptom of the menopause. But none of the books Gloria had read about the menopause, none of the endless conversations she'd had about it, had ever mentioned any of this. There had never been any warning that at some point in her mid-fifties, she'd be kissing another woman in her living room. And not just any woman. This was Mary and Alan's daughter. Oh, mother of Christ. No. No. No.

Gloria tried to pull away from Ash, but she was drawn right back to her, as if Ash's lips had suddenly gained magnetic powers. For the life of her, Gloria couldn't stop kissing Ash. She let one hand glide to the back of her neck, to feel Ash's soft skin there. The touch was exquisite.

Gloria concluded it could only be a case of temporary insanity. Only a little while longer, and it would all be over. Gloria would lock it all away and it would start to belong to the very recent past, then the somewhat further past, until it blended in with so many other unexpected things that had happened in her life.

But oh, good God, what was Ash doing? She kissed the corner of Gloria's mouth, her cheek, her lips trailing downwards. She found the sensitive skin of Gloria's neck and kissed her there. Gloria's tiny groan was growing louder. Her skin was hungry for this, her body so eager for another person's touch.

She lowered her chin, denying Ash further access to her neck. It had to be off limits. Gloria's temporary insanity would no longer be able to serve as an excuse if Ash continued doing what she was doing. If this was going to be temporary at all, and it had to be, Gloria would have to put a stop to it now.

Ash took a step back, her hands suddenly dangling uselessly beside her. Gloria hadn't completely snapped out of the spell Ash had put her under yet, because she reached for Ash's hand and held it in her own.

"Ash." She shook her head. "We have to stop."

Ash looked at the floor. She must know it too.

"I can't be kissing you," Gloria whispered, even though, now that she'd had a taste, it was all she wanted to do.

When Ash looked up, she appeared deflated, although a hint of hope still shimmered in her glance. Gloria didn't have the heart to squash that last dash of hope still alive in Ash, even though she had no choice. If she'd been so dead-set on kissing a woman, why couldn't she have chosen someone else? Why did it have to be Ash?

"You can do whatever you want, Gloria," Ash said, but there wasn't a lot of determination in her tone. She was a smart girl. She, too, knew that this was the last thing the two of them should be doing. And maybe Ash had been right earlier, when she'd claimed they couldn't resist it because it was wrong. Reverse psychology, that's what it was.

"No, I don't think that's true." Gloria let go of Ash's hand. She looked at her own empty hand.

"I'm not going to argue with you about anything like that right now." Gloria wasn't sure what Ash meant exactly. She would argue with her about it another time?

"It's getting late." Gloria put some distance between them. She felt her skin go cold as she did.

"I need to catch my train." Ash seemed to gather herself a bit more. She straightened her spine. "I'm glad we had that conversation." One last time, she locked her gaze firmly on Gloria's.

Gloria almost had to look away. Even though this was something they had done together, and it was only a kiss, Gloria somehow felt she had caused this. She shouldn't have flirted with a lesbian woman. What did she expect would happen? "Let's part on good terms, Ash, please." She found herself taking a step closer.

"We're on the best of terms." Ash's gaze softened a bit. "And you're a mighty good kisser, Gloria." She pulled those delicious lips of hers into a small, crooked grin. "I don't want to be a bitch about this. I don't want any bad feelings between us either." She sucked her bottom lip between her teeth. The sight of it made Gloria want to kiss her all over again. "I don't really know what to say right now because I'm not allowed to express what it is that I really want."

"I know." Gloria knew exactly what that felt like.

"We probably shouldn't see each other anymore. Not deliberately, anyway." Ash went all business-like on her. Her sudden matter-of-fact tone made Gloria's stomach twist. "No more texting."

"Okay." In the back of Gloria's mind a voice started screaming: "Not okay! Not okay at all!" She reached for Ash's hand again and Ash didn't pull away. Gloria took a step closer. "If I'm not going to see you again after this, then what's stopping me from kissing you again?"

Ash's earlier grin was back. She gave the kind of shrug that said, "Nothing at all."

And then Gloria was kissing Ash again. This time around, she could no longer claim a temporary loss of her faculties. They had both just decided this was a very bad idea. That they should go their separate ways. And they should. Gloria knew that they should. Not a single fibre of her being wanted it, but if Gloria had learnt one thing a long time ago, it was that the heart did not always get what it wanted. She had other matters to concern herself with than the desire beating in her heart, than the thrill chasing up her spine. She had two daughters who would never approve of this. She was friends with people who could make her life in this town miserable if they found out about this. Gloria wasn't about to give up the way she lead her life just because she enjoyed kissing Ash so much—and oh, how she did. She would just allow herself one more indulgence. One more kiss. And then it would stop. Forever.

Chapter Seventeen

A sh didn't feel as though she had a lot to lose, but she understood that it was very different for Gloria. She knew, in her bones, why this had to end tonight. It had been a nice fantasy. It had given her a few moments of divine distraction. Right now, it was giving her goosebumps across the expanse of her entire skin, because Ash hadn't been lying when she'd said that Gloria was a wonderful kisser. She put her hand on Gloria's throat and, under her thumb, Gloria's pulse beat wildly. Her own heartbeat thumped like crazy in her chest, as if to say: "If you stop, I'm not sure I will ever feel like this again."

Gloria leaned into the kiss with her entire body. Her fingertips dug into Ash's back. Her tongue danced inside Ash's mouth. Whenever she pulled back to take a deeper breath, for an instant, it felt like Gloria's lips didn't want to part from Ash's at all. They held on for one more delicious instant. A split second which held so much possibility, until their lips did break apart, and reality hit Ash hard in the face again.

But she would get over it. She would get on the train and not come home for a while. She'd got over far worse than kissing one of her mother's friends. If Ash played it right, this would be only a teeny blip on her emotional radar.

What it had taught her, however, was that Ash was ready to leave the sulking behind. She was done grieving for her marriage. It was over. Charlotte was never coming back—and Ash didn't want her to. But she did want this. She wanted someone to kiss, someone who would take away a day of stress with one single touch. Someone who could make her feel the way she was feeling now—the way Gloria was making her feel.

"Oh Christ." Gloria was the one who broke all physical contact between them. As if someone had given her an invisible cue, she stepped away from Ash. "If we don't stop now, I can no longer be held responsible for my actions." She had a wild glare in her eyes. Ash almost reacted to it—*almost*. She was tempted to close the distance between them again, but she didn't. Not because she didn't want to, but because she had to respect Gloria's decision. This wasn't Ash's call to make. They didn't have the same amount of skin in the game.

Still, it was hard for Ash to walk away. She took a breath and, for a split second, thought that she might have already found what she hadn't even started looking for yet. Someone new who made her feel like she was fully alive again, like everything was possible. Gloria had made her feel like that.

But it couldn't be Gloria. Ash had to take a moment to let that settle in again, because as she looked at Gloria standing there, her hair unruly and her lipstick smudged, the physical evidence of their attraction so glaringly obvious, it was so hard to walk away.

Ash had walked away before, but this was different. Leaving behind something that was already dead was a relief compared to walking out on something so exciting, so illicitly thrilling. Why did Gloria have to look so scrumptious? The top button of her blouse had come undone. Her neck had felt so delicate when Ash had kissed it earlier. For a few seconds, before she had rebuffed Ash's further advances, Gloria had tilted her head back, had allowed full access to the glorious curve of her neck, and Ash had wanted to spend hours exploring Gloria's skin, getting acquainted with what she liked and disliked.

"Ash," Gloria said. "You should really go now."

Ash nodded. "Yeah." She reached for Gloria—she wanted to kiss her one last time—but Gloria stepped aside, leaving the path to the door wide open.

Ash grabbed her stuff and walked to the door. She looked behind one last time. Gloria was looking away, as though she couldn't bear the sight of Ash leaving.

"Goodbye, Gloria," Ash said, her voice unravelling, like she was doing on the inside. She hurried outside. She looked around for any familiar cars, but the street was quiet. It was Sunday evening and a soft rain had started to fall. Most people were cocooning inside with their loved ones. Ash pictured Adrian and Lizzie and her nephews huddled over a board game under the gentle light of a lamp.

A few minutes ago, she'd been kissing Gloria. She'd been over the moon—under Gloria's spell. Now, she was walking away from it all and a heaviness descended on her shoulders. It coiled in the pit of her stomach. She braced herself against the rain, which started to come down harder.

What was Gloria thinking right now? Was she relieved that Ash had left? What had she meant that if they didn't stop, she could no longer be held responsible for her actions? Did she want Ash that much? Did she want to go further? Did she want to do any of the things that Ash didn't even allow herself to consider? Although, of course, in an unguarded moment here and there, she had allowed herself to consider them. She had pictured Gloria naked in front of her—and what she would do to her if she were. She had allowed herself to dream of waking up next to a smiling Gloria, her hair all wild like her smile could be, after a night of doing to her exactly as she pleased.

But in the distance the station loomed, lit up in the falling darkness. Ash would walk into its glowing light, take that train, and not look back.

Chapter Eighteen

After Ash had left, Gloria's glance had fallen on a picture of George. Maybe that was exactly what she needed right now—to be reminded of the woman that she was before she kissed Ash. She picked up the frame and held the picture close to her face. But however close she held it, George would never be there again. He was not coming back to talk some sense into her. She would have to do that all by herself.

Or could she talk to Sindhu about this? Fiona was out of the question, Gloria concluded, but Sindhu might be understanding. She might even mock Gloria to the point that she would start to understand how foolish she had been for even giving into the desire to kiss Ash in the first place.

She put down the picture frame and looked at the photo of her two daughters next to it. They came home using words like 'woke' and 'lit' and Gloria tried to keep up with this new vocabulary as best she could—she always did her best for her children —but she couldn't expect the same from them. She couldn't expect an eighteen-year-old and a twenty-one-year-old to be so 'woke' and so 'lit' to understand why their mother was kissing another woman. Or could she? Gloria tried to imagine telling them—but telling them what? So far, there really was nothing to tell. Yet, it was the prospect of having to tell her daughters that was holding her back the most. That had stopped her from letting Ash kiss her again and again.

Gloria replaced the photo and brought a finger to her lips, to the spot where, only minutes ago, Ash's lips had touched hers. The sheer exquisiteness of it had taken her by surprise. The way something had sparked deep inside of her. Gloria had expected to feel something, of course. A small flare of longing, or perhaps not even longing. More something along the lines she'd felt when she'd kissed the last man she'd been on a date with. His name was Robert and he had kissed Gloria, and what Gloria remembered most of all was how it had felt to want to be kissed. When Robert had pressed his lips against hers, she knew what he wanted: her. She hadn't felt the same desire for him, although being kissed by him had been pleasant enough.

With Ash, it was different. Yes, Ash's desire for her was impossible to ignore, but what had coursed through her more than anything else, was how much she wanted Ash. How the softness of her kiss, so light and tender at first, had woken her own desire. That had been the biggest surprise of all. It was probably the shock of that, that had made Gloria pull away in the end, that had made her ask Ash to leave.

Right now, she was of half a mind to run after Ash. To dash through the rain to the train station and demand that Ash come back home with her. But then what? They could keep it a secret for a while. But what about after that? When the secret had run its course? Ash would always be Mary and Alan's daughter. Gloria had two daughters of her own and the mere memory of them with their first boyfriends still made her feel a little uneasy. It was a visceral, parental anxiety that she hoped would go away once her daughters found their place in life, and someone to walk with them on their path.

Ash was much older, but Gloria had an inkling that such parental protectiveness never really went away. She remembered Alan at the party last week and how he had spoken about Ash, how much worry she'd picked up in his voice.

Simply put, it was all much too complicated. Gloria had made the right decision when she'd asked Ash to go. It was better to leave it at that. She'd always have the memory of the kiss. That was something. It erased the previous memory of her last kiss, the one with Robert. It obliterated the very last remnant of it. Ash's kiss had been superior in every conceivable way. How she'd put her hand against Gloria's throat. It made her swallow hard just thinking about it. She put her hand where Ash's hand had been. She felt her pulse pick up speed. Because there was also the undeniable fact that Ash was a woman. Gloria wasn't so sure she would be able to wait until Sindhu and Fiona came by tomorrow to talk about this. She was already planning to ask Sindhu if she could stop by earlier, but how would she make it through the next twenty-four hours with all but Ash on her mind? Without being able to properly process this?

But she would wait. She would deal with it. Because if she couldn't even deal with the next twenty-four hours of keeping her feelings inside, how on earth would she cope with cutting Ash out of her life completely, forever?

She checked her watch. On Sundays, there were only two trains going to London every hour. Had Ash made the previous one or was she stuck in the station, waiting another half hour for the next one? Gloria pictured her on the train, on her way home, moving further away from Gloria.

She glanced at the picture of George again. She tried to imagine him saying something to her but he'd been gone for so long, it was sometimes hard to properly recall what his voice sounded like. She could easily remember exact things he'd said like often-used phrases and the way he spoke to the girls, but new words were much harder to attribute to him. She shook her head at the frame and walked away. She went into the kitchen to clean up the plates and other things that were left scattered on the table, abandoned because they'd started kissing.

Chapter Nineteen

"I know exactly what you need," Lewis said.

Ash gave him a sceptical look. No one on earth could possibly know what she needed right now. Yes, she had just told him about kissing Gloria, but that didn't change much about Lewis's knowledge of the situation. Besides, Ash knew Lewis and she knew what he would say next. She held up her hand. "No. Whatever it is you're going to say, I especially don't need *that*."

"So. Bloody. Judgemental." Lewis shook his head. "You're not even giving me a chance."

Ash sucked on the paper straw in her gin and tonic. The blasted thing was going to mush already, but at least she could drink all the alcohol she wanted now. "Fine. If you have to say it, say it. But I'm not you, nor am I one of your gay-boy friends. What *I* need differs greatly from what *you* might need in my situation."

"Are you saying that I'm not capable of taking into account the subtleties of a woman's psyche?" Lewis sounded mock-offended.

Ash sighed. She wasn't feeling the banter tonight. She drank again. She couldn't get Gloria out of her head. Taking the train back to London had been but a symbolic gesture. The desire to take that train right back and knock on Gloria's door seemed to only grow stronger.

"Okay, listen to me." Lewis drummed on the table with his fingertips. "You want what you can't have. It's human nature. At least, don't beat yourself up over that."

Ash nodded. It was a surprising statement from Lewis. Yet, she still believed that what he was going to suggest next was that she have a one-night stand. While Ash had no moral objections against spending one night with someone, and she firmly believed that everyone should just do what they wanted, she wasn't a one-night stand kind of girl. Neither was she the kind to kiss someone she barely knew. Although she had kissed Gloria. But it didn't feel as though she barely knew her. That was the problem.

"Okay. I won't." Ash smiled at her friend, hoping that the smile on her lips would make something inside her smile as well.

"Taking that into account, in order to no longer want what you can't have, maybe you should just have it."

"What?" Ash knotted her brows together. They had made sure they'd eaten a decent meal before going out for drinks, but Lewis wasn't making much sense right now.

"One night, darling." Lewis shot her a triumphant smile. "To get it all out of your system."

"One night with Gloria?" Ash nearly spit out the words, so ridiculous did they sound.

"Yes," Lewis confirmed, as though he'd just made the most lucrative business deal.

"Out of the question." Ash drank some more, because when Lewis put it so adamantly, it sounded quite alluring. She needed to squash the images his suggestion created in her brain instantly, before she allowed them to take some sort of hold on her. "That is a truly bad idea."

"I don't think it is." Of course Lewis thought it a good idea. He had come up with it. No guy could be so in love with his own ideas as Lewis. Over the years they'd worked together, Ash had become the person to shoot down his most out-there ones —to be the voice of reason in the crazy town that Lewis's brain sometimes inhabited. "Purely from a psychological viewpoint, you can't fault it." He remained adamant.

"Maybe in theory, but this is real life. We are real people, with real emotions."

"What's the alternative, though?" Lewis asked. "You've met someone you like. You want more. Are you really going to deny yourself that?"

"It's not a question of denying myself." Even though Ash really wanted him to be wrong, Lewis was right on some level. Ash couldn't decide. She wanted him to be both wrong and right. She didn't know what she wanted. She was all over the place. "It's a question of nipping it all in the bud before it can become anything."

"Maybe you're looking at this all wrong." Lewis leaned over the small table. "Maybe you need to take off your romantic girl-goggles." He held up his hand, as though he already knew that Ash would protest. "You may think that if you and Gloria start some sort of torrid affair, you'll fall in love and want to be together forever. But do you know that the possibility of that occurring is actually quite rare? I'm not saying that it will never happen to you again, darling, because I'm sure that it will. But not with Gloria. Statistically, it's highly unlikely. So, for now, why don't you just let it be what it wants to be? Just go for it, enjoy it, let it peter out, and then move on." Lewis knocked back the last of his drink.

"Make her my transitional person?" Ash followed his example and downed her drink.

Lewis nodded and, without saying anything further, headed for the bar. This was going to be one of those nights.

While she waited for him to come back, Ash considered his words. They could make sense. For Ash to fall in love with someone again, a number of requirements would need to be met. She liked Gloria, but it wasn't very probable that she would fall head over heels in love with her. She had utterly enjoyed kissing her, and she did want more, but that didn't mean she'd be wanting to marry Gloria in a few years' time.

"Here you go." Lewis returned with two fresh gin and tonics. "What say you?"

"I say I've had too much to drink already." Ash sipped from her drink.

"You and me both, darling, but aren't we allowed to indulge once in a while? I spent all of Sunday listening to all the changes my mother-in-law suggested we make to the house... and you kissed your mother's friend." He winked at Ash. "We're allowed to take a load off."

"Have I told you that Gloria doesn't drink?" Ash said.

Lewis made a dismissive gesture with his hand. "Then it's a done deal. You will never fall for this woman, Ash. Just sleep with her already."

Ash shook her head at Lewis's ignorant remark. As if she drank so much it was inconceivable that she could be with a recovering alcoholic. But this was not the time to confront Lewis about that. This was, however, the time to consider the very last bit of what he'd just said.

Just sleep with her already.

Ash might not be a one-night stand kind of girl, but there was no use fooling herself. After that kiss, all she wanted was to sleep with Gloria. There was, however, one fatal flaw in Lewis's plan.

"You're just assuming she'll want to sleep with me as well."

"Of course I am, darling." The more cocktails he ingested, the more Lewis called Ash 'darling'. "Why wouldn't she?"

This sounded so ridiculous to Ash that she started giggling like a schoolgirl. "So many reasons, *darling*," Ash said.

"There's only one way to find out." Lewis tried to straighten his posture, but failed miserably. This was that one last drink too many. "Ask her."

"Sure," Ash played along. "I'll just text her here and now and ask if she wants to come over to spend the night with me some time soon."

Lewis nodded vigorously. "That's exactly what you should do."

Ash tried to shake her head just as vehemently. This was the worst plan ever conceived. If she ever had the great fortune of sleeping with Gloria, it would not happen after Ash had drunk-texted her. Ash wouldn't want it to happen that way; Gloria wouldn't stand for it.

"No, darling. But here's what I will do." Ash took out her phone. "I'm getting us an Uber so we can go home and sleep this off."

Chapter Twenty

"Did you swap shifts this weekend?" Sindhu asked as she poured herself a glass of wine.

"No." Once in a while, the craving for a nice glass of wine utterly overwhelmed Gloria. Tonight was one of those nights.

"You didn't reply to my text," Sindhu said matter-of-factly. "That usually only happens when you're working."

Gloria remembered the text message she'd only seen late Sunday evening, after Ash had left, when she'd been toying with her phone—and the idea of texting Ash. Gloria poured herself another glass of sparkling water.

"What did you get up to this weekend then?"

For the life of her, Gloria couldn't keep her eyes off the wine being tipped into Sindhu's mouth.

"This and that." She swallowed hard.

"Are you all right?" Sindhu looked at the wine glass in her hand. "Are you no longer okay with me drinking in your house? Because I don't have to."

"It's difficult today," Gloria admitted, because if she couldn't tell her best friend it was hard, then who could she tell?

"Okay." Sindhu got up and went into the kitchen with the

bottle and her glass. She came back with an empty glass and filled it with sparkling water. "Sorry about that."

"Don't apologise, please. Clearly, it's not you. It's me."

"That old chestnut." Sindhu sent her an encouraging smile. "Did something happen? Why are you having such a hard time?"

"Something *did* happen." Gloria took a deep breath. "Ash... um." She flicked an imaginary piece of dust from the armrest of the sofa. "Ash came over yesterday and..." Gloria shook her head, as though she herself couldn't believe it either. "We kissed. She kissed me. I kissed her. I don't even know. But we kissed." She pointed at the spot next to the dining table. "Right there, and..." The words died in her throat.

"Wow." Sindhu shuffled her feet. "Okay... back up a bit. Last week, you went to London and had dinner with her. This weekend, she came here? And you kissed? You're going to have to catch me up because I think I missed some of what happened in between."

Gloria told her friend about the flirting and the confusion and the impromptu dinner that had ultimately led to the kiss.

"My gosh." Sindhu sipped from her glass of water.

Gloria felt guilty for Sindhu having to put the wine away. It was easier than succumbing to all the other feelings of guilt running through her.

"Okay." Sindhu shifted her feet again. "I wasn't expecting that, so you have to give me a minute."

"Take all the time you need." Gloria was still processing all the events herself.

"You kissed Mary's daughter," Sindhu said next, making Gloria want to bury her head in her hands. "How old is she?"

"Forty-two," Gloria was quick to say.

"Hardly an impressionable young woman you could be seen as taking advantage of," Sindhu said in her matter-of-fact way.

"Hardly." More the other way around, Gloria thought. In

Ash's presence, she was the one who felt so much younger and up for anything. Completely under Ash's spell.

"And you decided to not see each other again?" Sindhu's demeanour relaxed a bit again. She stretched her legs and crossed her ankles. "Why?"

"Because she's Mary and Alan's daughter," Gloria blurted out. "And because she's a woman." She didn't know why Ash being a woman was of less importance to her. "Last I checked, I wasn't really into women in that way."

"When did you last check?" Sindhu even managed a smile now.

Gloria chuckled. "Last night, I guess. The result was not what I expected it to be."

"What was it like?" Sindhu's eyes narrowed.

Gloria sighed. "I'm trying not to think about that any longer."

"That good, eh?"

Gloria just nodded.

"Then you'd be a fool to end it before it's begun."

"No. I have to disagree with that." She wasn't only trying to convince Sindhu. Gloria needed some convincing herself. When she'd let Ash leave, it had immediately felt like the wrong decision. "I've lived in Murraywood all my life. I don't want to become *that person* in this town."

"What person?" Sindhu shrugged. It was easy for her to shrug it off. Her husband was still alive and she could go home to him after leaving here and return to her heteronormative, perfectly acceptable life.

"The one who runs off with her friends' child."

"Ash is *not* a child. She's in her forties. She's old enough to be divorced, for crying out loud. And she doesn't even live here." Why was Sindhu getting so worked up, anyway? What skin did she have in this game?

"I live here. I work here," Gloria said. "My girls come home here." When she said it out loud like that, it all made sense to Gloria again. The kiss would just have to remain that. Her life as she knew it was on the line. She'd worked so hard to put herself back together, to make herself strong again. She wasn't going to throw all that stability out of the window for a fling with another woman.

"I understand it's difficult, but there are other things to take into consideration." Sindhu's body tensed again. Was she about to give a speech? "What about your happiness? I'm not talking about the sense of normalcy you've managed to reach again after George died. The cruise control you operate on." She straightened her posture and looked into Gloria's eyes. "Don't you think you deserve a little more than that?"

"It's not a matter of deserving it or not." Something gnawed at Gloria as she said the words, even though they were sensible and reasonable—they were the embodiment of what she was trying to be. "Of course I deserve to fall in love again, but if I do, I don't want it to be complicated like this."

"Wow," Sindhu said on a chuckle. "I never said anything about falling in love."

Gloria shook off the comment. "You know what I mean."

"Yeah, I do. But I would be a bad friend if I told you that you're right, Gloria. It's my duty to tell you that this is worth pursuing."

"That's easy for you to say, though."

"Granted. Although not as easy as it would be to agree with you." She tilted her head. "Good thing Fiona's not here, because she would be saying all the things that you want to hear right now. But I won't do that."

Gloria had to agree about Fiona's expected stance on the whole thing. "Why are you so adamant about this?"

"Because... in every single person's life, there comes a time like this. A defining point. A time when you have to make a decision that can change the course of your life. This is it for

you. Or not. I don't know because I don't have a crystal ball."
She heaved a big sigh. "A few years ago..." Sindhu reached for
her glass of water, but she didn't drink from it. "We had this
consultant in at work." She briefly met Gloria's gaze. "I didn't
tell you about it, because... I don't know why. Maybe I should
have. But I felt like I already knew what you were going to say."

Sindhu had Gloria on the edge of her seat now. Was she
trying to say that she had fallen for another man?

"His name was Brian and we really hit it off. He was quite a
few years younger than me. Single. Not afraid to show how he
felt about me." She gave a nervous chuckle. "Nothing happened
in the end, but I still wonder to this day... you know?"

"Oh my God, Sindhu, why didn't you confide in me? This is
the sort of stuff you bring to your best friends." Gloria tried to
hide the disappointment in her voice.

"I was... embarrassed, perhaps? I don't know. It was on the
tip of my tongue many times, but I could never really say the
words. It felt as though if I actually spoke to someone about it,
it would become too real. I mean, I love Martin. We have a
great life together. We have our children. We'll be grandparents
soon. It was just a flare of passion. An escapist sort of fantasy
that I only allowed myself to indulge in theoretically. But you
don't have any of that standing in your way, Gloria."

"How many years ago was this?" Gloria wasn't going to let
this go so easily.

"About eight," Sindhu said. "You'd just joined AA and Sally
was going through a difficult time. You really didn't need your
best friend confessing to a silly crush on a co-worker."

Gloria shook her head. "Christ. Where's Brian now?" Of
course Gloria would have listened to her friend. She would have
been there for her.

"He woefully overcharged us and left, as consultants do."
Sindhu could heartily laugh about it now. Gloria laughed with
her until a silence fell.

"How long have we known each other?" Sindhu asked after a while.

"How long have we not known each other?" Sindhu and Gloria had been friends since they'd gone to Murraywood's secondary school together.

"Exactly my point." Sindhu drank and then pushed the water glass away from her, as though disgusted with it. "Go for what makes you feel alive inside, Gloria. Really. You will always be able to come up with a bunch of reasons not to, but if they pale in comparison to the reasons why you should, then what are we even debating?"

"I'm not sure that's the case." Gloria's pulse picked up speed. Maybe permission from a friend was all she needed to pluck up the courage to see Ash again. Or maybe what felt like permission was actually just foolishness multiplied by two. Maybe she was getting too caught up in Sindhu's enthusiasm and she shouldn't make her friend any promises tonight.

"Of course you're not sure, but you know what will pain the hell out of me when I go home later?" Sindhu rested her dark gaze on Gloria. "That you'll be sitting here, alone in your house, pining for Ash, too scared to go after something that could potentially bring you so much joy."

"Potentially..." Gloria repeated, because wasn't that the key word here?

"Text her," Sindhu said. "Tell her you want to see her again."

"What?" Gloria shook her head. "No."

"Then give me your phone so I can do it for you. I'm serious, Gloria. I'm not leaving here until you've texted Ash."

"You're very welcome to sleep in one of the girls' rooms. There's plenty of space." Gloria arched up her eyebrows. The thought of texting Ash, of the tiny sliver of contact with her, made her heart pound in her throat.

"I have no intention of sleeping. I'll just be nagging you the entire time." Sindhu tried a smile now. "Just do it. You think you have so much to lose, but you really don't."

"I'm not sure what that says about how you see me and my life."

"I think you're perfectly content. I think you could go on like this forever and just keep sailing life's inevitable ebbs and flows until the day you die. But what if there's something more out there? I know you're scared more than anything, after what happened to George. I completely and utterly understand that. Which is another reason why I stand by my advice. This is exactly why you need your friends in times like these. To take away some of that fear. Because no matter what happens, I will always be here, Gloria. I will always be your friend." She gave a small nod. "Tell me honestly... what's the worst that can happen after what has already happened to you?"

When did Sindhu become so philosophical? Was it reminiscing about her mid-life infatuation with Brian that had brought it about? One thing Gloria knew for sure; Sindhu would always be there for her. She had all the proof of that she needed. Should she trust her friend on this?

"It's just a bloody text, Gloria." Sindhu's voice was a bit sterner now. "I don't know if I need to manage your expectations, but it may very well turn out to be nothing."

Agitation curled in Gloria's stomach. *Nothing? After last night's kiss?* Gloria didn't think so. She glanced at her phone on the coffee table. She took a deep breath and reached for it.

Chapter Twenty-One

Ash wondered how drunk she actually was. When her phone buzzed, of course she had hoped it would be a text from Gloria, but when it turned out to be exactly that, she had started to question her sanity. Unfortunately, there was no one else she could ask whether her eyes were betraying her. She'd dropped off Lewis into Jonathan's arms half an hour ago. She was alone in her sparsely decorated flat. She had one mirror above the sink in the bathroom. Maybe she should check herself in that, see if she could ascertain her mental fitness from her mirror image.

Instead, she took a bottle of water out of the fridge and gulped it down. Then she looked at the text message again.

Can I see you again? Gloria xo

Gloria had signed the message. Did she think Ash had deleted her name from her phone already? Did she believe it would only take Ash all of twenty-four hours to forget about that kiss? Correction: those kisses. Those heavenly moments when their lips met, when their souls connected. *Oh shit.* Ash must still be quite tipsy.

But the message was real.

Lewis had said earlier it was unlikely that she and Gloria would develop actual feelings for each other. This was just some friskiness. Post-divorce horniness in Ash's case and mid-life madness in Gloria's. Maybe she should just get it out of her system and make Gloria her 'transitional person'. Then she could be done with the whole thing and truly move on. In fact, maybe a night with Gloria was all she needed. It could give her back the confidence she'd lost after the divorce. A night with a straight woman who hadn't slept with anyone in years... Ash knew how utterly arrogant it sounded, but she was convinced she could blow Gloria's mind. It represented an easy fix. The connection was already there. They had already kissed. Undeniable chemistry between them had been established. All Ash had to do was swoop in. All she had to do was say yes.

So she did.

I would really like that.

She tried to picture Gloria getting the message. What her face would look like when she read Ash's reply. Was it lighting up right this minute, the way the screen of her phone had done when the message came in? At least Ash was sure that Gloria hadn't asked her while under the influence of alcohol. Gloria was always sober. But did that automatically mean she was always doing the right thing? Of course not. Only yesterday, they had decided that seeing each other again was decidedly not the right thing to do, yet Gloria had instigated contact. Ash's phone buzzed again.

Friday evening? London?

Friday evening. The start of the weekend. Ash didn't care if she already had plans—she'd cancel them. They'd most definitely be work-related, because she didn't seem to have that many friends left after the divorce. It felt as if all the people she and Charlotte had known together, had taken her ex-wife's side —apart from Lewis. Lewis always took her side. Even if Ash had cheated on Charlotte for years, Lewis would still have taken her side. He was that kind of friend.

Of course Lewis could be full of shit as much as the next person, and he most certainly didn't hold all the answers to life's difficult questions, but Ash trusted him with her life. In this particular case, she also really wanted to believe what he had said. *One night.* The words pulsed like neon signs in her brain. Or a dirty weekend. No, no, no. That was Ash's problem. She always wanted to take things one step further than agreed.

It was one of Charlotte's eternal gripes with her. So Ash had learnt to rein in the impulse. When they were out, Ash had swallowed the 'one more drink' that always sat at the tip of her tongue. When she was working late, which she often did, following a foreign market or deep into research on a company that fascinated her so much she lost track of time, she had set a timer on her phone so she never left work later than nine, even though, most nights, she could easily have worked until midnight.

Ash shook off the memories and texted back.

Come to my place?

At first, she hadn't typed the question mark, because she didn't want it to be a question. She wanted Gloria to come to her flat. She didn't want to waste any time going out for alcohol-free cocktails and exchanging lingering looks over a long meal. But she didn't want to be too presumptuous. Even though Gloria had contacted her again, Ash couldn't just assume that they were after the same thing. In fact, it would be a grave mistake to assume that. But what could Gloria be after? Argh. It was only Monday night. Ash would be obsessing over that question all week. Her phone pinged again.

Does that imply bringing an overnight bag?

Jesus Christ. Gloria had picked up the flirting right where they'd left it, so it seemed. What had got into her? Whatever it was, arousal already hummed underneath Ash's skin. The memory of the kiss was still potent, the energy it had created still vibrant inside of her. When she closed her eyes and focused, she could feel Gloria's lips on hers again. Ash replied.

It's always better to be prepared...

After that, Gloria's text message flirting seemed to run out of steam. Or had she come to her senses? They exchanged a couple more texts of a more practical nature, agreeing on a time to meet, and Ash texting her address. But, at the end of the day, Ash had a date with Gloria in her calendar. The texting back and forth had sobered her up and she was too wired to go straight to bed. Gloria would be coming here, into her home. She scanned her living room and, as though she'd never really looked at it before, instantly noticed all its faults. The walls were too bare, the furniture too generic, the fittings too sleek. It didn't feel lived-in, like Gloria's house, where two children had grown up, where a family had lived.

The state of Ash's flat reflected the state of her life. She had only been living there for a couple of months. She hadn't taken the time to make it more cosy and warm. Because, these days, Ash didn't have to set a timer on her phone any longer in order to spend quality time with her wife. This place looked exactly like Ash imagined a recent divorcee's home would look like. It was what she was. Still, she made a mental note to order some patterned curtains and to hang up some of the pictures that were still in a box in the guest bedroom.

Maybe this whole thing with Gloria could kick her divorced arse back into gear and she could start really living again, instead of pretending to have a life.

Chapter Twenty-Two

G loria got off the train and walked out of the station, her overnight bag in her hand. Not for the first time, she asked herself what the hell she was doing. What had she allowed Sindhu to talk her into? But she could pretend this was all Sindhu's doing all she wanted. Deep down, she knew it wasn't true. Gloria wanted to be here more than anything.

She glanced at the throng of people as they made their way, snake-like, to the tube entrance. Briefly, she considered taking a cab to Ash's place, but she'd made the mistake of getting into a London taxi on a Friday night before—and had missed the first half hour of *Mamma Mia* because of it. Gloria followed the crowd and it felt like she was swallowed up and lifted to the tube platform, onto the train, and spat out at her stop. How did so many people bear living like this? Gloria couldn't face that kind of commute every single day, packed like a sardine into a tube carriage, with no protection against the smells, the sounds and the sights all those people created.

When she emerged above ground, she took a deep breath. The street was busy and she had to step aside to let a bunch of hurrying people move past. She looked up. Ash had told her she would notice her building immediately as she got out of the underground—and she'd been right.

It was taller than any of the other buildings around and one side was curved like a wave. It certainly looked sleek—and it screamed money. Gloria crossed the street and pressed the button with Ash's name on the large shiny panel next to the front door. She heard a buzz and the door opened. She felt a little out of place as she entered the lobby, which was like the entrance of the fanciest hotel. A bank of gleaming lifts was to her right. She half-expected the doors to open to a uniformed attendant who would press the right floor button for her, but Gloria was alone in the lift.

She was zipped up to the fourteenth floor so quickly, her ears hurt. When the doors opened, Ash greeted her with a wide smile. She stood leaning against the frame of the open door to her flat, looking quite satisfied with herself. Other than that, she looked exactly as stunning as Gloria remembered her.

"You made it." Ash stood aside and ushered Gloria inside. After she shut the door behind them, as if this could only happen behind closed doors, Ash took Gloria's free hand, pulled her near, and kissed her—not really on the lips but not really on the cheek either. As though she couldn't decide. Or maybe she didn't want to presume anything. "You brought a bag."

Once again, Gloria wondered if she had taken leave of her faculties. But she knew when it had happened. She could pinpoint the exact moment her body had decided that it wanted more of Ash Cooper. When Ash had kissed her once more, after they'd already decided that they should never kiss again. It wasn't just the defiance against the rule they'd just set, although that had been quite glorious in its own way. It was the way Ash had kissed her, as though, despite their decision, she also knew that a kiss like that could never be the last one between them.

Heat sparked beneath Gloria's skin as she put her bag down and shrugged off her jacket. She glanced around Ash's place. It looked very Ash-like. Glossy and angular. A little stark, perhaps.

"So this is where you live." Gloria was drawn towards the window and its view over the Thames. This place must cost a fortune. "Quite the bachelorette pad." She turned back to Ash.

Ash gave a low chuckle. "I can walk to work from here. That was really the clincher for me."

"Do you know your neighbours?" There were blocks of flats in Murraywood, of course. Some of Gloria's patients lived in them. But none of them came close to this extravagance.

"I only moved in four months ago."

"Is that a no?"

"It's not like back home. People don't necessarily greet each other, not even if they live in the same building." Ash was wearing another pair of skinny jeans with a colourfully striped jumper on top. She looked relaxed enough. "Can I get you anything? Water? Juice? Virgin mojito?"

"I'm fine." Gloria chewed the inside of her bottom lip. Just a few minutes in Ash's company were enough to have that charge running through her flesh again. They should talk, but Gloria didn't really know where to start. Or what to say, for that matter.

Surprise. I couldn't stay away from you.

"Let's sit," Ash said.

For all its luxurious fittings and breathtaking view, the flat was small, and it only took Gloria two steps to reach the sofa.

"You must have been surprised when I texted." Gloria tried to tame a strand of curly hair that kept falling in front of her eyes, but gave up on it.

"Yes and no." Ash sat next to her, but left enough space to be respectable—whatever that meant.

"I almost forgot how hard it is to get a straight answer out of you."

"That's as straight as it's going to get with me." Ash grinned as though she knew some sort of secret she hadn't made Gloria privy to yet.

"I told Sindhu about our kiss," Gloria said, her neck suddenly warming as though she was about to have a hot flush. "She had a real go at me when I said that we'd decided we couldn't see each other anymore after that."

"Yeah." Ash nodded as though she knew exactly what Gloria meant. Maybe she did. Maybe she felt the exact same way.

"So here I am."

"Here you are." Ash's grin had morphed into a wide smile. Her hair was just as sculpted as always. Her eyes sparkled. "I'm glad you're here. *Really* glad."

"It's not where I had expected to be tonight." Gloria stopped herself from reaching out her hand to Ash's. The tension between them was rising. Now she was sitting next to Ash, in the flesh, all she wanted to do was kiss her again. Feel Ash's lips on hers and see where it took them. Because ever since they'd texted on Monday night, Gloria had let her imagination run wild. At first, she'd tried to be chaste about it, until she'd had a chat with herself and asked who on earth she was trying to kid? Surely not herself? There was only one reason for Gloria to come to Ash's flat on a Friday evening, with an overnight bag and nothing planned for the entire weekend after. Once Gloria had settled on that, there was no stopping her fantasies.

Ash expelled some air, filling the silence between them. Gloria was usually very adept at turning uncomfortable silences into pleasant enough conversation, but this silence was of an entirely different nature. It was brimming with anticipation. With the question of who would make the first move. Did Gloria have to take charge? She had taken the first step when she'd texted Ash. But in her fantasies, it had always been Ash who had come for her. It made sense that way in her head. Still,

Gloria wasn't used to waiting for someone else to make the first move. She wasn't used to any of this.

Ash cast her glance to Gloria's face. She looked her in the eye. "It's been quite hard to not think about you all the time."

Ash was certainly direct. "What have you been thinking?"

One side of Ash's mouth quirked up. "Mostly that I want to kiss you again." She paused. "*Mostly*."

Gloria's lips tingled at the mere thought of Ash kissing her again. She was also intrigued by Ash's use of the word 'mostly'. What were the other thoughts Ash had been having? And how aligned were they with Gloria's? There really was only one way to find out. This was, in a sense, an exploration trip. She was here to explore her feelings. She was on an adventure. Perhaps even a joyride. But she would only know if she inched closer. So she did.

Ash met her halfway—the sofa wasn't very long anyway.

"I wasn't sure you'd want to kiss me again," Gloria said. She had no clue why. It was the truth, although not the entire truth. There was no denying the reciprocity of the feelings behind the kiss they had shared on Sunday. However, she'd believed Ash would have come to her senses by now. When she had texted her on Monday, a tiny, very afraid part of her, had hoped that Ash would be the wiser one. So that she wouldn't have to take the train to London to explore more of that red-hot sensation in the pit of her stomach, of the desire that had sprouted in her unbidden—although wasn't that how it always was with desire?

"I do want to kiss you again." Ash was sitting so close now, Gloria could feel the warmth of her breath.

Ash tilted her head to the right. Gloria bridged the last of the gap between them. With an inward sigh of relief, as though she'd finally found what she'd been looking for all her life, Gloria touched her lips to Ash's. It was as though no time had passed since they'd last kissed. All Gloria's good intentions were instantly erased, while all other intentions, all the endless images she had conjured up before falling asleep, sprang to life.

As if she'd never done anything else than kiss other women, Gloria opened her lips to Ash, and welcomed her tongue inside her mouth.

Chapter Twenty-Three

A sh caught her breath. Gloria had barely arrived and already a hot thickness seemed to make its way through her veins. But what had she expected—polite conversation from a safe distance?

She looked into Gloria's eyes. All that was raging inside of her was reflected right there, in Gloria's glance. Ash brought up her hand and cupped Gloria's jaw, ran her thumb underneath her bottom lip. Ash hadn't had a single bite to eat all day and it felt like every atom in her body was vibrating, not with hunger, but with desire for Gloria.

Ash moved her thumb upwards and skimmed it across Gloria's lip. Gloria opened her mouth another fraction. She flashed the tip of her tongue against the pad of Ash's thumb, and it was a jolt to Ash's system. All the lust she'd managed to keep at bay, all the pent-up feelings for Gloria she'd tried to rationalise herself out of, were congregating in the pit of her stomach, starting up a fire that could only be put out in one very particular way. Ash needed to have Gloria. She craved to touch every last inch of her skin. And this desire was not fuelled by her previous arrogance or even by the misguided notion that one night with her would ever be enough.

Ash tilted Gloria's face towards her and kissed her again. Softly at first, but not for long. Her yearning was too strong for a gentle kiss. She couldn't keep her tongue in check when she let it dart into Gloria's mouth. Her hands were already travelling down, one of them resting on the skin of Gloria's neck. But Ash had to ask. She had to know for absolute certain before she could completely lose herself in this—in Gloria.

She pulled away. "This is why you came here, right?" She managed to squeeze the words out despite the lust in her throat.

"I want you." Gloria's voice was clear, almost calm. "I want this," she said.

Ash briefly stood, never losing eye contact with Gloria, and straddled Gloria's lap. She swallowed hard. Ash's intimate life had been so totally taken up by thoughts of the divorce and her marriage falling apart, there hadn't been an inch of room left for desire. Feelings like this had been banished from her life while she did penance for the failure of her relationship with Charlotte. She hadn't met a single woman who had made her feel a fraction of what she was feeling now. It was as though the months— years—of passion that she had denied herself were now catching up with her. And it was all directed at Gloria.

Ash pushed Gloria's head against the backrest of the sofa. She kissed her while she let her hands—and lust—wander freely this time. She didn't need permission anymore. Her lips travelled down Gloria's neck—and Gloria didn't push her away this time. Her fingertips dugs into Ash's back as she drew her near.

A deep throb built between Ash's legs. Was Gloria feeling the same? This was her first time with a woman. Ash tried very hard to feel some reverence for that, but she had too much red-hot lust coursing through her veins. She wasn't sure how gentle she could be with Gloria when she was feeling like this. When her entire body had transformed into a means to an end. When all she could think of was exposing Gloria's skin to her gaze, seeing her breasts for the first time, touching her tongue to her nipples.

Ash tried to take another breath. *Oh, fuck it.* She hoisted her sweater over her head and tossed it away. Then she went straight for the buttons on Gloria's blouse.

She could feel Gloria watch her. She continued undoing the buttons, but looked at Gloria. Her grin was lopsided. Her eyes sparkled. What had she thought about on the train over here? Had her mind been suffused by images like this? Had she predicted this? Or had she practiced caution? There was no sign of caution on Gloria's face as she reached behind Ash's back and unhooked her bra.

The grin was no longer there when Gloria stared at Ash's naked breasts. It was more a look of concentration. Or something else. Ash didn't know. All she knew was that the pulse between her legs was picking up speed and intensity.

She parted the sides of Gloria's blouse. Her bra was pitch black against her cream-coloured skin. Ash wanted to touch the swell of Gloria's breast, but her access was blocked by Gloria's hands, reaching for Ash's breasts.

Gloria exhaled deeply as her hands connected. She scooped Ash's breasts into her palms hungrily, her thumbs flicking Ash's nipples.

She cast her glance up at Ash for a split second, but then focused all her attention on Ash's breasts again. Ash knew she had to give her this moment. She had to keep her own desire in check. She and Gloria were doing this together but they were not in the same stage of their journey. Ash tried to be aware of that, but if Gloria kept playing with her nipples like that, kept moving her soft hands over her breasts like that, she wasn't sure how long she could extend her that courtesy. Because Ash's need was so much higher than she had deemed possible. She

135

couldn't remember when she'd last felt her sanity hang in the balance if she didn't do something about the ramped-up lust in her flesh. Her hands trembled when she dragged the back of her fingers against the side of Gloria's bra—a garment that urgently needed to come off.

When Ash had dreamed of this moment, she had always— always—let Gloria come first. But now that it was happening, she wasn't sure it would be possible. Ash might not be physically capable of holding it back, so hot was the want bubbling beneath her skin. Every time Gloria touched her—and her hands were all over her now—the desire was ramped up.

Then Gloria pushed herself towards Ash and, with Ash's breasts still cupped in her hands, she flashed her tongue over Ash's nipple. Electricity shot up Ash's spine, its sparks not fading, but collecting at the junction of her thighs. Ash had falsely believed Gloria would be timid, simply because she had never done this before. But Gloria was not timid by nature and her nature very much shone through right now. Ash glanced down at Gloria's luscious crown of curls, obscuring the view of Gloria's tongue on her nipples. Ash wanted to see. She always had done. She wanted to see everything. If she could, she'd catalogue every last sensual act Gloria bestowed on her body, but her mind was racing too much with lust. If only Ash could get that first crash of desire out of the way. Until she did, she wouldn't be in her right mind—she wouldn't be able to give Gloria exactly what she wanted to give her and in the manner that she had envisioned it.

So Ash flicked open the button of her jeans, as though, at this very moment in her life, it was the only viable choice she had.

She'd do it herself if Gloria didn't.

"I need you to—" Ash believed she said, but she wasn't sure she had produced any sound. It was irrelevant, because one of Gloria's hands had moved from Ash's breast to the zipper of her jeans. She lowered it, then looked up at Ash. Gloria caressed Ash's nipple.

Ash realised her tight jeans would only be an impediment to what she wanted to happen, so she quickly stood up, wriggled out of them, and slipped back into her position on top of Gloria. "Please," she begged. Because this wasn't normal speech. This was flat-out begging. A hoarse demand wrung from her throat.

Ash watched how Gloria's hand slipped inside her underwear. The panel of her knickers was moist with her desire and when Gloria's finger connected with her clit, even with the barrier of the fabric, Ash's breath caught in her throat.

Gloria started circling Ash's clit very slowly, while she kept her nipple locked between her thumb and forefinger.

"Oh fuck," Ash groaned, when Gloria's lips found her other nipple again, and sucked it into the hardest peak.

Ash's clit pulsed against her knickers. She bucked forwards, wanting to catch more of Gloria's touch there. In response, Gloria's finger retreated. But only for a few seconds. Then, Ash felt it slide under the fabric of her underwear, and all the way down. She sat up a little straighter so she could feel as much of Gloria's caress in her current position.

She steadied herself by placing a hand on Gloria's shoulder. It felt like Gloria had completely latched onto her, tethered herself to Ash.

Gloria's fingers slithered through the wetness that had gathered between Ash's legs. Ash's only regret was that she couldn't see Gloria's face, but she would make up for that later. She had other things on her mind right now. Like dealing with the lust riding through her veins, trembling in her flesh.

Gloria circled her clit again and this time, there was no fabric to lessen the impact of her touch. All the lust that had been building in Ash's flesh pooled at the point of contact between her clit and Gloria's fingers. Ash didn't resist. This was exactly what she wanted. It was what she needed more than anything. To quench this desire, this sense of agitation under her skin, the lust that had morphed into unease because she couldn't possibly have what she wanted. Well, she was having it now. Gloria's fingers slid against her clit. Her tongue was busy with her nipple. Ash pressed her fingertips deep into Gloria's flesh as she rode the very first climax that Gloria had given her. She had no way of knowing for certain, of course, but she imagined it wouldn't be the last. Not by a long shot.

Chapter Twenty-Four

✿

"Did you just—?" Gloria had to ask.

Ash sat panting on top of her. "Bloody hell," she gasped. She smiled down at Gloria, then nodded. "Oh, fuck." Her smile transformed into a grin.

Gloria felt as though she'd barely walked in the door—and already this had happened. Had she really made Ash come? Because she'd been worried about that. Not overtly, not in a way that she would admit to her mirror image when she questioned herself, but in the back of her mind, it had nagged at her. Sure, Gloria was a woman and she knew perfectly well how everything worked. But still.

As it turned out, she needn't have worried for one single second. She flashed Ash a generous smile back.

Gloria glanced at the hand she had just withdrawn from Ash's knickers. Her fingers glistened with Ash's wetness. The sight of it made her nipples strain against her bra. Everything about Ash was just so deeply sensual. The fact that she had just come on her finger, moved Gloria deeply. It wasn't just incredulity. It was so much more than that. But Gloria pushed those feelings to the side for now. She'd have plenty of time to process later. Right now, she needed to focus on something else.

She glanced at Ash, then back at her fingers. Ash's eyes glittered with satisfaction, or something else—Gloria couldn't read her mind. She could, however, read the excitement that crossed Ash's face when Gloria brought her hand to her lips and slipped her still-wet fingers in her mouth. She sucked Ash's thick juices off.

"Oh, fuck," Ash said again. "Give me a breather, please."

Gloria slipped her fingers from her mouth. "Take all the time you need." She couldn't help but smile again.

"I'm so fucking hot for you," Ash whispered, as though she'd already taken the time Gloria had just granted her, and was ready for another round. Maybe she was.

"I noticed." Underneath the desire that pulsed through her flesh, Gloria sensed a feeling of invincibility coursing through her. Ash might have had the first orgasm, but Gloria had received something far more valuable. This sort of satisfaction had become completely foreign to her. Gloria hadn't had the faintest inkling that making another woman climax would make her feel like this.

"It's not how I thought our evening would progress." Ash kept straddling her, kept gazing at her from her vantage point above Gloria's face.

Gloria brought her hands to Ash's behind and cupped her butt cheeks. She could do that now. So many boundaries between them had been shattered already. "How did you think it would go?" Amusement coloured her voice.

"Not like this," was all Ash said.

"Did you want to play a game of cards or something? Monopoly?" Gloria teased.

"If you tease me now, I guarantee that you will pay for it later." Ash finally managed to put a bit of edge back into her voice.

"Can't wait." Gloria didn't know she had reserves of sexual confidence hidden inside her like that. It was also true that she really couldn't wait. Nervousness about showing her body to Ash, and qualms about how it would react under her touch, took a backseat to the flagrant lust prickling her skin. Her nipples still stood tight against the cups of her bra. Deep inside her, an unfamiliar warmth had started spreading.

"You say that now." Ash's cheeks dimpled with mischief.

Gloria responded by pulling Ash to her again, one hand remaining on her behind, the other in her neck. Oh, the soft heat of Ash's skin. It radiated off her. Although it was nothing compared to the wet hotness Gloria had encountered when she'd slipped her hand inside Ash's underwear. The thought sent a wave of heat straight to her clit.

"I'm done talking now," Gloria whispered in Ash's ear.

Gloria felt Ash's chin bob against her neck as she nodded. "I haven't even shown you my bedroom yet."

Gloria wasn't entirely sure she still had the strength in her legs to make it to another room. But the big window was a little disconcerting, even though all she could see through it from this angle were clouds and water. A touch more privacy might be worth it.

Ash moved off her and extended her hand to Gloria. She led them into a room of which the window was already covered by a closed curtain. Gloria didn't have time to give Ash's bedroom a once-over. Ash closed the door and pushed Gloria against it. Her naked breasts pressed against Gloria's, which were still covered by her bra.

As though reading her mind, Ash said, "Let's get that off you." With sudden tenderness, she reached behind Gloria's back, her fingers light and feathery on her skin.

After the bra was disposed of, Ash took a step back, as though wanting to inspect Gloria's body.

"You're beautiful." Ash sounded as though she'd never

meant anything more in her life. Then she gently cupped Gloria's breasts and kissed her.

Gloria melted into the kiss. All the agitation that was still coursing through her evaporated. She was half-naked in Ash's bedroom. It was crystal clear what was going to happen next. Ash had just told her she was beautiful. Ash had just ridden herself to a swift climax on Gloria's fingers. Even though, in any other room in the world, this might be the wrong thing to do next, right now, in Ash's bedroom, it felt like the only right thing. The only logical conclusion. Gloria knew with unparalleled certainty that she wasn't doing this with Ash because it was forbidden, she was here because she wanted Ash so fiercely, no amount of reasoning could stop her.

"Come." Ash tugged her gently towards the bed. Before they lay down, they stepped out of the rest of their clothes, leaving only their knickers on.

Gloria lay on her back; Ash on top of her. Ash found her ear, and whispered, "I'm going to make you come so hard."

Gloria believed every single word of that statement. Already, her clit was pulsing eagerly. Then, as though suddenly snapped back into the here and now, Gloria remembered that she no longer possessed all the physical advantages of Ash's youth. She might not get wet. Did she have to tell Ash about that?

"What's wrong?" Ash sounded worried. "Was that too forward?"

"No, Ash. Not at all. But... I'm in my fifties." She cleared her throat. "Do you have any... lube?"

Ash grinned, as though what Gloria had just said didn't faze her in the slightest. "I do." Her grin softened into a smile. "But don't worry about that now."

"Okay." It was as easy as that for Gloria to put her trust in Ash.

Ash planted a soft kiss on Gloria's cheek. Her hand meandered down, over her neck, to her breast. Lazily, Ash circled a fingertip around Gloria's nipple.

Gloria's nipple tightened. Her reaction was unmistakable. Of course it was, because it was inevitable. To be touched like this was such a treat. She glanced down at Ash's hand. Her fingers were long and graceful. There was a tenderness about Ash that her everyday demeanour wouldn't necessarily suggest. Her skin was so deliciously tan against Gloria's—kissably tan. God, how Gloria wanted to kiss every last inch of Ash's skin. How she wanted to explore her the way Ash was exploring her now with her finger. She only lightly grazed the hard peak of Gloria's nipple every so often. The warmth that had started to spread from somewhere deep in Gloria's core was turning into a blazing fire.

It wasn't just Ash's action, the soft, divine touch of her finger. It was having this kind of attention bestowed on her that was igniting the fire beneath Gloria's skin the most, that was sending pulse after pulse of deep heat between her legs. This kind of affection had been absent from Gloria's life for such a long time, she had no idea her body craved it that much. She had forgotten, pushed it away—despite the couple of half-hearted attempts at dating she had made. She had pretended this was no longer something that was on the cards for her. And it had been easy. It truly hadn't been difficult to give up this physical, this sensual side of her. Because she'd also believed that there was no-one out there who could make her feel like this. And now, Ash was merely skating a finger along her skin and Gloria was almost beside herself.

Ash slipped off her and kissed her neck again, then trailed a path of moist kisses to her other nipple, which she promptly sucked between her lips.

Gloria's back arched. Even her skin felt hungry for this, tightening into goosebumps.

Ash's tongue swept over Gloria's nipple while her hand glided down. She traced a few zigzags over Gloria's belly, then drew a straight line just above the elastic of her knickers. Ash's finger sliding closer to where all the heat in her body seemed to be pooling right now, made Gloria gasp for air. Because that was what it felt like now. Like her desire was so big, so ramped up, that it had knocked the wind out of her with its sheer force.

Ash's finger slid down her inner thigh. God, why was Gloria still wearing her underwear? She wanted to be totally naked with Ash. She wanted the intimacy that came from that.

Ash kissed Gloria's nipple one last time, found her gaze, then resumed her path of kisses on the way down. She kissed and licked Gloria's skin, which grew a million times more sensitive every single second, until she had somehow ended up between Gloria's legs.

With her gaze firmly fixed on Gloria, Ash slid her fingertip from where it had been driving Gloria crazy on her thigh, to just next to her clit. And still those damn knickers were in the way. Ash didn't seem to mind. She circled Gloria's clit over her underwear and it felt as though Gloria suddenly wasn't wearing them anymore.

Her lips parted and she emitted a low groan. Gloria tried to keep eye contact with Ash, but not all of her facial muscles wanted to cooperate with that intention.

Ash kept circling her clit, and Gloria felt it strain against the material. Never in her life had she wanted a piece of fabric off her more. But Ash was taking her time. She was in no hurry —she was obviously enjoying this.

Then, Ash bent forwards, breaking eye contact, and before Gloria had time to process any of what was happening, Ash's hot mouth was on her clit. But still the knickers were in the way. Oh fuck, Ash was licking her and Gloria was so aroused by now she might as well not be wearing underwear anymore. Ash's tongue was so hot and heavy on her, Gloria was gasping for air again. It was suddenly everywhere. Gloria had no way of knowing if her knickers had been made so wet by her own arousal or by Ash's mouth, but the moistness was rendering the protective quality of the fabric useless. Still, Gloria wanted nothing more than the touch of Ash's tongue directly on her flesh—no barriers between her throbbing self and Ash.

The wet hotness disappeared from between her legs and was replaced by the coolness of air. Ash's finger hooked underneath the gusset of her knickers as she shoved them aside. Gloria glanced down and she saw Ash looking at her down there. She seemed utterly entranced. The rush of air elicited a new kind of arousal from Gloria, which only added to her already sky-high anticipation. Her blood hummed with desire. Her clit pulsed as if it might explode with want if it didn't meet Ash's tongue soon.

With her underwear still drawn to the side, Ash leaned forwards again. It took another few seconds. First, there was Ash's hot breath, then, at last, Ash's tongue touched down. Gently, at first, but not for long. As though Ash was also over-come with the soaring fire that raged in Gloria's flesh, she licked Gloria—as though she had suddenly lost all restraints again, like earlier, on the sofa, when she had unbuttoned her jeans.

Ash's talented tongue swept along Gloria's heat, slid inside her, and lapped mercilessly along her clit.

Gloria fisted the sheet. Her toes curled. Ash had been right. There truly was nothing to worry about. Ash's platinum-blonde hair moved ever so slightly between Gloria's legs. By the sight of it, it was impossible to tell the tumult Ash's actions were causing Gloria. The fire had spread—had taken over and pillaged her. It had imploded from within Gloria's bones and left nothing but hot, raw desire in its wake. A need so deep, it caught Gloria by surprise. Then, there it was, not unannounced, but astonishing nonetheless. Her muscles spasmed. Her hips rose to push her sex against Ash's mouth. Gloria came under Ash's tongue. The fire turned into bone-deep satisfaction, into a gratitude that was impossible to articulate into words. All she could do was pull Ash into her arms and hold her so close there was not an inch of space left between their bodies.

Chapter Twenty-Five

A sh checked her alarm clock for the umpteenth time since Gloria had fallen asleep next to her. It was late when Gloria's body had finally relented, when she'd pleaded with Ash to let her get some much-needed rest. Ash had been reluctant, because despite all the physical activity she and Gloria had engaged in, she knew she wouldn't be able to sleep. Having Gloria awake in her bed was not a problem. Having her asleep next to her was.

Because now there was only darkness and Gloria's soft, steady breath, reminding her—as if that was even still necessary —of the question growing ever bigger in her mind: *what is this?*

Walking away from Gloria would not be easy. Not from this. She couldn't explain it. Nor could she excuse herself for inviting Gloria over. She should have ignored her text message. But it had been so easy, so seductive, to say yes. Especially after Lewis had planted the one-night thought into her head. Ash didn't do one-night stands for the very simple reason that she wasn't capable of them. She needed so much more than a few exchanged glances, some sultry looks and flirty banter. She had never understood any of that. So how had she put it in her head that sharing one night with Gloria would ever be enough? That notion had flown out the window as soon as Gloria had stepped inside her flat. It had been solidified when Ash hadn't been able to stop herself from straddling Gloria and—for crying out loud! —coming when the woman had barely been inside her home for fifteen minutes. What was that all about? How had her body betrayed her like that? She was meant to be the one with all the swagger. She had already pre-excused herself that bout of arrogance. She needed it, to take away some of the tenderness that naturally seemed to exist between them.

And oh, to have Gloria come all over her tongue like that. To have her clasp Ash's head between her strong thighs. How was she supposed to forget about that? And now, as she turned on her side and lay there, looking at Gloria and how she slept so soundly, so free of worries, so beautifully, she was certain that, unless Gloria fled her flat for some reason tomorrow morning, they would do it all over again—and again.

Gloria's curly hair was strewn over the pillow. Ash had to stop herself from touching it, from reaching for the soothing softness of it. How had all of this even happened? Had there been a logical sequence of events that had made it possible or could this be attributed to some form of temporary madness, accidentally shared by two people both in need of something very particular at the same time? Had Gloria seen her need? Her pain? Because Ash had seen none of that in Gloria.

She focused on Gloria's breath and tried to steady her heart rate by breathing in the same rhythm. It wasn't working. Ash's heart was beating inside her chest like a caged animal trying desperately to get out.

So she just kept looking at Gloria, at whatever features she could make out in the feeble light of the night. The upturned tip of her nose. The soft curve of her lips. One arm underneath the pillow, the other in front of her, as though still, even in her sleep, wanting to capture a piece of Ash.

Lewis's words turned and tumbled in her head.

It's highly unlikely you will fall for each other.

Yeah right. But Ash had believed him, because she'd needed an excuse, and any excuse would have been enough. Ash reckoned she'd fallen for Gloria on the night of her mother's party, when she'd danced with her. Or maybe when she'd watched her go around the floor with Uncle Jim and she could have sworn that Gloria had looked at her in a way that conveyed something... It was impossible to tell what exactly now. But it had been the beginning of this. Like when, under the right circumstances, the tiniest seed can grow into the biggest tree.

❧

Ash woke with a start. When had she fallen asleep? And how? The last thing she remembered was her heart pounding furiously, its relentless beat keeping her awake. Had her body surrendered and taken her mind with it when it drifted into sleep? Ash shook the thought from her. She knew from many nights of experience what the darkness of her bedroom did to her thoughts. They turned to a blackness that usually fled in the bright light of the morning. Especially on this glorious morning. Literally glorious, because Gloria was lying beside her, already awake, a wide smile on her gorgeous lips.

"Finally," she whispered. "I've been awake for hours."

Ash didn't believe her. "Then why didn't you get up?" Ash's stomach growled. She hadn't eaten anything all day yesterday. "Bring me breakfast in bed?" She scooted closer to Gloria, already so eager to bask in the warmth of her skin.

"I didn't know that was allowed. You have some funny eating habits, Ash. I wasn't even offered dinner last night." Gloria looked as though she didn't mind that all.

"I'll take you out to brunch." After all the calories they'd burnt last night, Ash could do with a large fry-up. "There's a great place just around the corner."

"Do you mean we have to leave your flat? This bed?" Gloria's hand cupped Ash's buttock.

"We don't have to." Ash suddenly didn't feel like leaving the flat either. "I have food in the fridge. I can make you eggs and toast and whatever else you want."

Gloria sucked her bottom lip between her teeth before she spoke again. "You looked so angelic when you were sleeping." With a tenderness that would have floored Ash if she hadn't been lying down, Gloria stroked her cheek with the back of her hand. "I kept wondering what you were dreaming of."

"Last night was a bit of a dream." Ash pushed her cheek into Gloria's caress, like a cat would do.

"It was special all right." Gloria huffed out something between a breath and a chuckle. "Fuck, Ash." A slight lift of her eyebrows. "You did ask me if that was what I had come here for, and I said yes, but I had no idea it would be like that."

Ash grabbed Gloria's hand and brought it to her mouth. She turned it around and kissed Gloria's palm.

"Ever since I've woken up..." Gloria sounded less confident. "I've been wondering if it was the same for you. I mean, this is very new for me. Maybe that's why it was so mind-blowing. So utterly incredible to be with you. I don't know. It has really shaken me, because... I somehow feel that was someone else last night, who did all those things with you. Yet, at the same time, I have strangely never felt more like myself."

Ash kissed Gloria's palm again. She pressed her nose into her hand and inhaled her scent. She smelled of sex, of the many orgasms they'd shared last night. "It was incredible for me as well." Under the sheets, Ash hooked her ankle behind Gloria's calf. "I don't know what this is between us either, but it feels so good."

"It's not something you regret the morning after?" Gloria

smiled at her now, as though she was already certain about Ash's reply.

"Fuck no." Ash kissed the inside of Gloria's wrist.

"We should probably have some sort of conversation." Gloria's hand cupped Ash's buttock with a bit more force. "And I really, really, really need to eat something now. Otherwise, I might start on you." Ash felt Gloria's body convulse against her as she laughed.

"Be my guest," Ash said, before finding Gloria's lips to kiss.

Chapter Twenty-Six

❧

After Gloria had showered, and entered the kitchen fully dressed—thank goodness for that overnight bag—she found a plate of scrambled eggs and toast waiting for her on the kitchen island.

Just like in the bathroom, most of the kitchen countertops were made of marble.

"Oh my God. You've made my wildest dreams come true." Gloria sat, piled some eggs on a slice of toast, and tried not to wolf down her breakfast. Missing dinner was one thing. Gloria worked in shifts and she was used to going long stretches without food. But it was as though sleeping with Ash had ignited a new kind of hunger in her. She couldn't remember when she'd last been so ravenous. Then again, she couldn't remember when she'd last had a night like last night. "Aren't you starving?"

"Fuck, yes," Ash said, but she didn't start eating yet. Instead, she addressed a tiny speaker that stood in the corner of the kitchen island, and said, "Alexa," making Gloria briefly wonder if there was someone else in the flat. "Play 'It's All Coming Back to Me Now' by Celine Dion."

The speaker repeated what Ash had just said, then started playing the familiar, dramatic notes.

A smile broke on Gloria's face. "Aw, that's so sweet of you."

Ash winked at her, then started eating as the long song played.

Gloria swayed to the rhythm as she ate. It was a perfect couple of minutes, because it allowed her to bask in last night's afterglow without having to think about any of the consequences. Every time her mind wandered, she focused on the music and the lyrics and Ash sitting next to her.

"She's very candid in this song," Ash said after the music had died down.

"What do you mean?"

"When she says 'there were things I'd never do again, but then they'd always seemed right', just before she reminisces about 'the nights of anal pleasure, it was more than any laws allowed.'" Ash sat there grinning.

"You've clearly misunderstood the lyrics." Gloria reached for Ash's naked knee sticking out of her robe. "Or you have a one-track mind."

"Hey, I analyse things for a living and I'm not easily fooled," Ash said drily. "I'm pretty sure that's what she really means. It makes perfect sense in the context of the song."

"No, Ash, it really doesn't." Gloria stared at Ash, at her perfect face. Her hair was tousled the way it had been when Gloria had arrived at the Coopers' last weekend, but it only made Ash look more friendly. She had a little bit of egg stuck to the side of her lip and it only made her look more endearing.

Ash shrugged. "I bet you, though, that next time you listen to that song, you'll think of it differently."

I'll think of you, Gloria wanted to say. But it felt like too much somehow, although she was already planning to play the song on repeat on the train journey back.

"What are your plans for today?" she asked, instead.

Ash gave her the kind of once-over that conveyed exactly what she had in mind as her most important activity of the day. "Depends on you. Are you staying?"

"I—I could." Gloria had packed two changes of underwear. She hadn't given it too much thought as she had put them into her bag. It could have just been a spare one. It didn't have to mean anything. Yet, it did mean something. Everything even remotely Ash-related meant something.

"You mean stay another night? Spend the weekend?" Heat seemed to be shooting off the skin of Ash's knee.

Gloria nodded as she squeezed Ash's knee a little tighter. She guessed there was a small chance that Ash wanted Gloria out of her hair, so she could do her normal weekend things, but it was unlikely after the night they'd shared.

"It's entirely up to you." Ash turned to her. "But I won't say no to that. I *can't* say no to that." Her robe fell all the way open. Maybe Ash had already been so certain that Gloria would stay and that was why she hadn't bothered to put on any clothes. Maybe she wasn't planning on getting dressed all day. Gloria could most certainly live with that.

Gloria raked her gaze over Ash's body. Her skin looked a shade paler in the morning light that flooded the flat, despite it being overcast outside. "I can't say no to this." Gloria slipped her hand further up Ash's thigh. What she'd said to Ash earlier, about not recognising herself, was true. She wasn't the kind of woman who did this sort of thing. She'd had no clue how much pleasure the touch of another woman could give her. But she knew now. And she wanted more. She didn't just want to receive pleasure, but give it back as well.

"Then stay." Ash's breath hitched in her throat.

Gloria's thumb skated along her inner thigh. "Whatever will we do all weekend?" A nervous laugh escaped her. Because this was as far removed from a normal Saturday Gloria had ever had. Her fingers touching Ash intimately. Her mind on one thing only. Even though they'd done this for hours last night, Gloria wanted more. Maybe this weekend, during which they could do whatever they wanted, was all they would ever have. If that was the case, then Gloria would make the most of every single second.

Chapter Twenty-Seven

"Charlotte and I stopped talking," Ash said. She'd pulled up two armchairs to the window and now they both sat where Ash often sat on her own, gazing out at the lights across the river. "We used to tell each other everything. We were always chatting away. Always over-sharing the biggest intimacies." She managed a small chuckle. "You know, processing everything excessively like lesbians tend to do." Gloria would perhaps not know, because as far as Ash was aware, Gloria wasn't a lesbian. "Once we stopped talking... Once I found myself self-censoring before I said something to her, that was the beginning of the end." She hadn't talked about this in a while, but Gloria had asked. "It's like we drifted away from each other, onto different wavelengths, where it became harder and harder to understand each other, until it turned into sheer unwillingness to even try." She heaved a sigh. "I wish I had a clear-cut explanation like that she cheated on me. Or even that I cheated on her. That one of us met someone else. But it wasn't like that. It was just a very sad, excruciating example of two people growing apart." She took a deep breath. "Now, as to who's fault that was... that's a debate that will never be resolved, but I'm certainly willing to shoulder my part." At least she could talk about this without tears pricking behind her eyes now. That was something. And she was telling Gloria. That was a lot.

"Do you still see her?" Gloria asked before taking a sip of water. She had insisted that Ash open the bottle of wine she'd spotted in the fridge, but Ash had not relented. She wouldn't be drinking in Gloria's presence. Her liver could do with the break.

"No. Haven't seen her since that last time at the solicitor's office. After we'd successfully 'divided our assets' and the divorce was final." What an awful day that had been. Their time together reduced to a couple of autographs on a form.

"Would you have liked to have remained friends?" Gloria held out her hand.

Ash captured it in hers. She'd put the chairs close enough together. She didn't want Gloria further than an inch away from her for the rest of the weekend. They still had to talk about what would happen tomorrow night, when Gloria would be taking the train back to Murraywood.

"I think that was the issue. Near the end, we'd worn each other down so much, we weren't even friends anymore."

"Does she live in London? You must still mix in the same circles sometimes?"

"We don't. I make sure that I don't run into her. Not yet, anyway. London's big enough. She stayed in Hackney, where we lived together. I moved here."

"I'm sorry you had to go through that, Ash." Gloria's voice was so soft.

"In the end, it's all right. We weren't meant to be together. It was hard to find out and accept that, but now we can move on." Ash traced an invisible line from Gloria's wrist all the way to the tip of her index finger. "Besides, you haven't been without hardship in your life."

Gloria gave an unexpected deep belly laugh. "It's funny," she said. "But I think I'm finally doing what George made me promise I should do after he died. I'm finally having the fun he ordered me to have."

"In that case, I'm glad to be of service."

"Oh gosh, you have been of excellent service. Is there anywhere I can leave a review? Ten stars for the orgasms." Gloria's laugh was infectious, but there was a nervousness about it as well.

There was tension in the air because neither one of them knew what this was. They could enjoy it, they could revel in it, and repeat their sensual actions as much as their bodies allowed. But after that, Ash had no clue what would happen.

"Seriously, though..." Gloria's voice was almost solemn now. Maybe she was thinking of her late husband—a man Ash could scarcely remember. "Maybe..." Her tone was hesitant now. "Maybe, after George, a new man was never on the cards for me." Ash could feel Gloria looking at her. "Maybe the new man for me is a woman."

Ash knew how easily she was baited by statements like that. Because it was Gloria, she waited a beat before turning to her to speak. When she looked at Gloria, with all that hope and easy laughter on her face, Ash swallowed her words completely. Whatever she had been going to say next wasn't called for in the moment. It could wait or it could also just never be said. If there was one thing Ash had learnt from going through a divorce, it was that sometimes it really was better to hold your tongue, even though it took all the willpower you had.

"Can I ask you the million-dollar question?" Ash still held Gloria's hand in hers.

"You can ask me any question you want." When Gloria used that sultry tone, Ash wanted to cease talking instantly and straddle Gloria again, but this, she had to ask.

"What happens after this weekend?"

Gloria nodded pensively, as though she'd already given the

matter a great deal of thought and had only to find the words to express her conclusion. But no words came. "I don't know. I wish I did, but I have no clue."

"Do you see this as something that has to end when you leave tomorrow? Something finite?"

"How can it be?" Gloria quickly responded. "Do you think that's even possible?"

This gave Ash hope, although she was very much aware that it could be false. "All the reasons why we said it had to end last weekend still hold."

"No." Gloria shook her head vehemently. "So much has changed since then, Ash. I'm here, with you. You have made me feel things..." She paused. "I can't just go back to Murraywood and pretend this never happened. It means too much to me to be able to do that."

"But how do you see things progressing between us on a practical level? Do you want to come back next weekend?" Ash wanted to share Gloria's optimism, but she recognised the signs of two people not operating on the same wavelength—she had become an expert at that. Not to toot her own horn, but, of course Gloria was over the moon. This was all very new and exciting to her. But there was no proof she could ever feel about Ash the way Ash could feel about her. Ash could fall for her. She wasn't sure the same could be said for Gloria.

Gloria shook her head. "I can't next weekend. I'm working Friday and Saturday afternoon and Fiona's having a barbecue on Sunday." She let her head fall against the backrest of the chair. "And the weekend after, the girls are coming home for the Easter holidays. It'll be a week of cooking healthy meals and doing laundry for me. And spending time with my daughters."

"Best make the most of this weekend, then." Ash tried very hard to keep her voice from cracking, an overwhelming sense of disappointment running through her. But maybe a dose of reality was exactly what they needed. At least then they could start acting as though this would be for a limited time only. Gloria had a life in Murraywood. Ash had her life here.

"I can take the train on a weeknight, Ash. Or you can come to Murraywood. It's not that far." It wasn't just optimism in Gloria's tone any longer. Her words sounded a bit more strangled—a bit more pragmatic. "There's no rush, is there? To find out what this is?"

"No," Ash admitted, because she could do that. But she also knew what she would have to do come tomorrow.

Chapter Twenty-Eight

❧

F uck it, Gloria thought, and took Ash's hand in hers. It was the first time they'd left Ash's flat since Gloria had arrived on Friday evening. Some fresh air had been sorely needed. They'd had brunch at the place around the corner and were walking back towards the river. Because it was Sunday, the streets were much quieter in this part of town, so close to the City.

Ash slotted her fingers through Gloria's as though they'd been walking hand-in-hand along the streets of London forever. But to Gloria, too, it just felt natural, despite the secret thrill it gave her.

Ash pointed at a tall building on the other side of the next bridge. "That's where I work."

Whereas yesterday, the atmosphere between them had been tinged by sheer exuberance and the complete inability to keep their hands to themselves, today, everything seemed heavier, weighted down by Gloria's upcoming return home.

"Let's make a concrete plan to see each other again right now," Gloria said.

"Okay." Ash didn't sound very convinced. "I'm pretty free. I just have work to consider." Was that a sneer at Gloria's busier calendar? And how could it be that a woman like Ash, who was in the prime of her life, didn't have any social engagements lined up over the next few weeks?

"Do you have any previously made plans to come to Murraywood?" Gloria asked.

"No."

"Hey..." Gloria gave Ash's hand a tug. "It's going to be okay, you know."

"No, Gloria, it's really not. I understand that you're in fantasyland right now, but this—" She held up their joined hands, looked at them, and then dropped Gloria's. "This is not going to work. How can it possibly work?" Ash took a breath. She looked as though she had a lot more to say, but she fell silent.

"Maybe it won't," Gloria countered. "But don't you think we should try?" She glanced around, but, in the end, didn't much care who might or might not be watching. She curled her arm around Ash's waist. "Why are you so cranky this morning?" She leaned into Ash and whispered in her ear. "Did I not make you come hard enough?" The memory of Ash coming all over her fingers only hours ago sent a shiver up Gloria's spine.

This did at least elicit a chuckle from Ash. "I'm sorry." She shrugged one shoulder. "It's mayhem up here." She pointed at her head. "I wish I could just go with the flow, like you do, but it's not really my forte."

"I get it." Gloria stopped walking and pulled Ash a little closer to her. "It's a lot. And it's confusing. But we can talk about it. We don't have to dance around it. We don't have to pretend that later today, I won't be leaving. That's why I want us to make plans already for when to see each other next."

"I can't just swing by Murraywood in the evening to see you. Adrian lives a five-minute walk from your house."

"Come on." Gloria knew this wasn't about Ash bumping into her brother—not entirely, anyway. Although, of course, it would raise questions if she was spotted. "Anyway, I'll come to London if it makes you feel more comfortable. When I don't have the late shift." Since Janey had left for university, Gloria had taken more evening and weekend shifts. Her colleagues had often allowed her to make her schedule more child-friendly when her girls were still at home and she was now repaying the favour.

"I've only just put myself together again after losing Charlotte. I don't know what I'm setting myself up for with you, but I do know I'm not ready to get hurt again."

"Oh, sweetheart, I'm not going to hurt you." Gloria tugged Ash into a proper hug, not caring that they stood on the footpath near the middle of the bridge. "Why don't we go back inside?"

Ash nodded against her collarbone, but didn't move. Gloria gently nudged her out of her embrace and they walked back towards Ash's building. Their silence on the way over allowed Gloria to consider if she could still walk away from this scotfree. The conclusion was obvious. Of course she couldn't. Not after the weekend they'd just had. She understood Ash's confusion. She wanted more of Ash, too. She wanted to see that fire in Ash's gaze again before she leaned in to kiss her, before her head dropped down between Gloria's legs. Already, Gloria couldn't imagine a life without any of that. She'd gotten a taste and she didn't just want more—she needed more.

But they would need to take their time. See how things evolved. Take some practicalities of their daily lives into account.

Or maybe Ash was simply scared. Whereas Gloria felt energised by this weekend and by all the sensations it had evoked in her, perhaps it was having a very different effect on Ash.

"Coffee?" Ash asked as soon as they got in.

"Sure." Even though it was just past noon, Gloria could only drink one more of the ultra-strong espressos Ash made, otherwise she wouldn't get any sleep tonight. Although Ash had exhausted her plenty the past two nights. "Check your calendar. Let's figure this out right now."

"It's not so much about the calendar." The espresso seemed to have perked Ash up somewhat. "We don't need to have a weekend like this every week."

Gloria scrunched up her eyebrows. "You say that, but I could live with it."

Ash grinned and shot Gloria a look that said she might just agree with that, despite what she'd just said. "I don't want to be heavy-handed about this too soon, Gloria, but you have to understand where I'm coming from." She took a breath. "Despite what's been going on here this weekend, you are, in my eyes, still my mother's straight friend. I'm not one of those lesbians who enjoys torturing herself by falling for unavailable straight women. That's not what I do."

Gloria didn't immediately know what to say to that. She gazed into her empty espresso cup. "I'm not feeling very straight right now." The words tumbled from her mouth, as though she wasn't in full control of what she was saying. "I'm not out to hurt you, Ash." She spoke quickly, as though it could erase what she'd said before. But it was true. Gloria was feeling anything but heterosexual in Ash's presence.

"And I'm not exactly looking for a toaster-oven romance," Ash said.

Gloria narrowed her eyes. "I have no idea what that means."

"Of course you don't," Ash said cryptically. Gloria made a mental note to google it on the train later. "And that's the whole point."

"Maybe we're getting ahead of ourselves here."

"Maybe we are, but... I have to. I have no choice, Gloria. I know I can't make any demands of you because it's utterly irrational to do so. There are no answers right now. We just had sex. But that's the thing with me. I don't just sleep with someone and move on. The only reason you're here is because I have feelings for you. I know it's unfair to bombard you with them already. But... I'm not even ready for something new. Which is probably why I was enjoying this so much in the first place, because it could never really go anywhere. But now that I want it to, it feels like something I can't allow myself to get caught up in." Ash was speaking a mile a minute.

All the while, Gloria had simply been enjoying Ash's company. She was too busy being thrilled by the electricity between them every single time they touched—or even looked at each other. Of course Gloria liked Ash, otherwise she wouldn't be here, but the stakes seemed very different for her.

Ash suddenly chuckled. "Oh, fuck it, Gloria. I'm being such a lez about this whole thing."

"What do you mean?" Gloria smiled, even though she didn't really know why. It could be Ash's whimsical facial expression. Even when she was in distress, she was so bloody cute. She looked kissable from every possible angle. Gloria had to keep herself in check for now.

"My processor gets overheated sometimes." Ash pointed at her head again. "It's a very lesbian thing to have happen to you."

"Is it?" Gloria remembered a book she had found in Sally's room a few years ago, called *The Fluid Rainbow*. At first, she'd just thumbed through it, but a few days later, she'd actually sat down with the book, and had been surprised by how open-minded and utterly without judgement the young people interviewed for the book had been. Gloria hadn't given it much more thought at the time. She'd just been secretly pleased that Sally read books like that, and she was comfortable enough to leave them lying around in her room, knowing her mother could see. "What other 'lesbian things' can happen to you?"

"Are you mocking me?" Ash tilted her head. She set down her empty cup. "Do you really think that's the right thing to do now? Mock me while I'm being vulnerable?" Ash didn't look vulnerable anymore at all. It was as though the espresso, the mere three sips of it, had transformed her into suave, seductive Ash again.

Gloria chewed the inside of her lip. As if she'd known Ash like this forever—like the woman who could make her come like nobody's business—she already knew what would happen next.

Ash came for her. With her knees, she spread Gloria's legs apart and stood between them.

"I was sharing my innermost feelings." Ash kissed Gloria on the cheek, then went straight for her neck.

Gloria brought her hands to Ash's hair, which she had watched her style carefully that morning. It was all stiff from the product she'd put in it, preventing Gloria from running her hand through it freely.

"Even though," Gloria managed to say, "you have a rather questionable sense of humour, I want it noted for the record that I wasn't mocking you."

In response, Ash reached for her hand. "Come on." She gently pulled Gloria from the stool she was sitting on. "I have the perfect punishment in mind for what you just said."

⚜

How exactly they'd ended up, in a matter of minutes, stark naked in Ash's bed again, Gloria couldn't recall. It was a jumble of hoisted up tops and unhooked bras. Of tangled-up limbs and the warmth of skin on skin.

"I want you to lick me," Ash said, sounding like a completely different person than the woman Gloria had comforted on the bridge earlier. This version of Ash could make Gloria do anything she wanted. "I want you to make me come." Her voice was lower now, barely a whisper.

"It would be my absolute pleasure." Gloria looked up at her.

168

Ash was lying on top of her, her knee pressing between her legs. Gloria reckoned that of all the things she and Ash had done this weekend, she'd miss tasting her that way the most. It was so surprisingly intoxicating to sweep her tongue over Ash's wet heat. She started wiggling her way out from under Ash because, frankly, she could hardly wait.

"Nu-huh." Ash shook her head. "Not like that."

Heat rose from Gloria's core. Her heartbeat pulsed in her clit.

"Like this." Ash shifted from her, but only for a few moments. Then she straddled her—Ash seemed to be quite fond of the move—and inched herself, over Gloria's breasts, closer and closer to her mouth.

As far as punishments went, this one was already turning out to be rather glorious, and terribly exciting. Gloria couldn't wait to taste Ash again. To lick at her very essence. To coat herself in Ash's delicious wetness. Ash manoeuvred herself into position.

Gloria ran her hands from Ash's back to her behind. She pushed her own legs together. She could feel the pressure building there already. Quite honestly, she'd had no idea she had all of this still inside her. She wasn't old, but she wasn't young either. They'd taken plenty of breaks, but it still felt kind of like she and Ash had engaged in a veritable sex marathon this weekend. Maybe, a subconscious part of them did believe that this could only ever be a one-weekend affair, and they wanted to squeeze the most out of it—they were still squeezing now. But, on the surface, Gloria refused to believe that notion. As she flicked her tongue over Ash's wetness, she simply couldn't accept that, after today, they would never do this again. That she would never take Ash in her embrace again as she'd done earlier, when she'd looked as though she'd so desperately needed someone's arms around her.

Even though the problem Ash had expressed didn't have an

immediate solution, and they seemed to be in quite different places regarding their tryst, Gloria could recognise insecurity when she saw it. She was glad Ash had laughed it off earlier, although that certainly didn't mean Gloria intended to ignore it. But for now, this was what they had. This time together to be made the most of. They could talk on the phone. They could Skype and FaceTime like Gloria did with her daughters. Now, when Ash had all her confidence about her again, when they could push aside the thought of any possible consequence, this was what they did.

Gloria swept her tongue over Ash's clit. She inhaled her—devoured her, it felt like. But it wasn't enough. She wanted more. She brought her fingers to Ash's entrance and pushed inside her. Oh, Ash's warmth there was intoxicating but also soothing. To be inside another person like that thrilled Gloria to the core. The way Ash's muscles tightened around her fingers when the time came was simply divine. Everything she'd done with Ash the past forty-eight hours had been of a truly addictive nature.

Then, Ash shifted, only a fraction, but Gloria could feel even the tiniest of her movements so intertwined was she with Ash at that moment. At first, she thought Ash wanted to feel Gloria's finger inside her from a different angle, until Gloria felt Ash's hand part her legs.

Ash found Gloria's clit. Her finger connected and Gloria had to gasp for air. She already felt completely covered in all things Ash. She was also aroused beyond a point of no return—that, too, had surprised her. Her level of arousal at Ash's touch. The desperation with which she wanted it, and how she tilted her hips a fraction, so Ash's finger could skate along her clit the way she liked it.

Not that it mattered that much. The taste of Ash on her tongue. The soft heat of her pressed against her mouth. The warmth of her around Gloria's fingers. The insistence of Ash's touch between her legs. It was more than plenty for that fire to take hold of Gloria's every cell again, for that wave of pleasure to take her, dip her under, until she re-emerged exhausted yet invigorated, restored by Ash's touch.

Ash, too, was toppling over that invisible edge. Gloria could feel it as Ash's muscles contracted around her. She sucked Ash's clit between her lips and flicked with her tongue, while Ash clenched hard around her fingers.

Fifty-four whole years without this, Gloria thought, as she lay basking in the afterglow of her climax. What kind of life was that?

Chapter Twenty-Nine

"One last thing." Ash couldn't let go of Gloria's hand. She wished she had a car, however useless in a city like London, so she could drive Gloria home and stretch the last hours of this Sunday together until the last possible minute. "What did you mean when you said I had a questionable sense of humour?"

Gloria's gaze on her was warm, as was her hand in Ash's. "I told you that 'It's All Coming Back to Me Now' is my favourite song in the world and now you've ruined it for me with your lame joke about anal sex." Gloria scrunched her lips together.

"I'm sorry." Ash's apology wasn't for the silliness of her joke. She was sorry because Gloria was standing at Ash's front door, bag packed, her coat already on. She was mostly feeling sorry for herself because soon her flat would be robbed of Gloria's presence. Because of Gloria's work schedule next week, they hadn't found a good time to meet up yet. "I'll go in the cab with you." They'd been over this twice already. Ash shouldn't push, but she did, anyway.

Gloria shook her head. "I'll text you when I get home."

"Okay." Ash hadn't spent a full weekend with someone in her personal space like this in a very long time. Still, she wished it was a bank holiday weekend, so Gloria could stay a day longer.

"Is your brain doing that over-processing thing again?" Gloria kissed her long and soft on the cheek. "If it's meant to be, it will work out," she said, just as softly.

It was exactly this kind of thing that made Ash so crazy about Gloria. Ash also wanted very much to believe her.

"Okay," she said, again, and pulled Gloria towards her for one last kiss on the lips. Then she let her go.

"Read my lips, Ashley Cooper," Lewis said. "Take a day off work." He shrugged. "Besides, I'm your boss. If I tell you to take the day off, you will bloody well take it."

"Take the day off and spend it in Murraywood?" As far as Lewis's far-fetched ideas went, this one sounded very appealing and easy to achieve. "Holed up in Gloria's house so no one sees me?" She had to laugh. What else was she going to do?

"Why not?" Lewis asked.

Indeed. Why not?

"You're smitten. I can tell," Lewis said.

"I wouldn't go that far." Instead of hovering over the coffee machine like they usually did, Ash had gone into Lewis's office to process the weekend. She was also underplaying how she felt, because it made her feel so ridiculous.

"Ever heard of body language, darling?" Lewis eyed her intently. "You don't have to say it for me to see it."

"Aren't you a regular Sherlock Holmes." Lewis made sure he always stood out, but with his shiny suits and gleaming shoes, he seemed to sparkle even more on what was quite the dreary

Monday morning. It could only be due to Ash's perception of him—and everything else around her.

Lewis tapped a few times on his keyboard and looked at his computer. "You have seventeen days of leave carried over from last year, that is on top of this year's quota." He shot her a mock-steely glance again. "You're making *me* look bad by not taking the days off you are allowed, Ash. Like I make you work night and day for me."

"You don't have to convince me. I'll take a day. This week or next week. Or *both*." Ash was feeling frivolous. "I just need to check with Gloria when would suit her most."

"Good." Lewis nodded, then his expression turned. "Are you ready for my news now?"

"Always, darling." Ash could have perhaps thought of taking a day off herself. That it hadn't occurred to her spoke volumes about how rarely she took leave.

"Jonathan and I were in this new bar in Kensington on Saturday. This posh new place with chandeliers hanging from the ceilings and the plushest armchairs you've ever had a cocktail in. We were trying out the house cocktail, it's called a Paloma, and it's truly delicious, although quite lethal..." He waved his hand dismissively, as if knowing he was getting away from the point he was trying to make. "Anyway, we were sitting there, minding our own business, as we do. You know what we're like, darling. When suddenly, out of nowhere, Charlotte turns up in front of us."

Ash did a double-take. "Charlotte?" It wasn't inconceivable. Charlotte was living in London.

Lewis nodded. "She wasn't alone, Ash. And the woman she was with, was not a friend, if you catch my drift."

Why did it feel as though someone had just punched all the air right out of Ash's lungs?

"How do—d—did you know?" Ash tried to stabilise her

emotions by taking a deep breath—as if that ever really worked. During the divorce proceedings, she'd taken so many deep breaths, she must have amassed enough oxygen in her lungs to last her a lifetime.

"Because she told me," Lewis said calmly. "Made no bones about it either. She seemed... I don't know. Almost proud that she could tell me."

"Was she off her face, at least?"

"Hard to say." Lewis planted his elbows on the glass top of his desk. "But I thought you should hear it from me. In fact, if you need to take today off, feel free..."

Take the day off to do what? Try to find out who Charlotte was seeing? "Hell, no. I'm working." Ash tapped the tip of her foot against the leg of her chair. "Was it someone you'd seen before?"

Lewis shook his head.

"What did she look like?"

"Like any other lesbian," Lewis said on a sigh. "I don't know. She had nothing on you, Ash. *Nothing.*" He emphasised the last word.

"It's fine. It's completely fine. We're divorced. She can go out on the town with whoever she wants."

"Maybe it's good that you're both moving on." Lewis was tapping his foot now as well, making Ash aware of what she was doing, so she stopped. "You are both moving on, aren't you?"

"I have no fucking clue what I'm doing." Ash tried to tune into the warm glow being with Gloria all weekend had left under her skin, but it seemed to have dissipated.

"Let me tell you what to do then." Lewis's voice was uncharacteristically warm. "Call your lady friend. Set a date. Go see her. Be merry again." He opened his palms as if he'd just solved a huge problem—as if it was that easy.

"Thanks for telling me." Ash got up.

"I'm available for drinks tonight," Lewis said, as Ash exited his office.

The first thing she did after she sat at her desk was text Gloria.

Chapter Thirty

Gloria was studying the different kinds of ground coffee her local Sainsbury's offered. She'd drunk the same brand of coffee for years, for decades, but after tasting the coffee Ash had made for her with her fancy machine, she thought she'd try something new. From the corner of her eye, she noticed a familiar figure push a trolley past the end of the aisle.

Gloria put back the pack of coffee she'd been holding and hastily shoved her trolley in the opposite direction she'd just seen Mary head into. After the weekend she'd had, Ash's mother was the last person she wanted to see. Whatever would she reply if Mary inquired about her weekend? Gloria wouldn't be able to keep a straight face.

She reached the end of the aisle and looked left and right. Mary was near the freezers on the left side of the shop, so Gloria took a quick right. She hadn't finished her shopping yet and Sindhu and Fiona were coming over for dinner tonight. Then her phone beeped in her purse. She had to find a safe space where Mary couldn't see her before she retrieved her phone.

The cold hard light of the day had not come with the reality check Gloria needed just yet. Her body was still awash with residual hormones brought on by a weekend of sex. Gloria had woken to find certain body parts pulsing for no apparent reason, while others felt a bit tender from so much activity after such an extended drought.

That reality check came now, under the glaring, unrelenting lights of the supermarket, Mary roaming about somewhere close to her. Although she'd been the one to recklessly claim that if it was meant to be between them, it would work out, Gloria was very much convinced that nothing could ever work out between her and Mary's daughter. Because, right now, Ash wasn't the woman she'd spent the weekend having the most glorious sex with. She was very much Mary's daughter. And that was simply not what you did with a friend's daughter, no matter how mature and consenting they were.

Gloria decided to ignore the text and not waste any time. She needed to get out of the supermarket and get her car loaded before Mary turned up in the car park. If it was an urgent matter with one of the girls, they would call instead of text. At least, that was what she always asked them to do, despite her girls being of a generation raised on text messages. A ringing phone seemed almost like an affront to them, something alien and not to be taken into account.

God. Her girls. Gloria tried not to think of either of them taking up with one of her friends. She quickly filled her trolley, not caring too much if she forgot something. There was always frozen pizza. Sindhu and Fiona might frown upon her unimaginative food choice, but she was sure they would be far more disapproving over what Gloria was intending to tell them later that night. Because she had to tell someone. Sindhu would ask about it.

Oh bugger, here she was ready to fall apart in the dairy aisle. Every time she heard someone behind her, she cast a furtive glance, hoping it wasn't Mary catching up with her. She tried to look relaxed as she nodded at a few people she knew, made a bit of small talk about the weather with the lady at the till, all the while hoping to avoid the reckoning that would come if she had to face Mary.

When she was finally safe in her car and had driven out of the car park, she hurried home. Only in the driveway, did Gloria relax her shoulders and expel a deep breath. Mary had invited her to her sixty-fifth birthday party and this was how Gloria thanked her? By going up to London to sleep with her daughter? Gloria was beginning to wonder what had come over her. How on earth had she ended up in Ash's flat?

With a sigh, she reached into her bag and grabbed her phone. It was a text from Ash. Gloria closed her eyes. It had been easy enough to push reality aside while in the safe and very sultry confines of Ash's home, but now, back in Murray-wood, everything was different. Gloria couldn't deal with Ash's message right now. She needed a cup of tea first. And another cold shower, perhaps. And to never run into Mary or Alan again.

"What?" Fiona twirled the stem of her wine glass nervously between her fingers—maybe because it didn't contain any wine. Neither Sindhu nor Fiona had brought a bottle tonight. Gloria could only assume that, after last week, Sindhu had told Fiona that it would be better for them not to drink in front of Gloria. It had happened before, since Gloria had joined AA, where she had asked her friends to refrain from drinking around her, but not very often, and there had always been an underlying reason. "Can you say that again, please? I'm not sure I understood correctly."

Sindhu elbowed Fiona in the arm. "Come off it."

"What? You already knew and you didn't even tell me," Fiona said.

"I didn't know this had happened." Sindhu sounded vexed. "But I'm happy that it has."

"I miss one dinner and this is what goes on?" Fiona shot Gloria an incredulous look.

"You missing dinner had nothing to do with it," Sindhu said.

Gloria let them fight it out amongst themselves. She was happy Sindhu was taking the heat for her—she'd let her do so for a few minutes longer. Until Fiona had calmed down a bit. They bickered a while longer, then fell silent.

Gloria shifted in her chair. The small of her back still felt a bit strained from bending towards Ash so many times over the weekend. It was a pleasant ache. One that reminded her of how things could be, if there was no one around to judge.

"Does that mean you're a lesbian now?" Fiona asked.

Gloria chuckled. It was a question she had asked herself. Could one weekend with another woman turn you into a lesbian? She shook her head, because the question was valid but also irrelevant. She could just picture how Janey would roll her eyes at someone saying something like that. Good heavens. Janey. No matter how open-minded and fluid and averse to labels today's youth might be, Gloria's daughters could never find out about this.

"I really don't think so," Gloria said.

"But you enjoyed it?" Fiona asked.

"Oh, yes." Gloria couldn't keep the glee out of her voice. "It was just…" Either she couldn't describe how it had felt to be with Ash, or she didn't want to. It was their thing, their shared intimacy. "It was like a dream." *It was as near to bloody perfect as you could get.* "I mean, it was real," Gloria mused. "But, in a way, it also wasn't real. Like we were trapped in a bubble where that sort of thing was made possible, just for forty-eight hours, until it inevitably burst."

Because Gloria's bubble had well and truly burst, which was why she hadn't responded to Ash's text yet. She wanted to take a day off this week and come to Murraywood to spend more time with Gloria. Gloria wanted nothing more than to see Ash again, but she wasn't sure she could do it in Murraywood. She also had a busy week at work. She supposed she could go back and forth to London—so many people commuted into the City every single weekday—but she wasn't sure that she should. She wasn't sure she should postpone the inevitable. Their return to reality. "I saw Mary at Sainsbury's this morning. Or no, I didn't see her, because I hid from her. I slinked around the aisles like a fugitive hiding from the police because I didn't want to talk to her. This woman who has been my friend for decades. It wasn't a pleasant feeling."

"Oh, shit," Sindhu said. "She didn't see you?"

"I don't think so." Gloria sure as hell hoped not. "But it was just such a brutal reality check."

"Okay, let me get this straight," Fiona said. "You spent the weekend having sex with Ashley Cooper, Mary and Alan's daughter."

Gloria groaned. When Fiona put it like that, it sounded so awful, so crude, so unlike the time she and Ash had actually had together.

"Are you saying that you regret it?" Fiona continued.

"I don't regret it." It was physically and emotionally impossible to regret a weekend like that. "But I don't think it should be repeated. The ramifications are too... I don't know. I don't want to be that kind of person in Murraywood. For years, I've been George's poor widow. Now that I'm finally just Gloria again, I don't want to be the person who ran off with the Coopers' daughter."

"You make it sound as though Ash is a young and impressionable thing," Sindhu said. "She's in her forties. Very much a grown woman capable of making her own decisions."

"But still," Fiona said, voicing Gloria's thoughts exactly.

"Murraywood is where I've lived my entire life. It's where I work. Where George and I built a life together and where my girls have grown up. I'm inextricably linked to this town. Can you see me walking across the town green with Ash on a Sunday afternoon? Hand in hand?" Gloria scoffed. "On our way to Mary and Alan's for tea?" She threw up her hands in defeat.

"You're looking far into the future tonight," Sindhu said.

"It's the only way." Gloria sagged in her chair.

"How does Ash feel about all this?" Fiona asked.

"She texted me earlier to ask if and when she could come over this week." Gloria glanced at her phone, which lay untouched on the sideboard. "She wants to take a day off to spend time with me."

Sindhu's eyebrows rose almost to her hairline. "She's keen."

Gloria nodded and it was hard to ignore the small pang of pride rushing through her.

"She's actually falling for you?" Fiona asked.

"Is that so surprising?" Sindhu sounded very offended. "We are women in our prime."

"As long as we get a fresh hormone patch every week," Fiona said matter-of-factly. "Is that what this is? Maybe you need to get your levels checked, Gloria."

"Maybe." Gloria had no intention of doing so. "I don't know what to do."

"Do you want to see her again?" Sindhu asked.

"Of course I do, but it's not a good idea. The longer we keep seeing each other, the harder it will be to end it."

"You're absolutely sure you want to end it?" Fiona's question surprised Gloria.

"No, I'm not. But what's the alternative?"

"See how things shake out," Sindhu said. "At least let her come to Murraywood. See how it makes you feel." She inclined her head. "If you end it now, you won't have really given it a chance."

"You and your words," Gloria said. "You can make anything sound reasonable."

"No, I really can't. I understand that you're conflicted about this. It would worry me if you weren't. But, Gloria, the light is fully on in your eyes, and, as your friend, it is such a pleasure to behold."

"True," Fiona said. "Actually... I noticed you were walking a bit strangely earlier when you brought the food to the table?" She thought this so hilarious that she slapped a palm against her thigh.

"Maybe it's not as impossible as you think it is," Sindhu said.

"Maybe..." Gloria paused. "It's strange, because, over the weekend, it was mostly Ash who expressed her doubts about this. Like she was several steps ahead of me already. I didn't want to think about any of this when I was in London. Maybe it was easier for me, because I went to her. I was away from here, where I feel I'd be judged in an instant, and she was in her home. I don't know."

"Let her come here," Sindhu repeated. "See what happens."

"And keep us posted." Fiona seemed to be coming around to the idea of Gloria and Ash together. But that was all it could be to her right now. An idea. Until she saw Gloria and Ash together. How would she react then? Gloria could speculate all she wanted, but she actively put a stop to it. Since coming back to Murraywood, her speculations had become more negative than positive, and she wanted to hold on to the lovely memories she and Ash had made a while longer. For all she knew right now, it might be all they'd ever have together.

Chapter Thirty-One

❦

On Tuesday evening, Ash packed a bag and took the train to Murraywood. Gloria would be home around nine and Ash would be waiting for her. The train to Murraywood was half-empty. Most commuters were safely home already.

On the train, she listened to Gloria's favourite song on repeat. Even though she was well aware it was an action worthy of a lovesick teenager wanting to feel closer to the person they had a silly crush on, Ash didn't care. And maybe that's what this was. After her marriage, maybe she had some regressing to do. Some teenage lust to channel.

She had been worried when it had taken Gloria almost twelve hours to respond to her text. When her name had finally appeared on her phone screen, Ash had been utterly terrified that Gloria's reply would be a resounding no. That she would end it there and then, hence the long radio silence beforehand. But Gloria had said yes.

And now, here she was on her way and she came bearing gifts. She wasn't sure yet if Gloria would like this particular gift, but she would soon find out.

Ash turned up the collar of her coat when she walked

from the station to Gloria's house, as if it could magically hide her from view. It was a touch exciting to sneak around Murraywood like this. She mainly looked out for Adrian or Lizzie's cars. And her parents, who could be on their way home from a visit to her brother. Gloria's house might be conveniently located near the station, but it was dangerously close to her brother's. What would Ash even say if Adrian drove past her now? *Surprise, bro?* Maybe she should have worn a hat. But her family would recognise her anywhere, as she would them.

Murraywood was quiet at this time of the evening. The days were getting longer, but darkness had started to fall before Ash had got on the train. Ash spotted Gloria's car in the driveway. She was home already. Waiting for Ash.

Ash allowed herself a brief moment to imagine coming home from work, commuting to Murraywood, every evening— to Gloria, waiting for her like tonight. She shook off the thought as soon as she'd allowed it to enter her mind. One day at a time. That was her new mantra. They might not have tomorrow, but they had today.

Her heart racing like mad from the mere prospect of seeing Gloria again, Ash knocked on the back door. It swung open immediately. Gloria must have seen her walk up to her house. She was still wearing her nurse's uniform.

Gloria pulled her inside. "Did anyone see you?" she asked, before taking Ash into a tight hug.

"Not that I know of." It was the truth, but it didn't mean Ash hadn't been spotted without noticing.

Gloria nuzzled her neck, the tip of her nose moving against Ash's skin as she shook her head. "Christ, Ash."

Ash didn't know if she was sighing because she was relieved to see her or because Ash had managed to arrive at her house unseen. Maybe it was a bit of both. She threw her arms around Gloria and held her tight.

"I just got here. I should have picked you up at the station." Gloria's body remained rigid in Ash's embrace.

Ash put some distance between them, just so she could see Gloria's face. "Are you all right?"

Gloria heaved a sigh. "This was a million times easier in London."

"Yeah." Ash had never in her life visited Murraywood without seeing at least one member of her family. It was strange to be here for an entirely different reason. "But, look, I'm inside your house now. It'll be just fine."

"I'm going to take a shower." Gloria wriggled herself out of what was left of Ash's embrace. "Have you eaten?"

"You don't always have to ask me that, you know." She reached for Gloria's hand. "And I quite like the look of you in that uniform."

This, finally, brought a smile to Gloria's face. "Do you now?" She cocked her head. "I'm still going to shower and change." She just stood there. Was that an invitation?

"Do you want me to join you?"

"Oh," Gloria said, as though that had been the furthest thought from her mind. "Um, if you want to, but..."

"Hey." Ash pulled her close again. "It's going to be okay." It was funny that she had to be the one saying that tonight. Maybe they would have to take turns reassuring each other. "Go take your shower. Relax. Can I get you anything while you do? Do anything to make your life a little easier?"

Gloria chuckled. "I'm not used to so much attention."

Ash shrugged. She wanted to say something along the lines of 'best get used to it', but as much as she wanted to mean it, she couldn't. So she didn't say anything. She had an inkling of what she would do while Gloria was in the shower, however.

"I brought you something," she said. "You'll see what when you get out of the shower."

Gloria's eyes lit up. "A present?"

"Something like that."

"Will it help me relax?" She pushed herself further into Ash's embrace. "I know I'm a bit on edge. It's been a day and, well, you know…"

"I promise it will help you relax." Ash found Gloria's ear and sunk her teeth into her lobe for a split second. "You have my word."

"I want to open it now," Gloria said on a sigh.

Ash shook her head. "No." She released Gloria from her arms. "Go on." She gave a quick tap on her behind.

Gloria brought her hands to her side. "I'm so curious. Why are you torturing me like this?"

"Come on, show me the way. I'm going with you," Ash said, because this was the kind of present best opened in the bedroom.

Chapter Thirty-Two

❧

Even though Gloria knew she needed to relax, she'd never taken as quick a shower in her life. She had no idea what Ash's present was, but she had the distinct impression it was something that would satisfy her immensely. That was what the expression on Ash's face had conveyed, anyway. Gloria enjoyed the sensation of the hot water on her tense shoulders a few seconds longer, until she couldn't take it anymore.

As she towelled off, she had to hand it to Ash that bringing her a surprise was an excellent way of taking Gloria's mind off what was, basically, hiding Ash in her house. She remembered how she'd hidden from Mary the day before. How she'd flirted with the speed limit on her way home earlier so that Ash wouldn't have to wait outside her house and risk being spotted. Seeing Ash on the sly was thrilling but also exhausting. Gloria was ready for a few thrills because the secrecy of it all was starting to get to her.

Gloria wrapped the towel around her body and went into the bedroom. Ash was already under the covers; the lights were dimmed. There was no sign of any gift.

"You're not wasting any time." Gloria walked to the bed. "Are you that tired?"

"Come here." Ash threw back Gloria's side of the duvet. Her voice was different. Her glance was more solemn as well. Gloria didn't really know what was going on. She dropped the towel and hopped into bed with Ash.

"I was promised a present." Gloria made her voice sound extra petulant, but she didn't really succeed. To have Ash waiting for her like that when she got out of the shower after a long shift was a magnificent gift in its own right. Gloria didn't need anything else.

"Give me your hand." Ash held out her hand. Gloria took it. Ash slid both their hands under the covers. She put the flat of Gloria's hand on her belly, which was enough to jolt the fatigue from Gloria's muscles. Then she gently guided it down—Ash was feeling very forward tonight. Not that Gloria would make any pretence about the real reason Ash had come to Murray-wood to see her tonight. She figured they were both very much agreed on that. But they'd barely kissed and already Ash was pushing Gloria's hand between her legs.

Oh.

For a brief instant, Gloria had trouble processing what she was feeling. It was too incongruous with what she was seeing—Ash's seductive grin, her chest now uncovered.

Gloria wrapped her hand around the contraption Ash was wearing. It felt smooth and soft. She had to see. With her other hand, she lifted the duvet. Holy hell. The dildo Ash had strapped on to her hips was soft pink and rather large.

She glanced back at Ash, who didn't say anything. Gloria didn't know what to say either. This was all so new to her. New, but terribly exciting.

"Surprise," Ash whispered. She put her hand on Gloria's back.

"It is a surprise," Gloria admitted. She still had her hand

192

wrapped around it. Now that the first shock had subsided, heat started spreading underneath her skin.

"Take all the time you need to get used to it." Ash drew circles on Gloria's back. "I can also take it off and put it back on whenever you want."

Gloria looked back at Ash. "Keep it on," she said.

Ash nodded and flicked the tip of her tongue over her lips. "Does that mean you like your present?"

"I think so." Gloria bent towards Ash. "We'll know for sure in a while." Gloria gazed deep into Ash's eyes before kissing her. At every turn, being with Ash surprised her, made her feel more alive than the day before. She let go of the dildo—for now—and curved her arm around Ash's back so she could pull her near. The dildo prodded against her thigh as she did, and it only spurred on the heat beneath her skin. Being with Ash was worth taking a few risks for. As she pressed herself closer to Ash, the strap-on very present between them, she easily forgot about all the reasons why they shouldn't be doing this. They were replaced by all the reasons that they should. The main one being that Gloria—very simply—really wanted to.

"Do you want me to fuck you?" Ash whispered in Gloria's ear. She'd manoeuvred herself on top of Gloria. While they'd kissed and caressed each other, Gloria's hand had steered clear of the toy, as though she wanted to save that sensation for later, but it was always there, like a constant reminder of what would inevitably happen.

Gloria had never in her life been spoken to like that. If she had, she couldn't remember. It was the last thing she expected Ash to say to her. Maybe that was why it was so deadly arousing when she did.

Ash looked down at her. The lust blazing in her eyes was different from what Gloria had seen in them over the weekend. Ash was in her element, that much was clear. What she'd just asked wasn't as much a question as it was a statement she wanted Gloria to confirm. Not that there was any chance she'd say no. Ash's confidence, and the insistence that came with it, was another new thrill she was discovering.

Gloria nodded and just the simple action of moving her head up and down, of acquiescing to Ash in that way, of giving her another small piece of herself, unleashed another round of flames to lick along her skin.

Ash smiled so warmly at her, as though Gloria had just given *her* an unexpected present.

"Just a second." She rolled off Gloria and rummaged in her bag that stood next to the bed. She re-emerged with the bottle of lube she had used on Gloria over the weekend.

"Let me." Gloria sat up. Ash gave her the bottle. Gloria squirted a dollop into her palm and rubbed her hands together. Then, she allowed herself a long, luxurious look at the strap-on she'd felt bulge against her body as she and Ash had kissed and rolled all over each other.

She reached for it and the softness of it against her hands surprised her again. She rubbed the lube all over it, getting well acquainted with its shape in the process. Gloria had a lot of questions about this, but they would have to wait until later— until after Ash had fucked her.

Then, there was only the sound of the sheets rustling as Gloria lay back. As she spread her legs. As Ash found her place between them. She'd spread her legs for Ash before—so many times in the space of one weekend, Gloria could barely believe it when she thought about it—but this was different. Not only in the level of arousal it stirred in her, but in the measure of surrender Gloria so easily engaged in when it came to Ash. This woman she'd known vaguely for a long time and who had burst onto the scene of her life and had painted it, so suddenly, in such splendid colour.

Ash's finger brushed against Gloria's pulsing clit as she applied more lube between her legs, and Gloria nearly burst out of her skin with want. It was the desire, the red-hot lust she had for Ash, that made her feel most alive of all. That stirring deep inside her that could so easily, like something set on fire, spread to every cell in her body. Gloria wanted Ash with everything she had, with everything she was, and right now, it was much more exciting than it was disconcerting. Because it was disconcerting. It was incongruous with whom Gloria had believed herself to be for most of her life. It didn't fit into the path her existence had taken.

But it was there. Pulsing hotly between her legs, where Gloria could feel the lube dripping along her inner thigh, a sensation so unexpected but, once again, so utterly beguiling, that Gloria grew even closer to Ash. Because she might be in bed with another woman, but, somehow, she knew that that woman could only ever have been Ash. She couldn't picture any other person ever making her feel like this. She'd tried, but she'd never come close to anything like this. Her lust was completely wrapped up in her feelings for Ash and Gloria knew this wasn't just some tryst to make menopause more bearable. She didn't know what it was to Ash, that was impossible, and it was too hard a conversation to have for now, but to her, right now, it was everything.

Ash's fingers skated along her entrance, flicked along her clit again. Gloria glanced down at the glistening toy protruding from Ash's hips.

"Please," she begged, because she couldn't wait one second longer.

Ash shuffled closer. Gloria tried to watch, but most of what was happening was hidden from her view. Ash's fingers were replaced by the tip of the dildo. She let it skate along Gloria's wet folds, let it slide along her clit the way her fingers had done earlier. Gloria could see Ash's face, though. She looked so focused, so intent on only one thing: Gloria's pleasure.

The toy stilled against Gloria. Ash looked up, her eyes

hooded and intense. She locked her gaze on Gloria as she very gently slid the tip inside.

Gloria swallowed the emotion out of her throat. She braced herself for what was coming. The toy was warm and wet as it slipped further into her, as it brought Ash closer to her. Gloria spread her legs further. Ash's eyes narrowed as she pushed in further and further, filling Gloria in a way she hadn't been in years.

Ash leaned over Gloria, their gazes still firmly locked. And yes, the sensation of the strap-on moving inside of her was utterly divine—so divine it elicited a strange noise from the back of her throat—but it was the way Ash looked at her that made her swoon the most. It was a look that said that Ash wouldn't be walking away from this any time soon. Gloria looked back at her as best she could, between her eyes falling shut because there was too much pleasure to process, too much joy for her body to absorb. But she knew she didn't want Ash to go anywhere. They'd find a way to see each other, to make it work, because this was too good to not pursue.

Ash upped the ante. Her strokes went from long and slow to faster-paced and more frantic, but only for a few minutes, after which she slowed again.

Gloria had cried in this bedroom. At times, she'd thought she might very well die in it, that was how little strength she'd had to get up in the morning, to face another day of being a young widow. The bed had been replaced years ago, but the memories of this room would always remain, the good and the bad ones. By no means could what she and Ash were doing erase any of them; they could only add to them. What a welcome addition they were. For years now, Gloria had only ever been on her own in this room. What once was their room had become her room, and her room alone. Until now. Because after tonight, after this, a piece of Ash would always linger here.

Ash brought her lips to Gloria's ear, and whispered, "Sit on top of me."

Gloria's eyes went wide. What? She didn't want to stop now. She knew it was unlikely she would reach orgasm in this position, but it didn't matter one bit. Just the sensation of what Ash was doing, of what they were doing together, was more than enough for now.

"Come on." Ash was insistent—a quality Gloria liked about her. If it hadn't been for Ash's insistence, this wouldn't be happening at all. Ash had asked her to dance. Ash had invited Gloria to dinner. Ash had invited herself into Gloria's house. Ash had kissed her first, although Gloria had wanted to kiss her just as much at the time. Ash didn't wait for Gloria's reply. She softly retreated, leaving what felt like a vast empty space inside Gloria for an instant.

Ash lay on her back and Gloria, who only wanted that void inside her filled again as quickly as possible, followed Ash's instruction. In the end, Ash was the woman with the most experience when it came to any of this. And it was an area in which Gloria gladly relinquished control.

She sunk her teeth into her bottom lip as she positioned herself on top of Ash. It was easy to slide herself down, the strap-on filling her so deliciously now.

"I want you to come," Ash said.

Who was Gloria to argue with that? She shifted backwards slightly. Ash slid her hands up Gloria's thighs, until her thumb came to rest near Gloria's clit. She positioned it so that every time Gloria slid back and forth on the toy, it brushed against her there, and flared up the heat that was now building inside her at a ferocious pace.

Gloria looked down at Ash. What was she feeling now? Her lips were slightly parted. Tiny pearls of sweat beaded between her eyebrows. She was grinding along with Gloria. They hooked onto a rhythm. Gloria couldn't feel it, but she could guess that every time she rocked forwards, it must cause some friction around Ash's clit. She glanced down to see what Ash's other hand was doing, but she couldn't see. What she could see was the look an Ash's face. The contorted expression. The narrowing of the eyes. Her breath that became more ragged.

Ash hadn't only wanted to make Gloria come.

"Oh, fuck." The thought of Ash coming like this spurred on the rolling wave of heat inside Gloria. To be able to look into Ash's eyes at a moment like this. To see her in this uncontrolled state of utter bliss.

The heat inside her got the better of her and with a sequence of loud screams, Gloria came.

Underneath her, Ash screamed and came with her.

Chapter Thirty-Three

"What ever shall I bring you next time?" Ash asked. "I feel like I've played my biggest trump card already." She looked at Gloria over the rim of a steaming mug of coffee.

Gloria was only wearing a robe, which she hadn't bothered to close properly. She leaned against the kitchen counter and fixed her gaze right back on Ash. "You strike me as very resourceful. I'm sure you'll figure something out." She grinned and Ash could tell it was one of those involuntary grins that were impossible to hold back, no matter how hard you tried. Ash had been suffering from the same affliction since she'd arrived last night—apart from the times Gloria had made her come. A slice of bread popped out of the toaster. "Are you sure you don't want breakfast?"

Ash just nodded.

"I'm positively famished after last night. I never knew sex was such hard work." Gloria retrieved the slice of toast and let it cool off.

Ash let the memories wash over her. It had been utterly glorious to use the strap-on on Gloria, but what had been even more delightful was when Gloria herself had discovered the joys of using it on Ash.

Robe still half-open, Gloria walked to the table. Ash couldn't keep her eyes off the strip of naked flesh coming her way. This was now officially much more than a one-night stand and there were no signs of her desire for Gloria letting up any time soon.

"What are you going to do when I'm at work?" Gloria sat.

Ash shrugged. "Go through all your stuff? Read your diary?"

"I don't keep a diary, so you can put that idea out of your head." Gloria buttered a slice of toast.

"I didn't really give it that much thought when I made my plan to come over."

"Are you going to see your parents?"

"It feels really weird not to, being in Murraywood. But it would also be very strange to just turn up at their house like that, out of the blue." Ash sighed. "I would also feel very bad lying to them about the real reason I'm here."

"On Monday, I narrowly avoided running into your mum at Sainsbury's." Gloria looked away. "I hid from her, Ash. Can you believe that?"

"They can't know. I agree with you on that." Ash drank more coffee, hoping the caffeine would jolt her brain into a magical solution, even though she'd gone over it many times already, and she knew there wasn't a clear-cut way out of their conundrum.

"What are we going to do? Only see each other in London?" Gloria chewed on a piece of toast.

"Like once a month?" Ash knew she sounded too petulant. She hadn't meant to. As long as she could block out reality, she felt so wonderful in Gloria's company. As soon as she was faced with it—and the thing about reality was that it was very hard to avoid—a sense of impending doom settled over her.

"I have my life, Ash. I'm perfectly willing to change my schedule for you, but it doesn't just depend on me. The Easter holidays are coming up. I have my job, which is shift work and involves weekends a lot of the time. Before we know it, it'll be summer, and Sally and Janey will be home for three months. I'm sorry."

"How can it be so impossible?" Ash mused. She didn't want to give Gloria a hard time. "We are two adult women who are perfectly able to consent. What's so wrong with what we are doing that we have to hide it?"

"In theory, you're right." Gloria put down her slice of toast. Apparently their not-so-cheerful banter was affecting her appetite. "In practice, it's very different. It's hard."

"Is it too hard, though?"

"I don't know where that line would be drawn." Under the table, Gloria's bare foot found Ash's. "It just also very much feels like a discussion we shouldn't be having yet. What happened last night, you turning up here with that strap-on, and delighting the fuck out of me, that's what should be happening. And it is. Although the come-down the morning after is a bit harsh, I must admit."

"It's just, the other day, at my place..." Ash caught Gloria's foot between her ankles. "You sounded quite optimistic about... us."

"You'd just shagged my brains out for an entire weekend." That grin was momentarily back on Gloria's lips. "But then I had to come home and face the music, so to speak. Running into Mary and not being able to strike up a casual conversation with her brought all the doubts back to the surface."

Ash exhaled deeply. "I'm an analyst. Part of my job is assessing the risk of making an investment. I should be able to break this down and find a way."

Gloria chuckled. "We're human beings. With oh so many feelings. You can't analyse that."

"Maybe, but I can make a list. Maybe I'll do that while you're at work."

"What? Risk assess our potential relationship?" Gloria cocked her head.

"I know it sounds very cold and clinical, but it might help us to see some things written down in black and white."

"I want to keep seeing you. Don't forget to put that in your final report." Gloria freed her foot from the cage of Ash's ankles and ran her toes up Ash's calf.

"I'll do my very best to produce a favourable outcome for us, but, quite honestly, I have no idea how I'm going to go about it yet."

"You have all afternoon and all evening. But please make sure you have some energy for when I get home." Gloria hooked both her feet around the leg of Ash's chair and pulled it closer to hers.

"Do you want me to make you dinner?"

"The only dinner I'll be wanting, Ashley Cooper, is you." Gloria leaned in and kissed Ash on the lips. When she did that, it was so easy, so seductive to forget about the impossibility of their situation. But it also made Ash want to try really hard to find a way out of it.

Ash figured Gloria's back garden would be a safe place for her to sit. The living room was quite dark and Ash had grown used to an abundance of light flooding her flat. The absence of sunlight was making her even glummer than she was already feeling after the conversation they'd had earlier. Being trapped on her own in a house that wasn't hers wasn't helping. It reminded her of staying at Lewis and Jonathan's after the separation, but at least, in their house, she didn't feel as though she had to hide from the outside world.

In front of her lay a sheet of paper and a pen. Ash hadn't written anything down yet. That, too, reminded her of the divorce—whereas this whole thing with Gloria was supposed to do the opposite. Of course, when the time had come to make a decision about putting in the effort to stay together or breaking up with Charlotte, Ash had made a list of pros and cons. It had turned into a sad exercise with only one possible result. She didn't want to repeat that today.

She sagged into her chair and looked out over Gloria's garden, which backed onto a stretch of empty meadows, followed by a gorgeous view of typical English rolling-hill countryside. This view, she could get used to. Only, she couldn't. While the view was lovely, sitting in Gloria's garden made her uneasy. Theirs was a clandestine affair. There were no two ways about it. Ash didn't want her parents to know. Gloria didn't want her daughters and most of the town to know. Although Gloria had, apparently, very readily admitted the news of her affair with Ash to her best friends. That was something. A start.

She wrote it down on the paper, so she could make a start as well. It was hard to focus, however, because the smallest sound startled her. Ash hadn't wrapped her head around Gloria's work schedule yet, so it wasn't a far stretch of the imagination that a lot of her friends might not have done so either, resulting in someone turning up at Gloria's unannounced. Murraywood was the kind of town where people came in through the back door —at least they did at her parents' house. Everything was informal. What if someone stopped by and found Ash sitting in Gloria's garden? What would she say? There was no plausible explanation. Then Ash imagined telling the imaginary person the real reason she was there. Was it really that appalling? She didn't think so. It might be hard for people to accept at first, but they'd get used to it.

Ash put the pen down again. Gloria had been right. This wasn't the sort of thing you analysed on a piece of paper. None of what they had done together, the conversations they'd had and the love they'd made, had been theoretical. There was really only one way to find out how people would react.

By telling someone.

Her parents were a step too far at this point. But her brother wasn't. Adrian lived nearby. He worked from home a lot. He might even be home and if he wasn't, he would be soon. Aside from that, Ash was keen to see her nephews. Their care-free smirks and cheers were exactly what she needed.

As she headed out the door, her resolve started to crumble. Should she really tell Adrian without consulting Gloria before-hand? She would be pretty much outing Gloria without her consent. But then again, Gloria had already told Sindhu and Fiona about what had happened. Surely, she would understand Ash's need to talk things over with her brother. And with that, her mind was made up.

She didn't text or call beforehand. She just walked over to Adrian and Lizzie's house and knocked on the door.

"Are my eyes deceiving me?" Adrian pulled a silly face. "Is that my fair sister all the way from London town?" The silly smile disappeared from his face swiftly. "Is everything okay? Is it Mum or Dad?"

"Everything and everyone's fine, Ade," Ash assured her brother. "There's nothing to worry about."

"Nothing to worry about? It's before five on a Wednesday and your standing in my kitchen. Of course I'm going to be worried. Did something happen to you?"

"Where is everyone?" The house was very quiet.

"The kids always go to Lizzie's parents after school on Wednesdays. She's picking them up."

"Oh." Ash moved further into the kitchen. She was glad Adrian was home alone so they could talk in peace, but now that she actually had to say something, it was proving difficult.

"Is it something with Charlotte?" Adrian walked to the

fridge and took out two bottles of beer. He handed one to Ash. "Or work? Why aren't you at work, sis?"

"Day off." Ash gladly accepted the beer. "Charlotte's seeing someone else, apparently." While it had initially bothered her when Lewis had told her, Ash had given Charlotte and her possible new love interest very little thought.

"I'm sorry, Ash." Adrian shrugged. "I guess it was bound to happen. I'm sure you'll find someone as well." He sat at the kitchen table and Ash followed his example. "Whenever you're ready," he said.

This was her chance. Adrian had left the door wide open. "It's not about Charlotte." Ash chugged back a good amount of beer. "I may have met someone. I mean, I have, but it's early days."

"Say what?" Adrian's eyes widened. "Tell me."

"Honestly, I'm not sure you want to know." Ash tried to relax. She leaned back and drank some more.

"Why not? Did you fall for a man?" He wiggled his brows. "Will you bring shame on to the family name with your sordid heterosexual ways, Ashley?" He chuckled loudly.

"It's Gloria," Ash blurted out. "We've been seeing each other since Mum's party."

"Who?" Adrian genuinely looked as though, for a split second, he had no idea who Gloria was. "Gloria Young? Who lives around the corner? Sally and Janey's mum?" He fell silent, his face a mask of confusion. Then he shook his head. "Nah. You're pulling my leg with this shit. I won't be fooled that easily, sis."

"Bro, I'm telling you, I'm not having a laugh here. Why would I?"

Adrian raked his fingers through his thinning hair. He took a quick, nervous swig from his beer. "That's why you're in Murraywood on a Wednesday afternoon? Because you're having a secret affair with one of Mum's friends?" It sounded more like an accusation than a question. "Jesus."

Ash thought it better not to say anything. To give Adrian a little bit of time to absorb the news.

"Isn't she straight? She's been a widow for a long time, but..." He shook his head again. "How did this even happen?"

"Someone sat us next to each other at Mum's birthday party."

"Lizzie and I were at that table too."

"We just hit it off. She came to London. I took her out. One thing led to another..." It felt odd to sum it up in a few short sentences like that. It didn't do Ash's true feelings for Gloria justice at all.

"What you're actually saying is that you seduced her?" Adrian's voice had changed from hesitant to more forceful, like he was blaming Ash for it all.

"What? No. It wasn't like that at all."

"You're the lesbian, Ash. She's the straight woman. It's pretty obvious."

Ash rolled her eyes. Some things simply couldn't be explained. Adrian didn't look very receptive to any explanation she might give, anyway. Maybe this had been a mistake. As far as test cases went, it was a huge failure. And this was her little brother. A young guy who had been raised with an open mind, who had been taught not to judge on the first impression. *Yeah right.*

"Don't tell me Gloria came on to you out of the blue." He slammed his beer bottle down.

"Ade, please. Calm down. What you're focusing on right now is so beside the point."

He puffed up his cheeks and blew out the air audibly. "Is it serious?" He held up his hand. "Sorry. I was just... I wasn't expecting this at all. My reaction was not okay. I apologise."

Ash waved him off. "It's all right. It tells me everything I need to know."

"What do you mean?"

"Coming to Murraywood and not seeing any of you was doing my head in. Hiding in Gloria's house while she's at work." Ash shook her head. "It just... takes away a great deal of the joy of meeting someone and being with them those first few weeks. It's like I constantly need to look over my shoulder. Or check my behaviour in case I fall too deeply for her and there's no way back apart from hurting again." Ash didn't know if she was making any sense to her brother.

"So it *is* serious?" Was that what Adrian concluded from what Ash had just said? Maybe her brother could read her better than she could herself.

"Not really. How can it be? But, shit, Ade... I really, *really* like her. Like, a fucking lot." At least Ash could swear all she wanted around her brother. At least that made her feel a little better.

"Does she like you back?" Adrian reached for his beer again.

"I'm pretty positive that she does." Saying this made a grin appear on Ash's face. "When we're together, in private, it somehow makes sense. It just fits, even though we might seem like an odd combination. I can talk to her and she opens up to me and it's just... fucking heavenly to be with her."

"Shit, sis. You've got it bad." Adrian knocked back the last of his beer. Ash did the same. Because Adrian was right. She did have it bad. "What are you going to do?" he asked.

"It's not only up to me. I don't even live here, but... can you imagine me telling Mum and Dad?"

"I'm not keen to be there when you have that conversation," he said on a sigh.

"It's not that they would be angry. All I can imagine at this point is even more disappointment. Dad has barely put the divorce behind him. I couldn't bear the look in his eyes. He's so fond of Gloria. It's just... I simply can't see it happening."

"Do you think there's a chance it might last?"

"Very little, at this point. Not because of how we feel, but because it's just too complicated. It's not just Mum and Dad. She has two daughters. Gloria's entire life is in Murraywood. I can't make her feel ostracised in her own town. I won't do that to her."

"What are you saying? Are you going to break it off?"

Maybe it took her brother to ask the question in such a straightforward way to finally make her crumble. "I really don't want to, Ade." Tears burned behind Ash's eyes. "But what's the alternative?"

Chapter Thirty-Four

"No, no, no, not Ade," Gloria said. Her head was spinning. "Lizzie is my co-worker. She's his wife, Ash. Of course he's going to tell her and then how are we going to keep this quiet?" This was not the homecoming she had imagined. Frankly, what she had imagined was Ash naked in her bed, save for the present she'd brought the day before. Instead, Ash had broken the horrible news that she'd gone to see her brother and told him about them—without consulting Gloria first.

"He's not going to tell her. I trust him." Ash paced up and down the kitchen. "Besides, you told your friends. What's the difference?"

"I trust Sindhu and Fiona not to tell anyone. I've known them since I was little."

"I trust my brother. I've known him since he was born."

"Look, Ash, it's just that we didn't discuss any of this before-hand. Telling Adrian brings it all a whole lot closer to your parents knowing. The thought of which is majorly doing my head in."

"Mine too," Ash said.

"Maybe this is telling us something very crucial." Gloria's stomach tensed.

"I know what you're going to say, Gloria." Ash finally stopped pacing. She took a few steps in Gloria's direction. "But let's just, at the very least, have one more night together. I'm not taking the train back to London tonight. It's too late. I'll go first thing in the morning. But give me tonight."

"Of course, we have tonight." Gloria put her arms around Ash. She swallowed a knot out of her throat. "But after that..."

"It has to end." Ash's voice broke a little.

Gloria didn't know what to say after that. So she kissed Ash and Ash kissed her back, but so much desperation was wrapped in their kisses, so much of the loss she was about to experience was already manifesting itself inside her.

"There's so much I don't know about you yet," Gloria said, when they broke from their kiss, which had been more sad than arousing, if she was being honest with herself. "There's so much I want to know."

A lone tear dripped down Ash's cheek. Gloria wanted to catch it with her finger but she had no right to do that. Not anymore. Not when she was the cause of it.

"I'm sorry I told Adrian," Ash said, wiping away the tear herself, then pretending it was never even there. "I just wanted to test what it would be like to tell someone in my family. Ade was the only choice."

"What was it like?" Gloria had been so shaken by Ash actually telling Ade that she hadn't yet inquired about his reaction.

"He was a bit shocked at first, but after that, he was fine." Ash pulled up one shoulder. "Like he might accept it rather easily."

"Really?" Gloria could only take Ash's word for it, but why wouldn't Adrian accept it? He was Ash's brother and Gloria knew they had a great relationship. He might, in fact, be one of the only people in Murraywood to accept it.

"Well, yeah... he wants me to be happy. Just like I want that for him." Ash sighed. "But when we speculated about how it would be to tell Mum and Dad..." She fell silent.

Gloria pulled Ash near again. "Let's make a deal for tonight," she said. "Let's pretend, just until you have to leave tomorrow, that everything will be fine."

Ash huffed out some air. "I've been thinking about what you said when you left my place on Sunday evening. About how if it was meant to be, it would work out."

Gloria nodded. She had said that. But she'd said it after a weekend of the most earth-shattering sex of her life. She would say something like that under those circumstances—but the circumstances were very different now. "I know."

"Do you still believe that?" Ash asked.

"I want to, but... I can't change how things are. Maybe half the thrill of what we have is the secrecy of it." Gloria didn't really believe that herself.

Ash freed herself from Gloria's embrace and sat on a kitchen chair. It probably wasn't what she wanted to hear.

"I'm not sure I can pretend." When Ash looked up at her with all the sadness on full display in her glance, Gloria wasn't entirely sure she should even stay the night. "I—I keep telling myself that I don't know what this is, but, really, I'm just being in denial about it. I know very well what this is, Gloria. I'm falling so crazily, so madly, so recklessly in love with you, and it scares me to death, because... well, last time I fell in love with someone, I married and subsequently divorced her."

Gloria scoffed and the instant she did, she regretted it. Ash being so open and vulnerable with her didn't deserve that kind of reaction. But Gloria was just as scared as Ash. It was merely her own fear trying to find a way out, masked as insensitivity.

Gloria pulled a chair close to where Ash was sitting. She took her hand in hers.

"I know—" Ash started saying.

"Sweetheart—" Gloria said, at the same time.

They looked at each other. "You first," Gloria said.

"I know how foolish that sounds, but it's how I feel, and that's the God's honest truth." Ash's eyes glittered with the onset of tears.

"You met me at a very vulnerable time in your life. I'm no psychologist, but even I can tell that you're still getting over your divorce. Maybe... you're just clinging to this so much because it's something that makes you feel better about yourself after having felt so lousy for a long time."

Ash pushed her chair back. "I don't expect you to feel the same way. That's not why I said it." She was the one who scoffed now. "How could you possibly feel the same as I do, anyway?"

Maybe, Gloria thought, this was the only way for them to do this. To brutally rupture the beautiful but delicate connection that had formed between them the past few weeks. Rip off the proverbial Band-Aid and be done with it. Maybe any other, any gentler way would be too painful for too long. Now Ash was saying that she was falling in love with Gloria? Surely, that couldn't really be true. It was too soon. Too irrational. Too devoid of any of the logic Gloria had based her entire life on after George's death.

"I think you know that I have very strong feelings for you, Ash, but..."

"It's fine." Ash shot out of her chair. "I think I'll go now. I'll crash at Ade's." She fixed her narrowed gaze on Gloria. "Don't worry, I'll make sure Lizzie doesn't know anything."

"Ash, come on. Don't just run off like that." Gloria was all contradiction now. She didn't want Ash to leave, she knew that much, but she also knew that Ash staying would only delay the inevitable. "We're both adults here."

"That we are, but there is one big difference between us, Gloria, and I'm glad it's coming up now instead of later. I'm gay.

I'm a big old lesbian. I fall in love with women. I've done so my entire life. So of course I was going to fall for you because..." She took a quick breath. "Because you're a bloody amazing woman. How can I not fall for you? That's the question that should be asked here. Granted, I'm still a little sore from my divorce. Although Charlotte surely hasn't been biding her time to start over with someone else—" She stopped her rant abruptly.

What had Ash just said? Was Charlotte involved with someone new? "Oh, Ash." Gloria couldn't help herself. Open-armed, she headed towards Ash. "I'm sorry. That must have been so hard for you to find out."

"Bloody Charlotte," Ash muttered under her breath, while she accepted Gloria's hug.

Gloria held Ash close. Her own mind was in such turmoil, it seemed impossible to be certain whether what she felt was compassion or tenderness or, even, like Ash, that roller-coaster sensation of falling in love.

"Stay," Gloria whispered, because she couldn't send Ash away now.

If Ash was crying, her sobs were almost imperceptible. But when Gloria put a little bit of distance between them, the top of her uniform was moist near her shoulder where Ash had buried her face.

"Oh, fuck." Ash fished a handkerchief out of her pocket and blew her nose. "I'm so sorry, Gloria. I take it back, okay? Can I?" She painted on a smirk, as if she wanted to make light of what she had just admitted, as though wanting to convince Gloria that she'd just been ranting, foolishly spouting nonsense.

Gloria could so easily detect the insincerity in Ash's expression. She couldn't lie about something like that. "You don't have to take it back." Gloria finally allowed herself to feel flattered by what Ash had said. It wasn't every day that a gorgeous and accomplished woman like Ash told her that she was falling in love with her. Obviously, this was all new to Gloria and she didn't know what she was feeling. Maybe the novelty was too confusing, or maybe she was afraid to admit her emotions to herself. Or maybe, as Ash had just said, she simply wasn't capable of having such feelings for Ash because she wasn't inclined that way.

"At least don't think you need to have the same feelings as I do." Ash shook her head. "That's not why I said it."

"It's been such a whirlwind, Ash. You, um, you don't do things by half and the way you've lavished all this attention on me, the way you've made me feel so alive, so wanted, so completely in my body... it's nothing short of a miracle, really. But I have to be certain that I'm not confusing certain emotions here. You're right, I'm way behind you in this. How can I not be? I'm still getting over sleeping with a woman for the first time. It's not a small matter to me."

"How about we just take some time?" Ash's tone of voice had returned to normal. Her eyes seemed totally dry of tears. "A breather. This thing with you, Gloria, it's just so intense." She held up her hands. "It's how I get when I really like someone."

"What are you suggesting? That we don't see each other for a while?"

"We weren't going to, anyway. Your daughters are coming home for a while and I need to do some emotional stocktaking. Let's press pause for a few weeks. See where we stand after?"

"Will we be in touch?" A different kind of fear gripped Gloria, made her insides twist.

Ash blew out some air again. "I don't know." A short silence fell. "Maybe it would be best if we weren't."

Gloria was the one who felt like spilling a few tears now. How could she still be confused about her feelings for Ash? Hadn't she completely rocked her world the past few weeks? Made her question everything? "But this is not the end?"

"No." Ash sounded adamant enough, but still, there was a

quality about her voice as though she was retreating, protecting herself. "Let's meet up after your girls have gone back to uni. Then, we'll see."

"That's in three weeks," Gloria said.

"Yeah, well, we need the time." Ash still looked the same, but she didn't sound like the woman who had arrived at Gloria's house with a strap-on in her bag the previous night.

"But you'll stay tonight?" Gloria was almost too afraid to ask.

Ash's eyes had suddenly gone moist again. "I'm not sure I can." She gave a slight shake of the head. "I think it might hurt me too much if I did."

Just like that, Gloria had the wind knocked out of her as well. Although she understood that it was easier to say goodbye right now instead of early in the morning, after, perhaps, a sleepless night.

"You're going to Adrian's?"

Ash nodded.

"I can give you a lift."

"He lives literally just around the corner."

"He won't be expecting you. They might have gone to bed already."

"Gloria." Ash's voice was very insistent now. "It's fine." And with that, everything was said.

Chapter Thirty-Five

I t was a definite sign of how she'd been feeling that Ash hadn't invited any of her family over to her new place in London yet. At first, she had to get used to it—to inhabiting a space, no matter how small, on her own again. To not have obvious signs of someone else's life on display everywhere. It had also taken her months to unpack, to decorate, and now, to put the final touches to the shelves, the walls, and the windows. To make it feel like a home she could be happy in, even if it had to be on her own. It didn't help that everywhere she looked she saw a spot where she and Gloria had kissed or, even worse, had had their hands and mouths all over each other.

It was the weekend after she had said goodbye to Gloria—after they'd pressed the pause button. Ash had just put clean sheets on the guest bed because her mother would be staying over after she'd taken her out for a night on the town. It would be the first time her mum would see this place.

Ash hadn't even had a proper house-warming party yet. She made a mental note to schedule one, if only to chase away the ghost of Gloria. Because even though Ash loved telling herself that it was just a 'break', that they would reconvene in a few weeks and only then make their final decision, the fact that they had needed to take a break at all told her everything she needed to know.

On top of that, Ash had made a real spectacle of herself, what with telling Gloria that she was falling in love with her. What had she been thinking? It was true, but some truths, she knew, were better kept for oneself. Saying you had such strong feelings for another woman so shortly after meeting her was simply not done, no matter how strongly said feelings made their presence known every single minute of every single day. Ash knew very well it wasn't one of her finest, nor her suavest, moments. So she had begun, slowly but steadily, to prepare herself for the break to turn into a break-up.

Last night, when she couldn't sleep, Ash had even scrolled through Tinder. Just to have a look. Just to be reminded that Gloria wasn't the only woman out there. On the contrary. There were many other women who would be much more suited for a dalliance. The problem was that Ash wasn't even remotely interested in any of these other, more suited women.

Ash cast one last glance at the guest room and deemed it ready for her mother's scrutiny, although she also knew she didn't need to worry about that. Her mother wasn't the kind—unlike Charlotte's mother—to walk into her daughter's home and dispense a slew of criticisms. At least Ash didn't have to deal with Charlotte's parents anymore.

She checked her reflection in the mirror. Her mum would surely comment on how tired she looked. Ash could hear the concern in her voice already.

I haven't been sleeping because I'm in love with Gloria, Mum.

She couldn't even say it out loud. The thought was stuck in her head, where it should remain. She put on her coat and went to meet her mother at the train station.

"Can I ask you something, darling?" Ash's mother said, as though she needed to ask permission.

"Of course." They were on their second cocktail and Ash was happy to be out with her mum. Happy to spoil her with overpriced drinks and take her to the kind of glitzy places that didn't exist in Murraywood.

"It's just that... you seemed to have really picked yourself up the last few times we spoke. Like you'd finally moved past the worst of the divorce, but now, looking at you, I'm not so sure anymore. Are you okay, Ashley?"

"Charlotte has someone new," Ash blurted out, just like she'd done to Gloria. As though it was an excuse for her own behaviour and it could explain the dark bags underneath her eyes. "Lewis saw them together."

"Is it serious?" Her mum sipped from her fancy drink.

"I don't know. It doesn't really matter, though, does it?"

"But it has shaken you? I can tell."

"No, actually, it hasn't really affected me that much at all. It was a shock when Lewis first told me, but now I don't really care that much."

"Is it that you've stopped caring for someone you used to love so much?"

Ash glanced at her mother. She was the sweetest woman she'd ever met, and she knew that wasn't a given just because she was her mum. Could she ever tell her the truth? It didn't really matter now, anyway. "I don't know. I *was* doing better. I do feel like I've put myself back together again, but... I have my ups and downs."

"You need to give these things time. You and Charlotte were together for such a long time. It's only normal." Her mum shot her a wink. "You'll find someone again. If that's what you want, of course."

Ash shrugged. She was afraid that if she spoke, she might say too much.

"Is *that* what you want?" The cocktails must have gone to her mum's head, because she was pushing more than she usually would.

"I think so. Yes," Ash said. *I've already found someone.*

"Earlier, on the train, I read an article about how more and more people are single. Divorced. Widowed. Or not even that. There are many people these days who just prefer it that way."

"I don't know if I prefer it. I guess I'll have to see."

"Look at Gloria," her mum said.

Had someone just given Ash an electric shock? Because that was what it felt like when her mother said Gloria's name.

"She's been single for such a long time," her mum continued.

Ash couldn't help but be suspicious. Was her mum fishing? Had she heard something? God forbid, had Adrian said something? It wasn't entirely unthinkable.

"She had children to raise, of course. But still." It sounded more as though her mum was just thinking out loud.

Her mum gave her a look. If she did know something about her and Gloria, would this be the strategy she'd deploy to get Ash to spill the beans? Ash really didn't think so.

"My situation's very different," Ash said.

"And you don't live in Murraywood." Her mum chuckled. "If Gloria can't find a man in Murraywood, what would be the chances of you ever finding a woman?"

Ash narrowed her eyes. Either her mother's cocktail was really strong, or she really was testing Ash. She had to ask Adrian. Ash excused herself to go to the ladies' so she could text her brother.

Adrian's reply came quickly.

Who do you take me for? I haven't told a soul. Not even my own wife!

At the very least, it was good to have confirmation that Ash could trust her brother with a secret.

"I just got a text from Ade," her mum said when Ash joined her at their table again. "He's asking, on a scale of one to Adrian, how much fun I'm having with you." She smiled broadly.

Adrian was having a busy Saturday night of texting. "Tell Ade to leave you be and have your fun with me tonight."

"I will, sweetheart."

While her mum texted back, Ash noticed that she'd finished her cocktail. It was time to have some food before Ash started feeling as though she could confide as much in her mother as she could in her brother.

❧❧❧

"You've really spoiled me, Ashley. Thank you so much." Mary had just polished off the last crumb of her dessert.

"This was your birthday present, Mum. And it was my absolute pleasure."

"We should do this more often. Now that you live alone, I should come to London more and spend time with you. It's not long at all on the train." She was almost slurring her words now. It was past eleven. Ash's mum was an early riser who liked to go to bed before ten.

"You're always welcome at mine." Being with her mum was simply comfortable. She was easy company. And it took Ash's mind off Gloria—as long as her mum didn't inadvertently bring her up.

"I liked it when you came over for the weekend two weeks ago. It was just lovely to have you home. To take care of you. Because that's really all I've been wanting to do since you and Charlotte split up. Take care of you. Feed you. Do your laundry." She sat up a bit straighter. "Make sure you're okay."

"I'll come home more often, because I happen to love being taken care of by you." Ash chuckled.

"Next weekend? Your dad would be chuffed. He's going to want some time in the pub with you after this."

"I—I need to check my calendar." Ash wasn't sure she was up for a weekend in Murraywood. She didn't want to run into Gloria—or one of her daughters, although she wouldn't even recognise them.

"As much as we loved having both you and Charlotte staying over, it's not the same as having just you at the house."

"How's Dad taking all of this?" Ash asked. "I know he was very fond of Charlotte. Thought of her as a second daughter."

"Darling, you are our only daughter. Sure, we always got along with Charlotte. And both your father and I thought it horrible how her parents treated her when it came to her relationship with you. But you're our priority. You always will be." She heaved a small sigh. "All your father and I want is for you to be happy again. That's it."

Ash divided the last of the wine over their two glasses. She wasn't going to give her mother any details, but now that she was in such a sentimental mood, she might as well quiz her a bit.

"Hypothetically," she started. "Say I meet someone that you and Dad wouldn't necessarily approve of."

"Like who?" Her mother shrugged. "What would be wrong with this person that we couldn't approve of her?"

"I don't know... she could be too old or too young or..." *A family friend.* "Let's say, for instance, your former colleague Joanne took a shine to me."

"Joanne?" Her mother furrowed her brow. "Is she gay? I never knew."

"No. This is just a hypothetical scenario, Mum. I'm not saying Joanne is gay, but what if she were and she and I ran into each other and one thing led to another. Do you think you and Dad would still prioritise my happiness?"

"I'm not entirely sure I understand the question, darling." Her mother widened her eyes, then rested her gaze on Ash.

"I guess the question is whether my personal happiness is more important to you than what people might think about who I'm with."

"In this case Joanne?" Her mother shook her head. "It's just that I'm having a really hard time picturing you and her together."

"It could be anyone. Joanne's the first person that came to mind, because she never married." This conversation was turning increasingly absurd.

"You mean someone like Sandra. Someone I've known forever." Her mother leaned over the table in a conspiratorial manner. "I have thought that Sandra might be a lesbian, you know."

"Say that she is." Ash held up her hands. "Although I'm by no means claiming that she actually is. She's just one of those people that you read about in that article, someone who prefers to remain single." Ash had never gotten any vibe off Sandra and she didn't want to be the source of a silly rumour—she knew how those things could go in a town like Murraywood. "Say that Sandra and I, against all odds, fall in love. How would you feel about that?"

"Jesus, darling." If her mother was wearing pearls, she'd be clutching them now. "That's truly impossible to tell." She cocked her head. "You aren't trying to tell me something, are you? I saw Sandra just the other day. She didn't say—"

"No, Mum. As I said, purely hypothetical. I haven't seen Sandra since your birthday party. It's not a real thing." Oh, Christ, what had Ash got herself into now? What a convoluted mess. All because she was trying to get the answer to an impossible question. "Let's just leave it." Ash tried to cover her annoyance with herself with a sweet smile—the kind only her own mother could ever accept—and asked for the bill.

"I'll sleep on it, darling. I'm feeling a bit fuzzy in the head right now," her mum said.

Chapter Thirty-Six

Gloria couldn't get the smell of the roast she'd burnt out of her nose, even though they'd left the house, in search of a more edible meal in the local pub.

She hurried Sally and Janey along because it was close to the time that The Horse and Groom would stop taking lunch orders, although Gloria wasn't too worried. A few years ago, the landlady had an operation go wrong and Gloria had tended to a wound in a delicate place on Peggy's body for weeks. Since then, she had received more free drinks at the pub than she had paid for. Still, she didn't want to inconvenience them just because she'd taken her eye off the oven. Or she'd put it on too high. Or whatever else had gone wrong. Gloria had made hundreds of roasts in that very oven and never had it come out so pitch-black and sad-looking.

Sally had made a sarcastic remark about hoping that 'fresh patch Tuesday' would soon come around, while Janey had just shrugged the way girls her age still did.

When they reached the pub, Gloria rolled her eyes. On the blackboard outside it was announced that a football game would soon start on the big screen. Gloria couldn't care less who was playing, she just hoped they could have a meal in peace.

They found a relatively quiet table by the window, as far away as possible from the television screen. Of course they could still order the Sunday roast and the first round of drinks would be on the house at Peggy's insistence.

Since they'd both arrived home the day before, Janey in the morning and Sally in the afternoon, Gloria's daughters had more to say to each other than to her. They hadn't seen each other in weeks and now that Janey was also at university, Sally could suddenly treat her as an almost-equal again.

They had also both informed her, as though they had agreed upon it beforehand—which they probably had—that later today they *had* to attend a party at Craig's house. Who was Gloria to argue with that? This wasn't the first time her girls had come home from university. She knew the drill. She didn't care, either way. She was just glad to have this time with them. She was even content to hear them chat and giggle with each other, even if it meant they were ignoring her.

Right now, they sat there so poised and put together. It was hard to imagine the frail wisps of girls they'd been after their father had been ripped from their young lives so cruelly. Gloria had had her own grief to deal with, of course, because she had always, and always would, consider George the love of her life, but to witness her daughters going through that kind of loss had been the most harrowing of all. To be the mother of two young girls who had always had a father until they didn't—who had seen their father fall ill, become weak from the chemo-therapy, get better, with all the hope that came with his remission, only to lose him for good after—was devastating. If it was already so hard for Gloria to bear, she couldn't imagine what it was like for Sally and Janey.

But now here they were—on the other side of that grief. Time had done its job. They went months and months without mentioning their father. When Gloria had told them about a man she was seeing a few years back, they had encouraged her to go on the next date and the next. They weren't the kind of children who wanted to hog their mother, keep her solely to themselves because they'd already lost one parent. Gloria's daughters wanted her to be happy, she knew that much. They wanted for her what she wanted for them.

Speaking of—it was about time for the traditional come-home-from-uni grilling about her daughters' love life. Gloria could be in denial about that all she wanted, but she knew at some point her daughters would fall in love. They'd had plenty of all-consuming crushes already, but none of them had ever really turned into much more than that, as far as Gloria knew.

"Hello there, girls." Out of nowhere, Alan appeared next to their table. "I thought that was you, Gloria." He shot her a warm smile that Gloria found hard to reciprocate. Luckily, Alan focused most of his attention on Sally and Janey, whom he hadn't seen in ages.

She tried to follow their conversation, but, at the sight of Ash's father, her mind was too preoccupied with thoughts of Ash. The girls coming home had given her exhausted brain some respite from going over their last conversation again and again. At last, Gloria had something else to focus on. For that reason, she wished Alan, who was surely here to watch the football, would go back to his own table soon.

Alan looked behind him at the bar. "Ash is home this weekend. She's getting the drinks in." He waved at his daughter.

Someone might as well have sat on Gloria's chest. Her breath caught in her throat and her heart started racing. This was the exact reason she and Ash couldn't be together. Gloria took a deep breath to try to hide her distress.

"Hey." Ash sauntered up to their table with two pint glasses in her hands. She briefly caught Gloria's gaze, then offered the girls a wide smile.

Gloria hoped Alan wasn't expecting an invitation to join them.

"Kick-off's in two minutes, Dad," Ash said, mercifully.

"Oh, yes, of course. Right." Alan nodded at Gloria. "Enjoy their visit, Gloria. Trust me, they grow up so bloody fast."

Gloria tried very hard not to look at Ash, but her gaze was drawn to her like iron to a magnet. Her hair was casually combed back and not styled in its usual upward, high-maintenance fashion. She looked as though she might have also skipped the few meals she did occasionally allow herself.

"See you around, girls," Alan said. "And remember, always be nice to your Mum."

"See you," Ash said, and turned away from their table without saying anything else.

"Ash is a hedge fund manager, isn't she?" Sally said.

"Hm. What, darling?" It took all Gloria had to give her attention to her own daughter. Not only was she worried about Ash, and how forlorn she looked, but she could also feel a pang of unmistakable heat burrowing its way up from deep inside her. What was Ash doing in Murraywood, anyway?

"Mum?" Sally said.

"Yes, sorry." Gloria looked into her daughter's eyes.

"Two hedge fund managers came to talk to our economics seminar a few weeks ago. They looked nothing like her."

"That's 'cause she's a lesbian," Janey said.

"What does that have to with it?" Sally said.

"Excuse me a second." Gloria stood. "I need to use the loo."

She heard Sally and Janey bicker about Ash as she made her way to the ladies'. As much as she wanted to hear what her daughters had to say about Ash and how lesbian she looked—whatever that meant—Gloria needed a moment to herself to regroup. Seeing Ash had caught her by surprise. She hadn't been prepared for the emotional reaction to seeing her, nor for the physical aspect of it.

Gloria washed her hands and splashed some cold water on her face. She studied her mirror image. "Pull yourself together. Your daughters are home," she said to herself.

Then the door of the washroom opened. Ash walked in.

"I'm sorry, Gloria," she said. "I didn't know you'd be here. I'm just here to watch the football with my dad."

"I burned lunch," Gloria said. "I—" She didn't know what to say. Too many thoughts were racing through her mind, all of which, she knew for certain, would be stopped in their tracks immediately if she could just throw her arms around Ash. If she could just kiss her. "What are you doing home?" Gloria asked, as though she had an automatic right to know the answer to such a question.

"Mum asked me. I'm spending more time with her. With everyone in my family, actually, hence the football with Dad." Ash painted on a sheepish smile. "How are you? Happy to have your daughters home?"

"Ash... let's not do this. I—I can't." Gloria truly couldn't stand in the lavatories of The Horse and Groom and have a casual conversation with Ash.

Ash nodded as though she understood much more than what Gloria was saying. "Okay." She turned towards the door.

Gloria was already preparing herself for the deflation she knew she would feel at the sight of Ash closing the door behind her, when Ash turned around.

"I know it's not what we agreed, but, um, can I see you? Just to talk. Five minutes. Any time that suits you." Ash's gaze on Gloria was so piercing, so demanding that it seemed impossible to deny her request.

"The girls will be out later," Gloria said. "I'll text you." Something in her relaxed.

"Thanks." Ash didn't exit immediately. Instead, she stood there and sized up Gloria for an instant. A tiny hint of a smile appeared on her face. Was Gloria so obvious that Ash could just read it all off her face? She would need to check herself in the mirror again before she joined her daughters. They might have moved out semi-permanently, but those girls picked up on everything, like they were in possession of a sixth sense. And running into Ash had flustered Gloria.

Finally, Ash twisted the door knob and left. Gloria steadied herself against the sink. This was no way for a mother to behave, for a woman her age—like the silliest lovestruck teenager you'd ever come across.

Chapter Thirty-Seven

The voice in Ash's head was back in full force. She hadn't allowed it to dominate her thoughts, though, at times, it was hard not to let it.

What if this was more than just a silly fling?

Ash had borrowed her mother's bicycle, claiming she was going on a wholesome ride before returning to London later that night. It wasn't a complete lie. She just hadn't told her mum that her ride had a destination—and that destination was Gloria.

As soon as she'd spotted Gloria in the pub, Ash knew she wouldn't be able to go back to London without seeing her again. She hadn't come to Murraywood with the purpose of running into Gloria, because she knew her daughters were home, and she wanted to give her the privacy and time she needed. They had only planned to see each other again after the next weekend.

But when her mother had asked Ash to come home this weekend, Ash hadn't been able to refuse the offer. Partly because being in Murraywood diminished the physical distance between her and Gloria and, for some obscure reason, this mattered to Ash. And partly because she didn't have anything better to do. Not for lack of plans, but because her mind was all over the place. No matter how hard she tried, which might not have been that hard, Ash couldn't stop thinking about Gloria. The memories they'd made were seared into her brain. The intensity of them made them too powerful to ignore, let alone file away as something done and dusted, as a short but torrid love affair that was all over.

Ash hadn't needed to see Gloria in the pub to know that it could not be over—not for her, anyway. What had surprised her, was Gloria's reaction to seeing her. Gloria looked as though she'd been the one, and not Ash, who had revealed too much about her feelings when they'd last said goodbye.

Ash parked her bicycle out of sight against the back of Gloria's house. The door was open. All she had to do was walk in. Ash was met with a burnt smell that made her nose wrinkle of its own accord.

"As I said." Gloria walked towards her. "I ruined lunch. I burned the roast." She shook her head. "I'm still not sure what happened."

"I'm glad you did," Ash said. "If you hadn't, I might not have seen you at the pub." She glanced around. The house looked transformed now that Gloria's daughters were home. A sweater was flung over the back of a chair. A backpack lay next to the kitchen table. Five pairs of shoes were lined up by the doormat. All reminders of why they had taken this break from whatever it was they had going on between them.

"Seeing you... it left me so nonplussed." Gloria ran a hand through her hair. It looked longer and thicker than when Ash had left this house two weeks prior. Everything about Gloria, and her house, looked slightly different. More off kilter. Less like it was when Ash had spent the night. "I didn't expect it, of course, but what I definitely didn't expect was that it would throw me so much. That I would..." She brought a hand to her lips, as though wanting to stop herself from saying more than she already had.

"I miss you." Ash tried to gaze deeply into Gloria's eyes. "Maybe I'm not allowed to say that, but I don't know what the rules of this are, Gloria. But fuck, how I miss you."

Gloria dropped her hand. She met Ash's gaze with confidence now—or was it something else? "Come here, please." She stretched out the hand she'd previously held in front of her mouth.

It only took Ash a fraction of a second to bridge the distance between them. She took Gloria's hand in hers and Gloria pulled her even closer.

"You make me lose my fucking mind." Gloria let go of Ash's hands and folded her arms around Ash's neck. "How I want you... it's utterly insane."

Between Ash's legs, a wild pulse was igniting already. She had come here to talk to Gloria. To, maybe, if she was lucky, express some of her feelings. But Gloria had a different idea of how to spend their time together, it would appear.

Ash pressed her hands against Gloria's back. Oh, to feel her body pushed up against hers like that again. Gloria started moving. She took tiny steps, pushing Ash backwards, until she stood against the fridge.

"You make me do things I really shouldn't do," Gloria whispered.

Her face was so close, but Ash could still make out the need in her eyes. Gloria's breath came out ragged. That pulse between Ash's thighs was getting more and more out of control. But Ash waited. She wanted Gloria to kiss her first. She wanted Gloria to take that final step towards her. Once that had happened, all the hinges would come off. Ash would fuck Gloria right here on her kitchen floor if she had to—if they couldn't make it to a more private place. She had an inkling they wouldn't. Gloria's gaze on her was as wild as the thumping in

Ash's veins. There was no rhyme nor reason to this. Ash knew exactly what Gloria meant when she claimed that Ash made her lose her mind. Yet this wasn't a purely physical connection either.

Gloria flicked her tongue over her lips. The tiniest of groans escaped her throat. Then she slanted forwards and touched her lips to Ash's. She had taken the final hurdle. When Ash had woken up in her old bedroom this morning, she might have dreamt of this, but she'd had no way of knowing she'd be kissing Gloria before the end of the day. Yet, here she stood. She opened her lips to Gloria. She met her soft, warm tongue. She buried her hands in Gloria's luscious mane of hair. More than at any time during the weekend, she felt like she'd come home.

"I want you, Ash." Gloria said when they broke apart for an instant. "I'm serious." She looked at Ash with hooded eyes, as though her desire was getting the better of her already. She moved away from Ash, leaned towards the door Ash had walked through mere minutes ago, and slammed it shut.

"You have me." As soon as Gloria stood fully back in front of her again, Ash cupped her jaw in her palm. "I'm right here."

Gloria's hand rested on the waist of Ash's jeans. "Can I?"

Ash wasn't sure she'd be able to articulate anything else, so she just nodded eagerly.

Gloria flicked open the button and pushed Ash's jeans down. Ash tried to heel off her shoes without falling over, but she had the fridge against her back for support, and Gloria in front of her. Now that her trousers had come off, the thumping between her legs was quickly transforming into the familiar liquid heat, a want that originated deep inside of her.

Gloria kissed her again. The back of Ash's head was pushed against the fridge, such was the force of Gloria's kiss—of her need for Ash. All Ash could do in response was claw at Gloria's hair. Tug her as close to herself as she could get. Maybe this would be the very last time they did this. Even though Ash didn't want to believe that, it was always a possibility. But the Gloria whose hands and body and skin were all over her right now didn't strike her as a woman who would come to her senses any time soon—quite the opposite.

Gloria's fingers slipped inside Ash's underwear—exactly where Ash wanted them. She was throbbing for Gloria, reaching towards her touch.

Gloria pulled away from their kiss just as her fingertip reached Ash's clit.

Ash gasped. Gloria gazed at her with even more intensity than before. Ash expected Gloria to push her fingers deep inside her wetness next. She'd anticipated the move already. She was more than ready for it.

Instead, Gloria's face disappeared from her view. When Ash looked down, she saw only the dark exuberance of Gloria's hair. On her way down, Gloria had taken Ash's knickers with her. They rested at her ankles and Ash quickly stepped out of them.

The next, sublime sensation was the hot sweep of Gloria's tongue against her clit. Ash's knees buckled a fraction. She held onto Gloria's shoulders for support—she needed it. All the desire Ash had shoved aside the past two weeks now came unleashed—unbuckled, like her knees. It ravaged her from the inside and pooled between her legs, where it met the generous strokes of Gloria's tongue. There was no stopping this, just like there was no stopping how Ash felt about Gloria. How, at the pub, there was no stopping Ash from going after her when she saw Gloria go to the bathroom. So, of course, Ash came mere minutes later, uttering Gloria's name with the breath she could manage, digging her fingertips deep into her flesh.

"Oh, fuck." Ash sank to her knees and joined Gloria on the floor. "Jesus, Gloria." She cleared her throat because her voice sounded croaky.

"I know." Gloria dragged the back of her hand across her mouth. "It's utter madness with you. Like I'm someone else."

"A big old lesbian," Ash joked, even though she wasn't sure the current moment could sustain it. But Gloria smiled at her.

Then, they were both startled by an insistent knock on the back door—the one Gloria had forcefully closed only a very short while ago.

"Gloria." A woman's voice came from behind the door.

"Oh, God. It's Sindhu," Gloria pushed herself up. She looked around wild-eyed.

Ash scrambled to her feet and grabbed her jeans and under-wear off the floor.

Gloria gazed at the unlocked the door. "I'll try to get rid of her," she whispered. "You can get dressed in the downstairs bathroom."

Ash tiptoed out of the room, not knowing if she was allowed to come back in once she'd got dressed.

Chapter Thirty-Eight

Gloria opened the door and, in the short moment she was obscured from Sindhu's view, tried to make herself look presentable.

"Where is she?" Sindhu said. "Where's my favourite goddaughter?"

"They're both out. Some big party at Craig's, apparently." Gloria stepped into view. She didn't have a mirror. She already didn't feel like herself, not after what had just happened with Ash, so she knew there was a good chance she didn't look the way her friend was used to seeing her either. She tried to remember if Sindhu had told her she would stop by. She could have forgotten because after seeing Ash at the pub, Gloria had only been able to think of one thing.

"Are you all right?" Sindhu took a step towards her. "You look feverish. Your cheeks are all red." She shook her head. "You never blush, Gloria."

A bang came from the direction of the bathroom, loud enough to make them both look up.

"Is someone here? You just said the girls are out. If Janey were here, surely she wouldn't hide from her godmother?" Sindhu's eyes widened. "Wait." She clasped a hand to her mouth. "Did I interrupt something?" Her dark gaze on Gloria was relentless. "Is it... Ash?"

"She's just, um, in the bathroom." Gloria tried to take a deep breath. This was Sindhu. It wasn't one of her children who had come home early, nor was it someone who didn't know anything about what had happened between her and Ash.

"Are you going to introduce me?" Sindhu was smiling now. Maybe, to her, this was funny. Gloria was mortified. Thank goodness she'd at least had the wherewithal to close the back door.

Gloria put both her hands on the kitchen table and took a deep breath. "Just a second."

"Did I catch you in flagrante?" This idea seemed to amuse Sindhu greatly. "Maybe I should go."

Gloria wasn't going to admit that to her friend. It was bad enough that she'd asked Ash to hide in the bathroom. "Stay. Sit. I'll put the kettle on." Gloria walked to the hallway door and called for Ash.

She filled the kettle and tried to steady her nerves while she waited for Ash to appear. If this was what they would both end up wanting in the end, to be together out in the open, it was a good test for Ash to meet Sindhu.

"Hi." Ash walked into the kitchen all smiles. She dragged a hand through her un-styled hair. She looked a million times better than she had at the pub earlier today. As if the orgasm Gloria had just given her had also returned her vitality. Even the circles under her eyes seemed to have shrunk.

"Ash, this is Sindhu," Gloria said. Was that a hint of pride in her voice?

Hand outstretched, smile and gait confident, Ash headed towards Sindhu. It was an entirely new sensation for Gloria to introduce Ash to Sindhu. In the past, she had brought men to meet her friends, but it hadn't felt like this. And not only because it was much more conventional for her friends to meet the new man in Gloria's life. She knew that for a fact. Although she couldn't just dismiss the thrill of having her female lover stand in front of her best friend. This new sensation, however, which Gloria identified as a blend of pride and relief and, yes, something akin to love, was entirely due to Ash being Ash.

Ashley Cooper was not the kind of person you hid away in your bathroom when your friend stopped by for an unexpected visit.

"Lovely to meet you." Sindhu rose and Ash gave her two friendly pecks on the cheeks. To Gloria's surprise, there was nothing awkward about the exchange.

The water boiled and Ash said she'd take care of it, leaving Gloria to sit with Sindhu, who shot her a look Gloria wanted to read as 'Wow, girlfriend' but of course she couldn't be sure of what Sindhu was trying to convey.

Ash poured tea and mugs were distributed. As though she'd lived at Gloria's for weeks, she took the biscuit tin from the cupboard and arranged shortbread on a plate. Maybe Ash was occupying herself so she could compose herself.

"So," Sindhu said. "Is this back on, then?"

Gloria chuckled nervously. Sindhu never was one to beat around the bush.

"I think it's fair to say that we don't know yet." Gloria looked at Ash for confirmation. "I ran into Ash earlier in the pub and..."

Sindhu nodded as though she knew exactly what Gloria meant by not finishing her sentence.

"For the record." Sindhu looked squarely at Ash now. "I'm all for this. You have my unconditional support."

Gloria felt an altogether different warmth surge in her chest. Sindhu had always boldly claimed she would have Gloria's back, but to see her sit here with Ash and be so frank about it made it much more real for Gloria.

"Thank you," Gloria said. "For now, though, the best way you can help us is by not telling anyone Ash was here."

"Of course I'm not going to tell anyone." Sindhu all but rolled her eyes. "I just... want to encourage you. Weren't you on a break?"

Gloria sneaked a quick glance at Ash again. It was weird to have this conversation with her friend while Ash was sitting next to them. She felt double the pressure to say the right thing.

"We were," Ash said. "But, um, well... I'm not sure the break is working for us very well." She grinned at Gloria.

"Honestly," Sindhu said, "Gloria, if you could see yourself through my eyes now, you'd know how crazy it was to fight this. You look so... utterly content, albeit a touch nervous, perhaps." She sipped from her tea and took a biscuit.

"That may well be," Gloria said, "but in a few hours, Sally and Janey will walk through that door, and that changes everything. Again."

"They're at university," Sindhu said. "I'm not saying they don't care, because I'm pretty sure they want nothing more than for their mother to be happy, Gloria. But they're discovering this whole new world. Sally's graduating in a few months."

"Which may very well mean she'll move back home for a while, until she finds her feet." Sally had been very vague about her future plans. Either she had them and didn't want to share them with her mother yet; or she simply had no clue what to do with her life after obtaining her degree. Both were a strong possibility with Gloria's eldest daughter. She made a mental note to talk to her about this as soon as possible.

"How about I take Janey out this week for some goddaughter/godmother bonding and I put out some feelers?" Sindhu looked at Gloria expectantly. "Don't worry, I won't give anything away."

"That would be great. She's looking forward to seeing you."

From the corner of her eye, Gloria spotted Ash checking her watch.

"I have to go soon," Ash said.

"Oh, gosh," Sindhu pushed her chair back. "I'm impeding on your time together. I'm really sorry. I'll leave you to it."

Ash was the first to get up. "It's fine. I can't stay. I was only meant to be here for five minutes." Ash shot Gloria a quick wink.

Gloria stood as well. The heat that wink had produced beneath her skin was already making way for the sense of impending doom that Ash's departure created in her. She had no idea when she would see her again.

"I'll call you," Ash said.

"I'll, um, just go wash my hands." Sindhu excused herself.

As soon as she was out of the room, Ash's face broke into a huge grin. "I like her."

Gloria expelled a loud sigh. "I think she likes you too." She pulled Ash close. "Not as much as I like you, though." She kissed Ash on the lips.

"We should talk," Ash whispered, her words hot clouds against the skin of Gloria's neck. "Any time this week that you can talk to me on the phone, text me and I'll call you back as soon as I can."

"God, I wish you didn't have to go." Gloria wanted to stay in Ash's embrace for hours instead of the few minutes they were afforded.

"We're on a break. Remember?" Ash followed up with a small chuckle.

"Sod that." Gloria nipped at Ash's earlobe.

"Thanks for the you-know-what, by the way. I owe you." Ash hugged her more tightly.

"You don't owe me anything, Ash." Gloria inhaled deeply so she could commit Ash's scent to memory again.

"I really should go now." Ash freed herself from Gloria's embrace.

Gloria watched her collect her bike and round the corner of the house. This time, their goodbye wasn't nearly as fraught as the last time. Sindhu's sudden arrival, which was by no means ordinary, but still had a reassuring normality about it, had made sure of that.

"Is she off?" Sindhu returned.

Gloria nodded.

Sindhu walked over to Gloria and put a hand on her shoulder. "It's going to be all right, you know," she said. "I can just tell by looking at the two of you together. There's so much there, Gloria."

"I hope you're right."

"What happened today?" Sindhu sat back down.

Gloria poured them more tea and told Sindhu all about running into Ash and what had happened after, leaving out the more intimate details—those memories she would savour in private.

Chapter Thirty-Nine

Ash parked her mother's bike in the shed and took a deep breath. It was one thing to be rudely interrupted by Gloria's friend—if she'd knocked on that door a few minutes earlier, Ash would have been in the very midst of coming—but now she had to spend time with her parents while keeping a straight face. She'd had no idea Gloria was going to react the way she did. She'd expected them to talk—another one of those difficult conversations with no easy conclusion. She hadn't expected Gloria to come for her like that, to be all over her, to show her emotions so nakedly to Ash.

Ash tried hard to suppress a very persistent smile as she entered the living room.

"Must have been quite the bike ride, sweetheart," her mum said, barely looking up from the magazine she was reading.

"Hm." Ash thought it better not to say much at all. She hated lying, especially to her parents. She made for the stairs. "I'm going to get my stuff together." She checked the time. "Can you or Dad give me a ride to the station in an hour?"

"Your dad still isn't back from the pub." Ash's mum gave her a look. "He'll be in no fit state to drive you. I'll take you, darling."

"Thanks, Mum." Ash headed up the stairs.

"Ashley."

The tone of her mother's voice made Ash stop in her tracks. She hung her head over the railing. "Yes?"

"Can I ask you something?"

"Sure." Instantly, all sorts of thoughts spiralled in Ash's head. Had her mum heard something? Or worse, seen something? Did mothers really have such a strong intuition when it came to their children?

Ash's mum put down that week's issue of *The Economist*. Even before she had retired, she had always taken the time, every single week, to read it cover to cover. "I've been thinking about what you asked me last weekend when I was in London."

Ash was starting to feel awkward with her body half-bent over the railing like that. She went downstairs again and sat on the ottoman near her mum's favourite armchair.

"What's that?" Ash had said many things to her mum that weekend.

"That very theoretical hypothesis you put to me about you —hypothetically, of course—getting involved with someone like Joanne or Sandra." She cocked her head. "I hadn't given it any more thought. We'd both had a fair amount to drink by then. But I had Sandra on the phone the other day and that made the thought pop right back into my head. It made me wonder... Or no, I'm putting it wrongly. It made me realise that when you asked me, I was too tipsy to inquire about it further, while perhaps I should have."

Oh, shit.

"Were you trying to tell me something at the time?" Ash knew very well her mother wasn't born yesterday. She also knew that she wouldn't be questioning Ash if she didn't have strong suspicions about Ash seeing someone. But she had no idea how she could know about her and Gloria. She probably didn't. "Because, for the life of me, I haven't been able to figure out why you would ask me such a thing."

"I was just... fishing," Ash said. *Like you are doing now.*

"Fishing for what? I'm your mother. I know you've gone through hell and back with the divorce. I'm here for you, no matter what. I really need you to know that."

"I do know, Mum. You and Dad have been so supportive, even though I know it was hard for you as well."

"The hardest thing was seeing you like that. So defeated and hurt." She put her hand on her chest. "Honestly, Ash, we just want you to be happy. If that means you being with someone that might shock us at first, then so be it. As long as this person makes you happy, that's truly all that matters."

Ash squinted at her mother. She did know something. Had Adrian finally run his mouth? But if he had, wouldn't he have warned Ash before she came home this weekend? She'd just seen him at lunch and he hadn't said a word about it.

"It's still early days," Ash said, and it felt so damn good to tell her mother something. "I have met someone, but..." She shook her head. "I can't tell you about it yet, Mum. I just can't."

"Why not, darling?"

"You say that all you want is for me to be happy and I believe you, but, well, let's just say reality might be a bit more complicated than that."

"You're making me awfully curious *and* worried now."

"I know, which is why I didn't want to say anything in the first place." Quite frankly, Ash was bursting to tell her mother, to just get it off her chest. "Besides, we're taking things very slowly and it may not work out. If that's the case, I wouldn't want to have created a fuss over nothing."

"Over nothing? How can it be nothing if you like her so much?"

"How do you know how much I like her?"

Her mother briefly pursed her lips. "I have known you your entire life, Ashley. It might sound like a dreadful cliché but I know you better than you know yourself. The way you just walked in here, with your eyes sparkling and trying so hard to wipe that grin off your lips, that's not the same person who left this house an hour ago. That's not the same person who came back from the pub looking so lost, all I wanted to do was hug you and tell you everything would be okay, even though I didn't know what the hell was going on."

"Really?" Ash had thought she was hiding it so well. It must have been what Gloria did to her.

"Yes, darling. *Really*." Her mother paused. "Look... full disclosure. I have an idea of whom it might be. Your father called me from the pub earlier and told me who you ran into."

"Dad? What did he say?"

"Nothing much. But I'm your mother. Granted, I may have too much time on my hands now that I'm adjusting to being retired, but I still have all my wits about me. I can put two and two together."

Was her mum telling Ash that she knew about her and Gloria?

"I just really hate the idea of you feeling like you have to hide this. You don't. You really don't, Ash." Her mum curled her lips into the sweetest smile. "Was that your way of trying to tell me? When I was in London?"

"Oh, Mum. I don't know." Ash buried her head in her hands.

"Darling, look at me." Her mother's hand descended onto Ash's shoulder. "Please."

Ash looked up, straight into her mother's face. "I'm so crazy about her. I'm crazy about Gloria." Ash puffed out some air. Had she really just said that to her mother? Had she actually said Gloria's name?

Ash saying it out loud must have flustered her mother, because she didn't offer an immediate response.

"What about Gloria?" Her mum finally asked. "Does she, um, feel the same way about you?"

Oh, yeah, Ash thought. But she could only nod. The weeks of pent-up tension, of hiding, of insecurity about her feelings, were fast catching up with her.

"But, Mum..." Ash had to know. "How did you figure it out?"

"After your father called earlier, it just started making more and more sense." Her mother kept her hand on Ash's shoulder. "A few things added up, like they can do in retrospect." She hesitated for a moment. "I still have the very vivid image in my mind of you dancing with her at my birthday party. And the other week, I could have sworn I saw Gloria come into Sainsbury's, but then I got the distinct impression that she was hiding from me. Running, even. Then there was this off-the-cuff remark that Adrian made last week. Plus what you asked me in London. What can I say, darling? A mother knows."

"Ade? What did he say?" *Argh*. Ash knew it.

"Don't blame your brother. He probably has no clue he gave something away. But he does know about you and...?"

Ash nodded again. "I came to Murraywood last Tuesday and took the next day off, but Gloria had to work and I got so bored at her house, hiding, not knowing what to do with myself. I went to Ade's because he's basically her neighbour." Ash cast a quick glance at her mum's face. "I'm sorry for the subterfuge, Mum. I never meant to lie. I just... didn't know how to tell you. Or even if I should tell you at all."

"Did you just say you were taking things very slowly?" Her mother leaned back into her chair, finally removing her hand from Ash's shoulder.

"We were, but then I ran into her at the pub, and now, I don't know anymore."

"You were just with her?"

Ash nodded. "Gloria's friend, Sindhu, arrived while I was there."

"She knows?" Why was her mother not more perturbed by any of this?

"Yes. Gloria told her a few weeks ago." Ash sat up straighter. "Your reaction is much calmer than I had imagined it was going to be."

"I'm not saying I'm not a little confused by this, but... What am I going to do? Tell you, a grown woman, you have to stop seeing someone you're crazy about? What's that going to do for *our* relationship?"

"But still."

"How did Adrian react?"

"He was a di—" Ash caught herself just in time. "A bit harsh, at first. Surprised, I guess."

"Goodness me. *Gloria.*" Her mum sighed. "That poor woman has been through so much. I really do wish her all the happiness in the world, but, well, I hadn't expected her to find it with my own daughter." She shrugged. "I've known her forever, yet I never knew she was bisexual. I guess we don't really have that kind of friendship."

"I'm not sure she was very aware of it herself," Ash muttered.

The sounds of footsteps on the gravel startled them both. "Oh, Christ," Ash's mum said. "*Now* your father's home. He probably wants to see you before you head off."

"Let's not tell Dad."

Her mum shook her head. "Let's not."

"Thanks, Mum. And not just for keeping it from Dad for now," Ash said.

Ash sat in the passenger's seat of her mother's car. They'd left earlier than they'd had to, much to her dad's chagrin, giving them some time before Ash had to catch her train.

"I've always believed it's not for any parent to dictate who their child should love," her mum said. "I hope you know that."

Ash should have known. Her coming out had been the biggest non-event of her life. But it felt so great to hear her mother say that.

"Those things are easy enough to say." Ash glanced at her mum and gave her a big smile. "But when it comes down to it, it's not always the case. I guess I'm just lucky to have you as my mum." Ash remembered how she'd almost got angry when she'd told Gloria about Charlotte's parents and their persistent refusal to accept their daughter for who she was.

"No, darling. Luck has nothing to do with it."

Now Ash remembered that she'd inherited that stubborn attitude from her own mother.

"Did you expect me to be in tears?" Her mother brought a hand to Ash's cheek and pinched it, the way she did when Ash was twelve.

"I expected you to be disappointed in me again, especially after the divorce."

"Darling, I've told you time and time again that your divorce did not disappoint me. What was the alternative? That you stayed in an unhappy marriage? This isn't the fifties anymore, you know."

"But maybe it gives me a track record for picking the wrong person to be with..."

"Maybe Charlotte was the right person for you, but only for a while. Things change. People change. Look at me. I'm sixty-five. Retired. I'm not the same person I was ten years ago, mostly because I now, finally, know that everything is how it should be. I'm the woman I should be at this age, because that's who my life made me. Your father has always been a great companion. Ade has his family. You..." She flattened her hand on Ash's cheek. "You, I worry about so much. Not because you're single or divorced, but because you're... searching for something. At least, you were. But when you walked into the house earlier, you looked as though you'd very much found what you were looking for."

Ash pushed her cheek against her mother's palm. "Do you know why"—Tears stung behind her eyes—"even in the midst of all the divorce despair, I always knew, deep down, I was going to be okay? Because you're my mum and with a mother like you, how can I not be okay?"

"Darling, come on." Her mum made a sniffling sound with her nose. "You'll make me tear up."

Ash wiped the beginning of a teardrop from the corner of her eye. "Come up to the city again soon. I'll take you out again. I had a really good time last weekend."

"Maybe the three of us can go." Her mother pinched Ash's cheek again.

"Maybe..." Ash's glance fell on the dashboard clock. "Oh fuck. I have to run."

"Language, dear." Her mum winked at her. They quickly kissed goodbye and Ash hurried to her train.

Chapter Forty

M*um knows.*

Gloria kept staring at the message Ash had just sent her. Damn. Sally sat next to her on the sofa. Janey wasn't home. She didn't want to start texting frantically with her daughter right there, that would surely rouse suspicion. But, oh bugger, Mary knew. Ash must have told her. Just like she'd told her brother well before Gloria wanted anyone to know. Then again, she'd told Sindhu and Fiona.

"Are you okay, Mum?" Sally asked.

"I'm fine, sweetie." She stood. "I need to make a quick phone call." She exited the living room. The kitchen wasn't far enough from where Sally was sitting to have a private conversation with Ash. Gloria went into the garden and pressed Ash's number.

"She figured it out herself," Ash said, as soon as she picked up. "She's a fucking smart one, my mum."

"What did she say?" Gloria's heart hammered.

"She reacted so well, Gloria." Behind Ash's voice, there was the steady thrum of the train on the rails. "I couldn't believe it."

"She did?"

"Yeah. She had a real enlightened view about it all. Maybe turning sixty-five had something to do with it. She just wants me to be happy, no matter who with." Ash paused. "It's not as if you're the worst person in the world I could have fallen in love with."

Gloria's heart warmed upon hearing Ash's declaration of love, but not enough to overcome her fear of being overheard. She glanced around the garden. She listened for signs of Janey coming home, but all was quiet. Through the window, she noticed the flickering of the TV, but she couldn't see Sally. Her brain was trying to process this new information, on top of absorbing the day she'd already had.

"This is good news," Gloria managed to say.

"It's fantastic news. I mean, my mum's my mum, you know. She's as decent as they come, but still. Maybe we've blown people's reactions, or how we thought they'd react, all out of proportion. Sindhu seemed to be more than okay with it as well." Ash sounded near elated.

"I'm still trying to grasp the fact that Mary knows. What about your dad?"

"He's as clueless as ever."

"But how did she figure it out? Has she been spying on you?" Because that was the most disconcerting about it all. Gloria sometimes figured things out about her girls simply because she was their mother and she intuited them—or because she wasn't born yesterday. But this was different. They'd been careful. Gloria had gone out of her way not to run into Mary.

Ash told her how Mary had drawn her conclusion.

"She saw me hide at Sainsbury's?" Gloria had to chuckle at the slapstick of it all. "Oh, God. I'm not sure how I'll face Mary ever again."

"You will. And it'll be just fine."

"I hope so."

"We should probably also talk about, um, what happened this afternoon," Ash said.

"I know, but... Sally's inside."

"Not now," Ash was quick to say. "My train's about to arrive, but... soon."

"Jesus, Ash. It's been quite a day."

"Yeah. Go be with your girls now. I'll talk to you later."

"Okay." Gloria wasn't sure how to ring off. She didn't feel comfortable using a term of endearment, what with Sally who could come into the garden at any time. "Talk soon." She witnessed how her voice went all gooey and soft when she said goodbye, however. She stayed outside for a while longer. Had Ash actually admitted to her mother, as she had just said over the phone, that she had fallen in love with Gloria? Her heart wanted to leap all the way into her throat, but Gloria was also wary. Sure, Mary's reaction was wonderful, much more so than Gloria had dared to dream, but they still had a long way to go.

For a brief moment, Gloria allowed herself to envision going inside the house, sitting next to Sally, and telling her she'd met someone. She'd done so before, when she'd started dating Robert more seriously. Both girls still lived at home then and it had been impossible to keep something like that hidden. They'd met him and they'd got along well enough, but there had always been an awkwardness, a forced quality about it when they'd all spent time together.

Maybe because, in the end, Gloria's feelings for Robert hadn't been strong enough to take things to the next level. Or maybe because it happened too soon after George died. Or it could also have been that she didn't want her girls to see her with another man. Or maybe Gloria herself didn't want to be with another man. Her growing feelings for Ash were obvious enough. Or maybe it was a little bit of everything that had conspired against her affair with Robert turning into a real relationship.

And who was to say the same wouldn't happen with Ash? If anything, it was more likely, because Ash was a woman. Gloria didn't want to put her daughters through a journey of acceptance and getting to know her for nothing.

On top of all that, she feared their reaction more than anything. Mary was a woman in her sixties. She had told Gloria, at the very birthday party where she'd met Ash, how much she enjoyed this particular decade of her life. Sally and Janey were only at the beginning of adulthood. They still had so much to learn and experience. Gloria hoped she'd taught them kindness and open-mindedness, but these were girls to whom life hadn't been very kind, so who knew how much kindness they had left to offer in return?

"Mum." Sally appeared at the back door. "You've been out there forever. *Call the Midwife* is about to start."

"Thanks, darling." She went into mum mode, which was a safe and easy mode right now, at least compared to secret-lesbian-lover mode. "Have you heard from your sister?"

Sally nodded. "She's on her way. She'll be here in a few minutes."

Gloria curled an arm around her daughter's shoulder and they headed inside together.

The next morning, Gloria had just hung a load of washing on the line when Janey called from inside the house.

"Mum," she yelled. "Phone."

"Who is it?" Gloria cursed herself. She shouldn't leave her phone unsupervised in the house like that. Ash could text her. One of the girls could see and start asking questions.

"Mary," Janey said.

For an instant, Gloria considered asking her daughter to pick up, but she didn't want to be a coward like that. It had probably gone to voicemail already by now, anyway. Gloria had to face Mary at some point. She'd already rushed away from her once at the supermarket. Murraywood was a small town. She was bound to run into Mary. Especially now, as it appeared that Ash's mother wanted to talk to her.

She took her time heading back inside. When she picked up her phone, she saw the missed call appear on the screen. Even though she already knew about it, it still jolted her. The kids were going to start asking questions if Gloria kept talking on the phone outside. But this was another conversation she couldn't have with her daughters within earshot. Besides, she didn't owe them an explanation. Their mother was allowed just as much privacy as they were. She took the phone outside and, her palms going clammy, called Mary back.

"Gloria, hi." Mary sounded as though this was one of her regular calls—as though she didn't know. "How are you? Happy to have your girls at home?"

"It's great. Yeah." Christ. Gloria felt as though she'd been called into her supervisor's office to be berated for gross misconduct.

"Listen, um, you probably can't talk right now, but, can we meet? I'd like to have a chat."

Gloria could make up all the excuses in the world, but it didn't feel right. This was a woman she'd known since she was a child. Gloria and Mary had grown up in the same neighbourhood. Their parents had been friends.

"Sure. I can stop by yours this afternoon, if that suits you," she said.

"That would be lovely." If Mary was at all upset with her, Gloria couldn't tell from her tone of voice.

Gloria rang off. Should she call Ash? If Ash had known Mary

was going to invite Gloria over for a chat, surely she would have let Gloria know.

She looked inside the house. The girls didn't seem to care that she was spending so much time making private phone calls outside. They had other worries to occupy their minds, like passing exams —and which party to go to next. Or in Sally's case, Gloria imagined, what she was going to do after graduation. A thought suddenly hit her. Maybe Sally hadn't discussed it with her yet because she expected not to graduate that year. If Gloria's own mind hadn't been so occupied with all things Ash, she would have thought of this much sooner. She would have sat her daughter down already and asked her about it. Again, she made a mental note to talk to Sally. But first, she had another conversation to focus on.

Gloria pressed Ash's number. She'd be at work. They seemed to have an unspoken agreement not to call each other at work. Half the time, Gloria couldn't pick up when she was on a shift. If she did, she often couldn't talk freely. Ash's phone went straight to voicemail. Gloria left a message but didn't give any details. She texted Ash as well, hoping she could talk to her before she went to see Mary.

For the life of her, Gloria couldn't keep her eyes off that bottle of gin on the drinks trolley. Mary had taken her into the living room, whereas they usually had coffee and chatted in the kitchen. Gloria hadn't been able to get a hold of Ash. Even though she'd had a few hours to think about this, she sat in front of her friend totally unprepared.

She shifted in her chair so that the bottle of gin wouldn't be in her direct line of vision. But looking into Mary's face was no piece of cake either. Throughout this thing with Ash, this was one of the moments she'd dreaded the most. It was one of the reasons Gloria had felt they should have stopped seeing each other. But they hadn't stopped. And here she sat.

They had only made small talk so far, but the tension was mounting. The elephant in the room wasn't getting any smaller either.

"Look, Mary, I know this is all very odd," Gloria started. "I'm still adjusting to it as well, to be honest."

"Is it really that serious?" Mary asked. "I wish I could say I had a good night's sleep, knowing that Ash had met someone, but..." Her voice trembled. "You know I have nothing against you, personally, Gloria. It's just that Ash is very vulnerable right now. She's obviously crazy about you. I'm not sure she could take another bout of heartbreak."

"Heartbreak?" Gloria expelled some air. That was what Mary was worried about? That Gloria would break Ash's heart? She supposed it was a valid enough worry.

"You're not... I mean, I don't want to pry, but I've known you forever and yet I've never known you to be attracted to women," Mary said.

A little late to stop prying, Gloria thought. But, this too, was a valid question. All questions she could have foreseen, even prepared an answer for, if her mind had been able to find some calm since Mary's phone call.

The most confusing of all was that Gloria didn't know how to approach Mary now. As her old friend or as Ash's mother? They were vastly different entities in her head.

"I never have been until now." Gloria wasn't going to pretend otherwise. "But... I'm crazy about Ash as well." Oh Christ. This conversation was so surreal. Gloria looked away and her gaze landed on the bottle of gin again. Maybe she'd need to go to go to an AA meeting tonight—something she hadn't done in years. "I'm not using her or taking advantage of her. It's not like that at all."

"I know you as a sweet and kind woman, Gloria. A wonderful mother to your girls, but this is my daughter..."

"Mary," Gloria started to say, but she had no clue how to continue. This entire conversation was not something Gloria was ready to have. Mary wasn't supposed to know—not yet, anyway. "Look, I'm sorry, I know this must be hard for you, but it's hard for me too. This is very uncomfortable."

"If this is uncomfortable, then how do you see things with you and Ash progressing?" Was that a hint of derision in Mary's tone?

"I don't know." Gloria couldn't keep the desperation out of her voice. If only she could have spoken to Ash before she'd come here. She should have declined the invitation, she knew that much—oh, the cruel benefits of hindsight.

"You're my friend, Gloria. I've known you forever. You used to babysit Ash and Ade, for crying out loud. And now you're my new daughter-in-law?"

Gloria was ready to jump out of her chair. She tried to summon the endless patience she'd bred in herself while raising teenage girls on her own, but it seemed to have escaped her. "I know this is upsetting, Mary, but what do you want me to say?"

"I've only known for twenty-four hours," Mary said on a sigh. "I figure I'm going to need some more time to process this." She managed a small smile. "I wasn't sure you would come. That you would have the guts to. Not after you fled from me at Sainsbury's that day."

"I'm not sure I should be here. I have my girls at home and..." Some of the tension left Gloria's shoulders. If only she could see Mary as her old friend for a few minutes instead of her lover's mother subjecting her to an inquisition.

"Do they know?"

"No."

"Does anyone in Murraywood know?"

"Sindhu and Fiona." They were coming over for their weekly

dinner date tonight, but Gloria wouldn't be able to speak freely, because Sally and Janey would be there too. She heaved a sigh.

"Does Alan know?" Gloria asked.

Mary shook her head. "I think Ash should be the one to tell him, although it's killing me to keep it a secret from him. But I promised Ash that I would keep it to myself for now."

"I know it's a shock for you. It will be for Alan too. It was a shock for me as well, Mary. I didn't mean for any of this to happen. But it seems to have snowballed into something that... could become more serious." Obviously Gloria couldn't tell Mary how difficult it was for her to stay away from her daughter. "I do believe both Ash and I feel the same way about that."

"I'm not going to stand in your way. Ash is a grown woman. But she's also a recent divorcee and she hasn't taken the divorce well. It has really knocked her for six and she's only just recovering. I can't bear the thought of her getting hurt again."

"It's most certainly not my intention to hurt Ash."

"But... you've been single for so long and..."

Somehow, Gloria knew exactly what it was Mary couldn't say.

Mary took a deep breath and straightened her posture. "I'm sorry, Gloria. With what you've been through, you don't need a lecture from me on hurting others."

"You're worried about Ash. It's only normal."

"I am, but I should really accept that Ash is a big girl who can take care of herself and make her own decisions, including who she dates." She shook her head, her cheek lifted into a half-smile. "Look at me, giving you the third degree. That's not me. But this is all so unusual and I honestly don't know how Alan's going to take it. I wish I could say the man is entirely predictable to me, but when it comes to this, I find myself unable to foresee his reaction."

"He adores Ash," Gloria said. "At your birthday, he was telling me how much he worries about her."

"She was always such a daddy's girl. Still is."

"Don't you think that, if and when the time comes to tell him, he might simply be happy for Ash?" Gloria wondered who had suddenly given her the authority to be the voice of reason.

"In the end, yes, of course. It's the bit that comes before that worries me." Mary managed another smile.

"Maybe that bit doesn't matter all that much." And maybe, Gloria thought, this awkward chat with Ash's mother could make her see beyond the wall of denial and fear of judgement she herself had been hiding behind.

Chapter Forty-One

"Jesus Christ," Ash said into the phone. "I'm so sorry, Gloria." She loved her mother, but sometimes, like all daughters, she could just strangle her. "I had no idea she was going to summon you."

"It's all right. It had to happen sometime."

"Yeah, but not like that."

"We both live in Murraywood. I had to see her sooner rather than later."

Ash was trying to figure out how Gloria sounded. She couldn't really tell over the phone. What they really needed was to see each other, to look each other in the eye, and have a proper conversation about everything that had happened since Sunday.

"Is there any way I can see you this week?" Ash asked. "I'll hop on the train whenever you want me to."

"I was thinking about making a quick trip to London."

Ash's heart did a silly dance in her chest. "Really?"

"I think I should go to an AA meeting," Gloria said.

"Oh. Okay. Of course."

"Not because I think I might relapse, but to..."

Ash gave Gloria the time she needed to find her words.

"Just to recalibrate. Because it's been a crazy few weeks, Ash, and now all this."

"Do you have a regular meeting you attend?" Gloria hadn't really talked about that part of her life yet.

"Not a regular one. I haven't been to a meeting in, let's see... two and a half years. But I always know they're available to me when I need them. I think I need one now." Gloria paused. "I used to go to one near St Paul's. There are meetings closer to home, but I always felt more comfortable knowing I wouldn't run into anybody I know. I'll check the schedule. I can see you afterwards, but I won't be able to stay the night."

"No, of course not. And yes, I would love to see you." In the back of her mind, Ash was already making plans for getting the most out of her time with Gloria. "Do you, um, want me to join you at the meeting?"

First, there was silence on the other end of the line. "The meetings are usually closed," Gloria said.

"That's perfectly fine. I was just asking in case you wanted me to." Ash wished she could be with Gloria now. To wrap her in her arms and tell her how much she cared for her. "How are you feeling?"

"I've parked my car behind a patient's house because I know nobody comes here just so I could call you." Gloria sounded a bit deflated. "In a way, I'm glad your mother asked me over, because this sneaking around is starting to do my head in. I'm not ashamed of how I feel for you, Ash."

"Nor am I." On the contrary, Ash thought.

"I have to go now. Sindhu and Fiona are coming over later. Let's talk tomorrow."

"Can't wait," Ash said. "Be sure to give Sindhu my love." When she hung up the phone, her lips stretched into a wide smile.

Ash pulled Gloria into a warm hug, even though they were outside, for everyone to see. But they were in London, so it didn't matter.

"How was the meeting?" she asked.

"Good." An unmistakable smile bloomed on Gloria's face. "Not as good as seeing you, though."

"I know we don't have long, but..." Ash cocked her head. "I bought us some more time." She fished a car key out of her pocket.

"I didn't know you had a car." Gloria's brow furrowed.

"It's my friend Jonathan's. He's out of town. He let me borrow it. I can drive us to my place first, after which I can drive you home, so you don't have to get on the train and you can stay longer."

"Aw. That's very thoughtful of you." Gloria kissed Ash on the lips again.

"I can be nice when I want to." Ash took Gloria's hand and started walking, but Gloria didn't seem to be following.

"I'm not sure we should go to yours, Ash. We both know what's going to happen if we do and we really need to talk."

"I figured we could talk in the car." Ash tried her most seductive smile, even though Gloria was right. They needed a conversation more than all the other activities Ash had in mind.

"We can, but..." Gloria nodded at a pub a bit further down the road. "I need to eat something. I can't go days without food like you." This time, Gloria pulled Ash along, and Ash let her.

Once inside the pub, they found a nook that afforded them some privacy. They both ordered food and a bottle of sparkling water.

"Do you want to talk about the meeting?" Ash asked.

"No. I mean, we can if you want to. I know I haven't been very forthcoming about that part of my life, because I can usually deal with it so well these days. What I think we should talk about is what happened on Sunday, before Sindhu arrived... Ash, I—I didn't mean to jump you like that, but you do something to me that utterly stops me from controlling myself. It's been that way since the beginning. To feel that way about you and to then find myself across from your mother... Honestly, it's been a bit of a mind fuck."

Gloria obviously really needed the conversation. Or maybe she was still in a talking mood after her meeting.

"I know. I will have a word with Mum about that, by the way." The truth was that Ash hadn't called her mother yet to give her an earful. She had been so incredibly nice to her on Sunday, Ash could still hardly believe it. That she hadn't been able to extend the exact same courtesy to Gloria was, perhaps, normal. But Ash knew she couldn't let it slide. She would talk to her mother as soon as she'd spoken to Gloria. She may even stop by tonight, after dropping Gloria off.

"Don't. I know exactly where she's coming from and she mainly expressed concern for you, Ash. As though I'm some woman-eater who will chew you up and spit you out mercilessly after I'm done with you." Gloria chuckled.

"She's been a bit overprotective since the whole divorce debacle."

"In a way, I'm grateful I got to talk to her; it made me see a small light at the end of the tunnel. Our concerns about being together are logical and reasonable, but look at the people who know." She rested her beautiful gaze on Ash. "Sindhu, Fiona, Adrian and your mother. None of them have been ghastly about it. Maybe us being together won't be as badly received as we thought it would. Maybe all we, and anyone else, need is some time."

"Ever since Mum confronted me, I've been leaning in that direction as well." Her mother's words had made a world of difference to Ash, but Ash wasn't the only one in the relationship. "Either way, I've always been more worried about you. I live here, in this anonymous city, where I could go days without seeing anyone I know. Your life is very different."

Gloria nodded. "My daughters are my biggest concern." She focused her gaze on her glass of water. "On the train over, I actually wondered if I should tell them this week. They're not in final revision mode yet. They're home for a while longer, so we could talk. If I don't tell them now, it will be a while before I can. I can't tell them when they come home for summer revision. I don't want to distract them at an important time like that. I would need to wait until they're home for the summer." She sighed. "I don't know."

When it came to what to say to children, Ash didn't have much experience. She had two nephews who had grown up knowing from the start that their aunt was gay. "What's the worst that can happen if you tell them now?"

"It's easy to imagine the worst. I've done nothing else since I started seeing you. Now I'm not so sure it's the right way to think about it." She huffed out some air. "They'll be shocked more than anything. How can they not be? Put yourself in their shoes."

Ash nodded. "But shock doesn't last."

"If I do tell them... maybe you should come by before they're off again. So they can see us together for just a brief moment. So they can see it's a beautiful thing rather than a sordid image that they might conjure up." Gloria smiled.

"Anytime." This was suddenly all going pretty fast. "If you tell Sally and Janey, I should probably tell my dad. Word will start spreading and I don't want him to hear it from anyone else."

"Yeah... but, Ash." Gloria cocked her head. "This is all on the condition that we're all in. We're doing this. You and me. It's going to be an official thing. I know it's what I want, but is it what you want?"

Ash chuckled. "Don't you know by now?"

"Maybe I need you to tell me."

"I want to be with you, Gloria. You're all I think about. I've driven Lewis crazy with my non-stop chatter about Gloria this and Gloria that. I want you with an intensity that seems brand new to me. You've made me feel better about myself than I have done in years. I'm totally and utterly head-over-heels in love with you. So, yes, I want it. I want *you*."

"I knew when I saw you again at The Horse and Groom," Gloria said. "It hit me like a ton of bricks that I would be the stupidest woman in the universe if I let this chance go by. This opportunity at a new kind of happiness. No matter what anyone thinks about it."

Ash wished very much that they'd gone to her flat. She wanted to kiss Gloria for hours. She wanted to celebrate with a dozen orgasms shared between them.

She heard footsteps behind her. Their food was ready. Even though Ash hadn't eaten all day, she wasn't very hungry. Her stomach was filled to the brim with over-excited butterflies.

Chapter Forty-Two

"**A**re you all right?" Ash put a hand on Gloria's knee. "You look like you're about to be sick."

Gloria hadn't expected this trip back to Murraywood to be a white-knuckle ride. Maybe it was because she was so used to driving herself. Or maybe Ash was simply a terrible driver. The friend who'd loaned her his car must not have been in the passenger seat with Ash Cooper at the wheel before.

"Can you pull over, please?"

Ash barely looked in her rear-view mirror before pulling the car to a stop on the hard shoulder. Gloria couldn't fall apart on the motorway like this. Grateful though she was for the extra time with Ash, she wished she could have taken the train back home.

"What's wrong?" Ash sounded as though she genuinely had no idea.

"I hate to break this to you, sweetheart, but you are a terrible driver. I've narrowly avoided a panic attack at least three times since we left London."

"What?" Ash slapped a hand against the wheel. "Driving in the City is just different than driving in Murraywood."

"No, Ash, it's exactly the same. All the same rules apply." Gloria held out her hand. "I would like to drive." She wasn't going to waver on this. If she let Ash drive her home, she'd be in a right state. "Please," she added, because being polite never hurt anyone.

"Is it really that bad?" Ash sucked her bottom lip into her mouth.

"Yes." Gloria's stomach was settling somewhat.

"I don't do much driving. I might be a little out of practice."

"I really appreciate the gesture of wanting to take me home, but if you really want to put this extra time we have together to good use, I'll need to drive. If not, I won't be able to hold a conversation." Gloria threw in a smile. "And I would really like to talk to you some more."

"Smooth move." A smile appeared on Ash's face as well now. "How can I say no to that, despite you insulting my driving skills." Ash started getting out.

When Gloria crossed with her outside, she stopped to kiss her. "Please promise me you're not driving yourself back to London tonight. I wouldn't sleep a wink if I knew you'd be doing that."

"Jesus, Gloria. I'm really not that bad a driver."

Gloria just nodded—although it was not a nod of assent—and took her place behind the wheel.

"Where do you see us a year from now?" Gloria asked. She didn't add 'if this lasts', even though she was thinking it. She'd been driving for a good five minutes now and felt a lot better.

"Oh, wow. You're going in with the hard questions now that you're in charge of this car." Ash put her hand on the back of Gloria's head and ran her fingers through her hair. "Do you mean on a practical level? Like where we would live and things like that? Or just whether you'll ever be able to be a passenger in a car that I'm driving?" Ash chuckled.

"It's a very broad question. You can answer any way you like."

"Okay, but since you asked the question, you must have considered an answer to it already," Ash said. "So why don't you go first?"

One thing Gloria knew for sure, nothing would ever be straightforward with Ash. She liked answering a question with a question too much for her own good. Although this particular question might have come out of the blue for her. Gloria, on the other hand, once she had allowed herself to, had given the matter quite a bit of thought.

"Fair enough." Driving always allowed her thoughts to flow better. If only it could make the articulation of said thoughts easier. But she was the one who had asked the question in the first place and she really owed Ash an answer, especially because she was dying to hear Ash's vision of their possible future. "I suppose we will have got used to the commute between Murraywood and London by then." She briefly glanced at Ash, whose hand lay still on the back of her neck. "Don't worry, I won't ask you to move back to your hometown."

"I wouldn't mind it."

Ash surprised her by saying that.

"I've been back more often lately and I quite like it. I know Mum and Dad would love it, once they, you know, get over seeing you and me together." She softly caressed Gloria's skin. "Your work schedule wouldn't allow you to move to London and if we ever wanted to live together, me moving to Murraywood would be the only solution."

"This is all purely hypothetical, of course," Gloria quickly added. They were just dreaming. She needed to make sure Ash knew that.

"Yeah." Ash's thumb dug into a knot in Gloria's shoulder. "Sure."

"You'd be up for commuting?" Gloria briefly glanced side-ways again.

"It's not that far." Ash's tone was musing. "We'll be at yours in ten minutes from now."

"It's late now. There's hardly any traffic left."

"If I really can't get used to commuting, I can always retire. Live a life of leisure in Murraywood."

"Retire?" Gloria quirked up her eyebrows. "You're only forty-two."

"Trust me, in my line of work, a lot of people retire by the time they're forty. For some, it's like a badge of honour to have made enough to retire by that age."

"Are you serious?" Gloria knew Ash made good money. The building where she lived dripped with affluence. But she didn't have a clue Ash made that much that she could even consider retiring.

"I'm not sure I'd know what to do with myself. I couldn't just do nothing all day. You may think I'm a bad driver, but I'm an even worse cook." Ash snickered. "Or maybe I could learn to become a good cook." Her thumb swept over Gloria's neck again. If she kept this up, Gloria would have to park the car somewhere out of sight to attend to the growing need between her legs. "Or I'll just do some day trading from home. I don't know. The point is that there are always options."

"That's a great point." Gloria leaned her head against Ash's hand. They approached the exit towards Murraywood. It was the first time they had taken this exit in the car together. Gloria couldn't help but see the symbolism in that. She would talk to Sally and Janey about Ash this week. Ash was going to tell her dad. They were dreaming up a future. Ash had, indeed, made an excellent point.

"I don't want to pressure you, darling." Gloria was starting to feel like a broken record—a feeling she absolutely hated, but it couldn't be helped when you were a mother. "But you'll have graduated before you know it."

At least Sally was up. Gloria had shouted for her other daughter to come downstairs because lunch would be ready soon, but she'd heard no sounds come from Janey's bedroom yet.

"I genuinely had nothing to say because I hadn't made my mind up whether to do a masters or find a job," Sally said. "Otherwise, you know I would have talked to you, Mum."

Gloria nodded.

"But what I would really like to do next year..." Sally looked away, as though she was about to admit to the most shameful act.

Gloria braced herself.

"I'd like to take a gap year. I'll take a summer job to make some money, but come September or October, I'd like to travel for a while."

Gloria had been afraid of this. Two of Sally's friends had taken a gap year before they'd started university, but Sally hadn't given any indication that she would ever want to do that.

Gloria had always tried her very best to not make her daughters feel that they couldn't have what everyone else had—because they'd had so much taken away from them at such a young age already.

She'd had savings and George's life insurance, which hadn't been a huge amount of money, but had allowed for some breathing room. Both Sally and Janey had qualified for partial scholarships, but raising and clothing and putting two children through school still seemed to cost an arm and a leg.

"Where would you go?" Gloria tried to keep her voice neutral.

Ideally, Sally would be ready to get a proper job and start life as an adult. The second option—of her continuing at university to obtain a master's degree—would cost Gloria more, but she'd always told Sally that she would make it work. That she didn't have to worry about the financial side of things. Education was too important. This third option, which Gloria hadn't accounted for, threw her off guard.

"Australia. I could get a working holiday visa for a year."

Jesus Christ. Gloria was used to Sally being at the University of York, but her daughter backpacking through Australia for a year was most definitely not a prospect she was ready for.

"That's quite far, darling."

Sally nodded. "I know. I just feel like I need... something. It's hard to explain, Mum. Chances are, I'll be working an office job for the rest of my life. When I come back, I can get a job and start training to become a chartered accountant. But before I do any of that, I just feel like spreading my wings and doing it properly, you know?"

Gloria nodded. She might be able to understand, but every single one of her motherly instincts told her this was a bad idea. Although, for Sally, it might just as well be the best thing that happened to her. Gloria knew she'd need to get over her fear— because she knew that was the main factor here, again—quickly if she wanted to be a supportive parent. Sally only had one left. She couldn't ask her to share this idea with her father.

Upstairs, Janey's door finally opened, followed by the bathroom door being slammed shut.

"I know it's a lot to deal with," Sally said, suddenly sounding very mature. "We can talk about it more later."

"Have you told your sister about your plans?"

Sally nodded, confirming that Gloria was always the last to know.

"It would only be for a year, Mum."

A very expensive year, Gloria thought. "Do you know anyone who has done this?"

Sally nodded. "Fran, a girl in my year. She did it before she went to uni. She says it was the best year of her life."

"Did Fran break down the cost of this year abroad by any chance?"

Janey was ambling down the stairs now. Gloria had planned to have a proper conversation with her daughters over lunch, but the eldest had just told her she wanted to go to Australia for a year, while the youngest had only just rolled out of bed.

"Yep. It's very doable, Mum. I swear."

The cost of the airfare alone, Gloria thought. "Could you break it down for me?"

Sally nodded. Janey approached her and gave Gloria an unexpected kiss on the cheek.

"I don't know why, but I was utterly unable to wake up today."

"Maybe go to bed a bit earlier," Sally said, sounding like Janey's second mother.

"Blame Netflix," Janey said, as if it was the most normal thing in the world.

"Are you hungry?" Gloria asked. "I've made your favourite pasta."

"The one with chorizo and haloumi?" Sally asked.

"Oh, yes." Even now that they were grown up, Gloria could still take such delight in getting this kind of reaction to her cooking from her daughters.

"I could eat a horse," Janey said.

"For breakfast," Sally said.

Gloria listened to their gentle bickering while she drained the spaghetti and readied lunch. How she would miss this if Sally went away for a year.

Over lunch, the conversation had evolved in such a way that it sounded like a done deal that Sally was going to Australia come autumn. Janey egged her sister on as though it was also her dream that her older sibling would travel so far away—maybe she was already making plans of her own and she wanted Sally to pave the way.

But Gloria had her own news she wanted to share. Maybe now was a good time to do it. Sally sounded rather elated because she'd finally told her mother about her plans and Janey was, at the very least, well slept. They'd both just eaten one of their favourite home-cooked meals—although Gloria always sent them back to university with a large batch of sauce. If now wasn't the best time to break the news, Gloria didn't know when that time would ever roll around. Probably never. But not telling her daughters was no longer an option.

"Girls," she started, "I have some news of my own."

They both stopped talking abruptly, as though shocked already. Gloria didn't often have personal news to share. It was always the other way around. She noticed how Sally and Janey exchanged a glance. She ignored it and pressed on.

"I've met someone. I'm *seeing* someone, to be more accurate. It's, um pretty serious, so I thought you should know."

"Is that where you were on Tuesday night?" Janey asked.

"I went to a meeting in London on Tuesday." Gloria had been very clear about that, although, at the time, it had also been the perfect excuse. "But, yes, afterwards we did meet up."

"He drives a fancy Jaguar," Sally said. "That much I know."

Had she seen the car pull up to the house? She must have also seen how Ash took the wheel afterwards, although she'd just said 'he'. It didn't matter. Gloria's mind was racing because she was nervous. She took a deep breath.

"Ooh, did you snag yourself a rich guy, Mum?" Janey said, sounding so unlike herself, Gloria wondered how else the first year of university had changed her youngest daughter.

Sally rolled her eyes at her sister's remark.

Gloria had, apparently, snagged herself a rich woman. She was still processing that Ash had ever so casually mentioned that she could retire if she wanted to.

"It's not, um..." Damn, this was harder to say out loud to her children than she had anticipated. Just like facing Mary, this was the very moment Gloria had always dreaded the most. The few words she couldn't find in herself to utter. "It's not a man. She's a woman." Oh Christ. Gloria tried taking a deep breath. "I've been seeing a woman." She straightened her posture.

"Oh," Sally said.

"Really?" Janey's eyes widened to the size of saucers.

"You actually met her at the pub last Sunday. Ash Cooper."

"Wait," Sally said. "What?

"The fake blonde?" Janey said. "Who dresses like a boy?"

"It's called androgynous," Sally corrected her sister.

Androgynous. The word had never even occurred to Gloria.

"But... isn't she so much younger?" Janey narrowed her eyes.

"She's forty-two," Gloria said as matter-of-factly as she could.

"That's pretty old, actually," Janey responded.

Gloria tried to keep a chuckle at bay. Anyone over thirty was old when you were eighteen years of age.

"I would like you both to meet her before you go back to uni." Gloria finally dared to rest her gaze on her daughters. "Only if you want to, of course. I can imagine this is a lot to take in."

"We knew you were seeing someone," Sally said. "That was pretty easy to guess. All those secret phone calls in the garden." She twirled her fork around on her plate. "We didn't know you were seeing a woman, though."

Gloria nodded. "Is that a problem for you?" Her pulse picked up speed.

"It's just a little weird, Mum," Janey said. "I never knew that was what you wanted. What about Dad? Was that not real? Were you in the closet all this time?"

"No, darling. Absolutely not. I loved your dad so very much."

"Are you bi?" Sally asked.

"I'm not sure. I guess. If being married to your father for so long and falling in love with a woman ten years later makes me bisexual, then that's what I am, I suppose."

"Are you really in love with her?" There was a definite incredulous note in Janey's voice.

"Yes." Gloria might as well say it out loud now. "I really am."

"She looks pretty cool," Janey said. "Not like your other friends."

She is pretty damn cool, Gloria thought while fully allowing herself to chuckle at her daughter's comment.

"Is she in love with you?" Janey asked, as though that was most surprising of all.

"I very much believe that she is, darling." Gloria relished the sensation of pride blooming in her chest.

"How long have you been seeing her?" Sally had been quiet for a while.

"A few weeks."

Sally nodded in response, then fell silent again.

"If you have any questions, I'm here, okay?" Gloria slowly exhaled. There was no obvious damage to assess, although, of course, she had no idea what was really going on in her daughters' heads right now. "You can ask me anything." She tried to find Janey's gaze, but she was studying her nails very intently.

Sally looked at her. "You raised us, Mum. This isn't a problem for us. At least it isn't for me." She elbowed her younger sister in the arm.

Gloria's chest swelled with a different kind of pride now. What Sally had just said hit the nail on the head. She had brought up her daughters to not even think twice about their own or someone else's sexuality—largely due, in fact, to Ash coming out to Mary and Alan at such a young age. Neither Mary nor Alan had ever spoken about their gay daughter any differently than they did about their straight son. They had set an example for her, although Gloria had always believed that she would need that unprejudiced kindness for one of her daughters, rather than for herself.

"I don't have a problem with this either," Janey said. "Half my dorm is LGBT or at the very least Q."

Gloria found that hard to believe, but she wasn't going to argue about it now.

"Was that her car she was driving?" Sally asked.

Gloria shook her head. "She borrowed it from a friend."

"Oh." Sally looked disappointed.

"I'm so glad I told you." Gloria broke into a wide smile. She wanted to call Ash and tell her they'd just taken another step towards what they previously thought impossible. "Will you think about when you'd want to meet her in a more official way?"

"Last Sunday, when she was at the pub, you made it seem like you barely knew her," Sally said. "Was that because you were trying to hide it from us?"

"That was one of the reasons." Gloria wasn't the type of mother who believed in being best friends with her daughters, yet she felt that she could maybe share this with the girls. "This hasn't been so easy for me. You know, to find myself falling for a woman. I never expected it. It's all so new and confusing."

"Is this a secret?" Janey was eyeing her phone. Now that her girls knew, there was no more keeping this affair private.

"Ash hasn't told all of her family yet, but I think she will soon. Until then, it would be good if you kept this to your-selves." And not tell everyone at the next Easter holiday party you're going to, Gloria added in her head.

They both nodded, then Janey cocked her head. "Isn't she a bit too hot for you, Mum?" she asked in all earnestness.

Gloria burst into a girly giggle.

"What kind of a question is that?" Sally's gaze shot daggers at her sister.

"Mum's... Mum," Janey said in her defence. "And Ash... I don't know. She looks so cool and woke."

"Do you know what, girls? Why don't you ask her yourself." She stood and hugged them both, kissing them on the top of their head. "Thank you for being so lovely about this."

Chapter Forty-Three

Now that Gloria had told her daughters, Ash was under pressure to tell her dad. Sally and Janey had taken it well, but they were young adults. Ash's dad was a man in his late sixties who had known Gloria since before Ash was even born.

It also wasn't fair on her dad that both her mother and her brother already knew, and he didn't. If she waited too long, he might actually get more upset about being the last to know than about the actual news.

When she woke up on Saturday morning, after arriving in Murraywood late on Friday, her mother theatrically announced that she was going to the store, leaving Ash alone with her father. She all but winked at Ash when she closed the door behind her.

"I'll be in the garden if you need me," her dad said. "Unless you want to give your old dad a hand?"

"You do know I have the exact opposite of a green thumb. I'll probably end up killing whatever it is you're planting."

"Excellent for pulling weeds, dear." He already had the doorknob in his hand.

"Dad, I need to talk to you about something."

"Oh." He looked at his hand, then let go of the doorknob. "Sure." He poured himself and Ash more tea from the pot Ash had made earlier. "Does it have something to do with why you're here every weekend now? Not that I'm complaining. Just observing."

"Yes. It has a lot to do with that, in fact." Ash swallowed. She took a sip of tea. "I'm seeing someone... Someone who lives in Murraywood."

Her dad did a double-take. Ash could see the wheels in his head turning. "Who?" He really had no clue. "The only other lesbians I know here have all been married forever. Unless they've broken up, but I haven't heard anything about it at the pub..."

"It's Gloria, Dad." Ash bit the inside of her cheek in suspense. "She and I are, um, an item now."

"Gloria?" He scratched his cheek. "Nah. That can't be. Gloria Young, you mean? *Our* Gloria?" He squinted at Ash as if that would allow him to read the truth off her face. "But she's..." He shook his head. "Is it the first of April? Are you and your mother playing a prank on me?"

"No. I know it's hard to wrap your head around. Believe me, I've had some trouble with that as well."

He scratched his temple. "But... Gloria, she's—" He didn't get much further than that.

"We tried to end it, but... it was too hard. We've come to believe that being apart is much harder than being together."

Her dad stared into his teacup. When he looked back up, his thick grey eyebrows were knitted together. "Back up a minute, Ash. Does your mother know about this?" This was exactly what he used to say when Ash tried to get something out of him as a teenager.

"She guessed it. Last weekend. Ade knows as well."

"How long has this been going on?"

"Almost two months. It started not long after Mum's birthday party."

"And Gloria... She's, I mean, she's really into this? With you?"

Ash tried hard not to giggle. "Yes, Dad." *If only you knew how much.* "She really is."

"What you're telling me is that Gloria Young is going to be my new daughter-in-law?" He was the one chuckling now.

"I'm never getting married again," Ash deadpanned.

"Well, yes, in a manner of speaking." He nodded. "I hope this isn't my fault." He paused. "At your mother's party, I had a few too many, and I might have said something to Gloria about being worried about you after the divorce. Maybe she took my plea too literally, even though it was never my intention that she herself do something about it."

"Oh, Dad. It has nothing to do with that."

"You love her?" His tone changed.

"I do." Warmth bloomed in Ash's chest.

"I've always said that anyone you fall in love with is someone I will welcome into our home with open arms. That hasn't changed. If anything, I already know Gloria." His Adam's apple bobbed as he swallowed hard.

Ash puffed some air out of her cheeks. "Thanks, Dad." Some more air followed. "That's a relief to hear."

"What did you think I was going to say?"

Ash shrugged. "That you thought I had lost my mind or something."

"Not after all the heartache with Charlotte. And Gloria... with George. Your mum and I attended their wedding. For some reason, I've always remembered that. That funeral still gives me nightmares sometimes." He slanted his head. "Besides, what else have I always told you?"

Ash drew a blank. Was she supposed to remember some deep life lesson her dad had imparted on her after watching a football match with him at The Horse and Groom? He was usually a man of few words and he didn't dispense advice often, so maybe Ash should have remembered. Or maybe her dad wrongly remembered saying it to her—maybe he had wanted to share some wisdom with her, but had never actually done so.

"What?" Ash asked, because she didn't want to start inventing things.

"You can't tailor your life to what others want of you. This includes us, your parents. You can only ever live your own life."

Ash had no recollection of her dad saying that to her. Maybe he had said it in his speech at her wedding, but Ash didn't want to remember that. She shook her head. "Can you believe that Gloria and I almost ended it precisely because we were afraid of what everyone else might think?"

"I can very well believe that. Although you should never have feared our reaction. What did your mother say?"

"She was lovely about it. Just like you."

"That's what I thought." He blew some air through his nose. "That doesn't mean I'm not somewhat shocked, though. I might need to whisk you off to the pub later."

"That will have to wait until tomorrow, I'm afraid. I'm having lunch at Gloria's. *With* her daughters." Ash's stomach twisted into a nervous knot.

"She told them?"

Ash nodded.

"How did they react?"

"Pretty well, apparently." Ash could only go on what Gloria had told her over the phone. She hadn't seen her yet. She would only really know how well Sally and Janey had accepted the news once she spent some time with them.

"Maybe we should have them all over for Sunday lunch before the girls go back to university," he said.

Ash could hug him. But they weren't tactile like that. Her dad buying her a pint and openly talking to her about Gloria in the pub was how he would express his acceptance, as he had always done.

"Maybe it's a bit too soon for that." Suddenly, it seemed like everybody knew. Their secret was out. Before any official family dinners took place, Ash wanted to evaluate how their relationship would progress now that it was all out in the open.

"We'll ask your mother," he said.

"Sure." Ash leaned back in her chair, relaxed, and peered at her father. She'd feared telling him the most. But the fear, it turned out, had all been in her and Gloria's heads. But wasn't that the thing with fear? It made you see things in a twisted fashion, made you afraid of events that might never happen. Made you almost give up on something as glorious as love.

Heart knocking against her ribcage, Ash waited for Gloria to open the door. When Gloria pulled her into an immediate, fierce hug, Ash knew that her daughters must not be home yet, or else biding their time upstairs.

"It's so good to see you," Gloria whispered in her ear. "I missed you."

"I told my dad." Ash had borrowed her mother's bicycle again and on the ride over she'd felt lighter than she had in weeks, as though her legs were pedalling of their own accord, just because she was on her way to Gloria and it was no longer a secret. When she'd set off, she'd shouted at her dad, who was bent over a flower bed in the garden, that she was off to see Gloria. The simple straightforwardness of doing so had given Ash that extra spring in her step.

"What did he say?" Gloria ushered her further into the kitchen. Something smelled good.

Ash tried to remember her dad's exact words, but she could

only paraphrase. "That I should never tailor my life to anyone else's expectations but my own."

"How deep for Alan," Gloria joked.

Ash reached for her again. "I can't believe I was so afraid of telling him." She shook her head. "He's my dad. I should have known he would be fine with it."

"It's not just that. I mean, I'm sure he will be fine with it and that is his message to you, but beneath the surface, he must be doing some serious recalibrating. But this wasn't just about telling other people, Ash. Not for me."

"Where are your girls?"

"I sent them on a last-minute run to the shop so I could have you to myself for a bit." Gloria curled her arms around Ash's waist.

"I'm a bit nervous," Ash admitted.

"Don't worry about it too much, sweetheart. They already think you're too cool for me." Gloria pushed her nose against Ash's neck.

"Well, who am I to argue with that?" Ash kissed Gloria on the cheek. Sally and Janey could walk through the door any minute. She'd already sort of seen them in the pub, but she didn't want the first image of her in their home to be in a passionate lip-lock with their mother.

Gloria sighed before releasing Ash from her embrace. "Sally wants to go to Australia next school year. She wants to take a gap year."

"Sounds like fun."

"Oh, I'm sure it would be fun..." Gloria shook her head and waved it off. "We'll talk about that some other time." She sauntered to the stove and took the lid off a pot. "What else did Alan say?"

"He wants you and the girls to come to Sunday lunch." Ash followed Gloria and leaned her hip against the kitchen counter. How different this Saturday was from any other Saturday she'd had since the divorce. Standing in Gloria's kitchen, watching her put the final touches to a meal Ash would share with her and her children, chatting about her dad.

"When?"

"I told him it was a bit too soon."

"The girls are here for another week." Gloria turned towards her with a wooden spoon in her hand. "Here. Try this."

Ash obliged. "Delicious."

"And I didn't even burn anything today," Gloria said triumphantly. Surely, she must be a tad nervous as well. If she was, she wasn't showing it.

Then the back door burst open and the girls walked in.

Ash stood straight, as though gearing up for a military inspection. Here we go, she thought.

Chapter Forty-Four

꧁꧂

Gloria picked up a piece of lamb chop with her fork. She cast her gaze over the table. The food was going down well. Conversation was a little slow, but not too awkward. It could all have been so much worse. But it wasn't.

"I hear you want to go to Australia," Ash said to Sally.

Gloria didn't know why she'd mentioned that to Ash earlier. But she and Ash were together now. They were a couple. At least she thought they were. They'd expressed their feelings for each other. Ash had told her she was in love with her and Gloria had, soon after, realised she felt exactly the same about Ash. They were telling people. Ash was having lunch with her and her daughters. Of course she was her partner. They *were* together. Ash and Gloria. It still sounded strange to Gloria, yet it felt so right. She'd told Ash about Sally wanting to go to Australia because that was the sort of thing one shared with one's partner.

"If Mum will let me." There was a bit too much defiance in Sally's tone for Gloria's liking.

"Why wouldn't she?" Ash asked.

Gloria tried to send her a look that conveyed Ash was

supposed to be on her side, but Ash was giving Sally her full attention. She was probably trying to ingratiate herself with Gloria's eldest daughter. Gloria could hardly blame her for that.

"Because it's either carry on studying or get a job," Sally said.

"That sounds fair enough, I guess." Ash found Gloria's gaze. Gloria gave her a quick smile.

"It may sound fair, but, often," Sally said, "there's a third option that no one has considered yet."

"It's because of money," Janey interjected. "When you're a single mother, it doesn't grow on trees." She said it in the tone Gloria had often used over the years—more often than she perhaps should have.

"I can imagine." Ash nodded.

"But she's not single anymore," Janey said.

Gloria couldn't believe what she was hearing. It very much sounded to her as if on their way back from the shop her daughters had cooked up some sort of scheme to embarrass her in front of Ash.

"Excuse me?" Gloria fixed her gaze squarely on her youngest daughter.

"Why shouldn't we benefit from this as well?" Janey's eyes were narrowed, as though she was ready to pounce again. Had Gloria read her own child so wrongly?

"Janey." Sally stepped in, making Gloria believe they weren't in on this together. "Stop it."

"I'm so sorry, Ash," Gloria said. "Janey, apologise to Ash right now."

"Apologise for what?" Janey put down her cutlery.

"It's fine. I don't need any apologies." Ash painted an obvious fake smile on her face.

"I'm not hungry anymore." Janey first pushed her plate away from her, then her chair away from the table. She stormed off, her feet pounding on the stairs.

"Come back here," Gloria shouted, then caught her breath. She hadn't shouted at one of her girls like that in a long time. It wasn't the way they dealt with things in this family—or so she believed. She probably had some stress of her own to deal with.

"I think she's having a little trouble with this scene." Sally swept her hand over the table. "Don't hold it against her, please, Ash. She'll be fine later."

"I understand that this might not be easy for Janey," Gloria said. "Or you, Sal. But to go off in such a huff over that? We weren't even talking about her."

"It must have triggered her," Sally said. "There are a bunch of posh girls in her year. The kind with room for a pony or two on their estates back home."

"She's never said anything about that to me." Whenever Gloria found out something like this about her children, that they hadn't been able to come to her with an issue they had—no matter how small or big—she felt like someone was throwing salt into a gaping wound. Motherhood was as much Gloria's pride and joy as it was her eternal weak spot.

"Duh," Sally said. "She's not going to tell you, Mum. You've always done everything you could to make us feel we had everything we needed. Sometimes even everything we wanted." Sally pulled her lips into a grin.

She's told me now, Gloria thought. She gazed at the door Janey had just stormed through.

Ash cleared her throat as if to say something, but she remained quiet.

"Jesus," Gloria said. "I'm sorry about this, Ash." She did her best not to call Ash by any pet names in front of Sally. "This wasn't really the family meal I had envisioned us having today."

"Don't worry about it." Ash's voice was soft. "It's all good with me."

"I'll just go up and talk to Janey for a minute," Gloria said.

"Leave her for a bit, Mum. She'll need a while to calm down," Sally said.

"Okay. Thanks, sweetie. I will." Gloria thought it wise to take her daughter's advice on this.

"So, is the topic of Australia completely taboo now?" Ash asked. "Because I've been there. Twice. Where do you want to go, Sally?"

Gloria decided there and then that she would somehow make it happen for Sally. If it was what she really wanted to do, it was her job as Sally's mother to facilitate it, not stand in the way. Sally hadn't made it sound as though all she would do when she got down under was lie on a beach and learn how to surf. She'd get a working visa. She'd pay her own way as much as she could. Who was Gloria to get in the way of that?

Janey still hadn't come down. Sally had gone out to meet a friend. Gloria and Ash were clearing up the kitchen.

"I'm mortified by Janey's behaviour," Gloria said.

"She's not even nineteen." Ash was drying a plate. "I was a much bigger brat at that age."

"Nah, I don't think you were." Gloria cocked her head. "Mary would have said something about that."

"I'd like to believe my mother didn't share everything about me with you." She grinned at Gloria. "I'd like there to be some mystery left between us."

Gloria sighed. She wasn't ready for banter with Ash yet. "It's not just that Janey's behaviour is inexcusable, but what she said was very rude. She made it sound as though I'm with you for your money. Like I'm a gold-digger or something."

Ash chuckled. "I know you're upset. But to me, it's like it didn't happen. I've forgotten about it already." She put the plate down. "I know why you're with me, Gloria." She took a step closer until her face was less than an inch away from Gloria's. "It's the sex," she whispered. "It's all those delicious orgasms. And the fact that I'm so cool, of course." Ash's lips split into a grin.

Ash wasn't too far off with her assumptions. Gloria couldn't help but laugh. "You're cool and hot all at the same time. Who can resist that?"

"Clearly, not you." Ash leaned in and gave her a lingering kiss on the lips. "In all seriousness, though. I *can* contribute. For all the money I make, I care very little about it. I used to. It used to give me such a thrill. And a good investment still does, but I have nothing to spend it on. It just piles up and for what?"

Gloria moved her head forcefully from left to right. "No way."

"I understand that you would react that way now, but think about it," Ash said. "Or look at it like this: nothing would make me happier than to spend money on making your life easier."

"That's very generous of you, Ash, but now you're actually saying exactly what Janey said earlier. Why shouldn't she and Sally benefit from me being with you?" This was turning into a ludicrous conversation.

"Why shouldn't they?"

"You're not their mother. I'm the one who takes care of them."

"I'll give you a loan then." Ash clearly wasn't willing to let this go. "With a negative interest rate."

"Just... stop it." Gloria leaned away from her.

"What?" Ash pulled Gloria close to her again. "You'll take the orgasms I give you, but not my money?" If this had come from anyone else, it would have sounded ultra-arrogant and obnoxious. But Gloria knew Ash wasn't like that. "I'll pay you future rent for when I inevitably move in with you." Ash's tone had descended into a lower register again. "I care much more for you than I do for anyone or anything else, Gloria. I want to make your life as pleasurable as possible."

Gloria was just about to let Ash kiss her again properly, when she heard hesitant footfalls on the stairs. Gloria quickly took a step back. This wasn't the time for Janey to find them all over each other. "Hey," she said, trying to sound casual, when Janey entered the kitchen.

"I'll give you two some space," Ash said.

"No, Ash, it's fine," Janey said. "Stay."

Purely on instinct, Gloria was already spreading her arms for her daughter. "Come here, baby," she said. "It's all right."

Janey let herself be embraced by her mother and Gloria revelled in the fact that she could wrap her arms around her daughter and hold her close. She wished she could do more for her during this transition from girlhood to adulthood—but all she could do, it felt like, was give Janey a hug from time to time and try to assure her that everything would be all right. So she did.

Chapter Forty-Five

Ash was in the pub with her dad, watching Chelsea lose, when her phone buzzed in her pocket with a message from Gloria.

Can you meet me in the alley off Brooke Street at 5? Maybe we can go for a drive?

A drive? What where they? Teenagers who had just got their driving licence? But Ash understood. As long as her daughters were home, Gloria's house was partly off limits. They could hardly meet at Ash's parents' house for a private conversation either. She texted back that she'd be there.

"Gloria?" her dad asked.

Ash just nodded. It had all been a bit much this weekend. Telling her dad. Spending time with Gloria's girls. Her mother now asking about Gloria in front of her father. Adrian quipping about it over Sunday lunch. These were all positives, in the grand scheme of things, but Ash needed some time to process. Watching the football with her dad beside her was a good way to do that. He wasn't going to ask her any invasive questions about her love life—especially not while the game was still on.

She thought about what he had said to her the day before, about how he and Ash's mum had attended Gloria and George's wedding.

"Can I ask you something, Dad?" Ash kept looking at the screen, but from the corner of her eye she saw her father nod. "What was he like? George?"

"George Young?" He sipped from his pint. "Decent bloke. Always up for a laugh. Could spin quite the yarn."

Ash glanced sideways at her father. She probably wasn't going to get more out of him. There was no point comparing herself to Gloria's deceased husband, either way.

"Were you drinking buddies?" she tried.

Her dad nodded. "That man could drink anyone under the table. Even me. If you can believe it." He tore his gaze away from the match. "Are you worried about something?"

Ash shook her head. "Just curious."

"You can never win against a dead man, Ash, but just like any of us, he was no saint. No one is."

Excited sounds on the TV snagged their attention. A Chelsea player was on his way to the goal. Her dad tensed beside her. The man in blue was tackled and the hope for a late equalising goal thwarted.

"Bugger."

"They're not exactly on a winning streak, are they?" Ash said.

Her dad shrugged. "But they're our team, so we support them." He held up his glass to Ash, who clinked hers against it.

They watched the rest of the match in silence. The score remained the same.

"I feel like I'm getting just as intimately acquainted with your car as I am with you," Ash said.

"It's well deserved on the part of my car. The old thing has served me well over the years." Gloria caressed the steering wheel. "I needed to see you."

"For any particular reason?" Warmth bubbled beneath Ash's skin already.

"I missed you." Gloria turned fully towards her. "And I won't see you for another week."

"Says who?" Ash gazed into Gloria's eyes. They were the lightest of blue.

"Don't tease me. I'm only getting my fresh HRT patch on Tuesday." Gloria played with Ash's fingers.

"I could come to Murraywood one evening this week and have dinner with you and the girls. I'll sleep at my parents' house." Ash looked at their intertwined hands. "I'd best get used to a spot of commuting."

"As long as you take the train and don't borrow your friend's car."

"Your near-hysterical reaction to my driving skills was greatly exaggerated, you do know that?" Ash was still a little offended by that. She just had a different driving style to Gloria's—more sporty, less like mothers drive.

"I would love for you to spend the evening. And who knows, the girls might be out."

"Were they suitably impressed with me after I left yesterday?" Ash joked.

"I wish I could have been a fly on the wall when they discussed all things Ash Cooper in their room, but I wasn't, and I'm not the sort of mother who eavesdrops on her daughters, so..." Gloria smiled. "But I think they liked you." She grabbed a fistful of Ash's shirt and pulled her closer. "What's not to like?"

Ash chuckled. "It seems we both made the mistake of

projecting our inner worries onto our families. I guess I was using my parents as a way to avoid falling in love again."

"And I was using my daughters as an excuse too, in a way." Gloria paused for a second. "Maybe there was a subconscious part of me that wasn't as comfortable dating a woman as I thought. There's a difference between theory and real life." She pulled Ash even closer. "But any discomfort I might have felt is well and truly gone now." She pressed her lips to Ash's for a kiss that seemed to go on for minutes.

Ash slowly pulled her lips away from Gloria's. "When was the last time you had sex in a car?" She held Gloria's gaze.

"Probably before I was married." Gloria's lips lifted into a grin. "And never with a woman."

"Are you ready for another first time?"

"Try to stop me now." Gloria's voice had lowered into a whisper. "You're not packing by any chance?"

"Packing?" Ash burst into a giggle. "Where did you hear that?"

"I read it on some lesbian website," Gloria said matter-of-factly. "Is that not how you say it?"

"I don't know. I've never been in the habit of announcing that sort of thing in public." Ash shook her head. "But no, it didn't really seem like an appropriate prop to bring for the weekend."

Gloria found her ear. "Next time we meet like this, pack some heat, baby." She lingered near Ash's ear. Her breath was hot on Ash's skin. Her lips touched down softly. Her tongue traced a moist line down Ash's neck. "That thing you said a while back." Gloria's lips were back hovering over Ash's ear. "About how you were falling in love with me?"

Ash could only nod. Gloria's hand had crawled underneath her shirt.

Instead of lips, Ash felt Gloria's teeth graze against her skin. "It's safe to say I'm in love with you too."

Chapter Forty-Six

✿✿✿

Gloria straddled Ash in the too narrow car seat. Ash's fingers were buried deep inside her. This really was transporting her back to her younger self, even though twenty-year-old Gloria would never have done this with another woman in a car parked in a secluded Murraywood alley. It would never even have occurred to her. Today, however, as soon as Ash had got into her car, she very quickly knew that this was going to happen. That there was only one way this was going to go. Being near Ash made Gloria hyperaware of her body, as though awakened after a long hibernation. Gloria was fully awake and always ravenous for Ash. The intensity with which she wanted Ash could knock her for six. But she was done wanting for a while. She was having all of Ash and then some.

Gloria rode Ash's fingers the way she had ridden that strap-on a few weeks ago. The bruises she incurred while bumping her arse against the dashboard and her knee into the hand-brake, she would celebrate as victory marks later, alone in bed.

She glanced down at Ash. Their gazes and their bodies locked to each other, Gloria thought about what she'd said to Ash earlier. She was in love with her. She'd done the falling already. She'd done that weeks ago. Because Gloria was not in the habit of wanting another human so fiercely while being unmoved by them. The truth was she'd fallen for Ash long before she was able and then willing to admit it to herself. And look at her now. This sneaking around in her car might make her feel like a younger version of herself, but Gloria would still turn fifty-five in August.

She looked forward to it, not only because she would spend it with Ash, but also because all the pain, all the hurdles life had thrown at her, all the detours she'd had to take to arrive at this moment, had been worth it. Gloria wouldn't be the person she was now, on the cusp of fifty-five, without all the valleys her life had been forced through. There was no doubt this was a massive peak, just as there was no doubt that more valleys would follow. Because that was how life was.

But life was also this. Ash's glorious fingers inside of her. Ash's dark gaze on her. But most of all, how Ash made her feel. So full of life and desire. So hopeful for the future—a future with Ash by her side. It was hard to believe that it was the very image of that future that had almost scared her out of accepting her feelings. But that was another thing about life—it always took time. Just like it had taken years to blunt the hard edge of pain that had settled inside Gloria after George's death, she had needed time to adjust to this. To Ash. To the fact that she was a woman. To her own desire getting away from her, forcing her to make decisions her common sense couldn't always agree with.

Gloria had gone on the date that couldn't possibly be called a date back then. She'd gone to London for a weekend of ravishing Ash. She had done those things despite herself, or maybe just because she was herself. Because she was growing into this new version of herself. She'd needed Ash to break through the final barrier.

And now, they were together. They were here. Gloria felt the now familiar heat rev up in her belly. She felt it as soon as she merely flicked her gaze at Ash. A fire of aliveness, some-times of acute need. But all her needs were being met right now, because nothing else existed in the world for Gloria. It was just her and Ash. Intertwined. Ash coaxing pleasure from her. Gloria giving herself to Ash. Their bodies contorted in awkward positions just because they wanted this so much, because there was no other way for them to be in this moment but all over and inside each other.

Gloria stilled herself and let Ash's fingers take her there—as they had done so many times before. That, too, had changed her. It wasn't just desire, it was the consistent meeting of that desire that made Gloria look at herself differently in the mirror. What she had at first lost because of all the insecurity and the doubts that came with falling in love with a woman, she had gained in confidence because of all the gifts her body—and Ash's body—had bestowed upon her. She knew, down to her core, that it was no small thing for a woman her age to feel like this.

Because of their surroundings, Gloria hadn't expected it, but a tear rolled down her cheek as she came, as Ash found that spot inside her that tipped her over, that drove her a little bit madder while at the same time calming her down.

Ash's thumb was there to catch her tear. She licked it off her finger as she gazed up at Gloria.

"I love you," Gloria stammered. She breathed in deeply so she could say it again properly. It deserved to be expressed better. "I love you," she repeated, and wrapped herself all over Ash.

Chapter Forty-Seven

A FEW MONTHS LATER

❧

A few weeks ago, Alan had told Gloria he saw a touch of Ash in Sally, even though, of course, they were not genetically related. Maybe what he was really trying to say was that he saw a bit of himself reflected when he interacted with Sally. He treated both girls as though they were his granddaughters by blood and, at times, he seemed almost as sad as Gloria that Sally was leaving for Australia in a few short weeks.

Adrian was manning the barbecue. Lizzie looked completely enthralled by something Sindhu was saying. Mary poured wine for herself and a few others who needed a top-up.

Where was Ash? Gloria cast her gaze around the garden. Maybe she was fetching something from inside the house. Gloria's eyes landed on Sally again, who was sitting a little forlornly at the other end of the table. Maybe she was having seconds thoughts. No, that would be the kind of wishful thinking Gloria didn't allow herself as a mother. She wanted her girls to do whatever they wanted, within the realm of possibility, of course. When Sally had first told Gloria about her dream to take a gap year so far abroad, Gloria hadn't considered it within that realm. Until Sally and Janey had formed an alliance with Ash and, together, they had soon become a triple threat to Gloria's sanity.

In the end, Gloria had set aside her motherly pride and let Ash pay for a couple of things towards Sally's gap year. Although it wasn't just a matter of pride. More than that, it was a matter of letting Ash into the intimate circle Gloria and her daughters had constructed since George's death. Taking money from Ash was more a symbolic gesture than anything else.

Gloria spotted Ash in the kitchen doorway. She was trying to beckon Sally inside. It was Gloria's birthday party, after all. It would be foolish of her to assume Ash and the girls hadn't been up to something behind her back. Sally had finally caught Ash's drift and hurried inside.

"Here it comes." Fiona elbowed Gloria softly in the arm.

Gloria looked at the door again. The three of them walked out of the house carrying a giant cake with a picture of something made in icing on top. From where she was sitting, Gloria couldn't make out what the picture was.

"Happy birthday to you," everyone was singing.

Gloria rose. Her heart swelled. There had been a few unexpected additions to the family since her last birthday. As in-laws, the Coopers were quite full-on. On a few occasions, Gloria had even found herself doing the school run for Ash's nephews, what with them living around the corner from her. Ash had all but moved in. The lease on her flat in the City would soon be up. For a brief moment, they'd considered keeping it so they could go on a last-minute trip to London whenever they wanted, but, in the end, the cost was too ridiculous for a single mother who had pinched her pennies for such a long time to even consider. Besides, Ash always seemed so much happier in Murraywood, surrounded by her extended family.

"Happy birthday, dear Gloria. Happy birthday to you!"

Everyone stood around the table now, clapping. The cake was huge with candles all around the edges. The picture on the cake was one of Gloria and her girls with a plane in the background and the shape of Australia drawn beneath it. This image puzzled Gloria. Surely, no one in their right mind would think presenting the birthday cake was a great occasion to rub it in that Sally was leaving so shortly after Gloria's fifty-fifth birthday.

"Here you go, Mum." Sally offered her a small rectangular box. "This is from the three of us."

The three of us. When one of her daughters said something like that, Gloria could hardly believe it. Her family was back to being a foursome now.

Gloria tore off the ribbon and removed the lid from the box. There was an envelope inside, which she opened as quickly as her fumbling fingers would allow.

From the envelope, she unearthed three plane tickets to Sydney. She checked the date. Departure on the twenty-first of December.

"No way." She glanced at Ash who had the biggest smirk on her face Gloria had ever seen—and Ash had proved quite skilled at smirking. "We're going for Christmas?"

"The three of us," Janey said, referring to yet another constellation of their family. "To see Sally." Her voice was bursting with excitement.

"The Coopers have been briefed," Mary said, a smile in her voice. "We'll have an early Christmas party before you take off."

Alan had come up behind her. "No one deserves it more than you, Gloria," he said.

Oh Christ. Tears stung behind Gloria's eyes. She wasn't going to cry in front of her family and friends. She bit them back. But when Ash came up to her and threw her arms around Gloria, a few tears escaped from her eyes anyway.

"Happy birthday, my love," Ash said.

"You're going to have to stop spoiling me soon," Gloria said through her tears. "I might get used to it."

"Wait until you find out what I have planned for our private celebration," Ash whispered. "I'm not done spoiling you yet."

Chapter Forty-Eight

"There were nights of *endless* pleasure," Gloria shouted in Ash's ear. Ash grinned and turned to her, but Gloria had her gaze locked on the stage again. She'd been near ecstatic since they'd arrived at The O2.

Ash had driven them to London, in the car that she now owned to commute between work and Murraywood on the days when she didn't want to take the train—with herself safely and skilfully behind the wheel, thank you very much. She had told Gloria they were having dinner with Lewis and Jonathan in the City, but really, Ash had secretly scored tickets to the Celine Dion concert Gloria had been moping about missing since they'd had their very first meal together. In Ash's business, it was easy enough to know a guy who knew another guy who could arrange last minute VIP seats to a sold-out event. Connections like that were one of the perks of being in finance.

"Jesus," Lewis shouted in her other ear. "Your woman is going mad."

"I know." Ash grinned at her friend. "I scored big time tonight."

"Are you sure she's not a gay man trapped in a middle-aged

woman's body?" He quipped. "A very shapely body, of course," he added with a wink.

Ash shook her head. Lewis could make his jokes all he wanted. Ash was having the time of her life as well. She was here with Gloria and her best friend. Gloria's hand firmly intertwined with hers. During the time they'd been together, Ash hadn't had much choice but to appreciate Celine Dion's discography. She was enjoying the concert and the company and all the prospects the future held for her—for them.

"Do you know who else is here tonight, darling?" Lewis really couldn't keep his mouth shut. Ash wished that he would keep quiet just this once as she was enjoying the song, which she and Gloria sometimes—jokingly or not, Ash wasn't sure— referred to as 'their song'.

"Charlotte and her new woman. Apparently, Gretchen's very fond of Celine as well."

Unlike a few months ago, Ash didn't flinch any longer when her ex-wife's name was mentioned. She couldn't react to it entirely stoically yet, but she would get there at some point. Or maybe she wouldn't. Because Charlotte would always be her ex-wife, but that didn't mean Ash had to suffer every time she came up in conversation.

"Good for her," Ash said. "How do you know?"

"Instagram, darling." He pulled a face as if wanting to assure Ash that he and Charlotte were not on speaking terms and wouldn't be as long as Ash didn't expressly give him permission.

The song was coming to an end now, much quicker than Ash thought it would. It seemed the live version was a lot shorter than the album version. Still, one glance at Gloria was enough to convince her that it had been long enough to be effective. She sat there beaming, taking in the last few notes, then shot out of her chair, dropping Ash's hand in the process, to join in the raucous applause.

When she finally had eyes for Ash again, Gloria said, "That was one of the best moments of my life."

Ash pulled her close. "I aim to please," she half-shouted into Gloria's ear.

"I didn't really think I could love you more, but I seem to have reached a whole new level of Ash-fondness."

"Good to know what it takes." Ash kissed Gloria on the cheek. "That's excellent information to have." She might have been the one to give Gloria a surprise gift, but the pleasure was all hers. To see Gloria so lit up, so perfectly pleased and, granted, so utterly infatuated with her, was the biggest gift anyone could ever give Ash. "Apparently my ex-wife's here as well," she said.

"How does that make you feel?" Gloria briefly furrowed her brow.

Ash shrugged. "I'm here with you," she said. "I don't have any room left inside me for any feelings of resentment or hurt towards Charlotte."

Gloria curved her arm around Ash's shoulders and pulled her close. Ash felt her lips curl into a smile against the skin of her cheek. "The power of lo-o-ove," Gloria sang into her ear, going high and extremely tone-deaf on the last note.

"It's also good to know that you still can't sing to save your life." Ash wrapped Gloria into a full body hug, ignoring Lewis's wolf whistles and not caring that they were standing in the middle of a crowded arena. When she curled her arms around Gloria, and she could do that now no matter where they were, it always felt like it was just the two of them in the whole wide world.

About the Author

Harper Bliss is a best-selling lesbian romance author. Among her most-loved books are the highly dramatic French Kissing and the often thought-provoking Pink Bean series.

Harper lived in Hong Kong for 7 years, travelled the world for a bit, and has now settled in Brussels (Belgium) with her wife and photogenic cat, Dolly Purrton.

Together with her wife, she hosts a weekly podcast called Harper Bliss & Her Mrs.

Harper loves hearing from readers and you can reach her at the email address below.

www.harperbliss.com
harper@harperbliss.com

Made in the USA
Las Vegas, NV
10 December 2021

36931917R00184